Advance praise for Theresa Alan and
The Girls' Global Guide to Guys

"With *The Girls' Global Guide to Guys,* Theresa Alan delivers a brisk, funny, keenly observed portrait of a woman who wants more out of life than a soul-killing job and a tepid romance—and finds it on exotic shores."

—Kim Green, author of *Paging Aphrodite* and
Is That A Moose In Your Pocket?

Praise for Theresa Alan's *Spur of the Moment*

"The players come across as real—kudos to Theresa Alan for accomplishing this feat. The sensitivities of Ana and the uniqueness of each member of the troupe as she perceives them make for a solid character study with overtones of a family drama and chick-lit tale."

—*The Midwest Book Review*

"Alan shows that she's capable of handling sensitive issues with an effectively gentle touch."

—*Romantic Times*

And praise for her sensational debut *Who You Know*

"Alan does a masterful job . . . As the three women face the trials and triumphs of life, they assist each other in ways that only best friends can—through unconditional love, unrelenting humor and unwavering support. Reminiscent of *Bridget Jones's Diary* and *Divine Secrets of the Ya-Ya Sisterhood,* Alan's is a novel to be savored like a good box of chocolates."

—*Booklist*

"A delightful chick-lit."

—*The Midwest Book Review*

"A gorgeous book, superbly written with compassion and caring. *Who You Know* should absolutely be number one on everyone's list."

—*Rendezvous*

Books by Theresa Alan

WHO YOU KNOW

SPUR OF THE MOMENT

THE GIRLS' GLOBAL GUIDE TO GUYS

Published by Kensington Publishing Corporation

The Girls' Global Guide To Guys

Theresa Alan

KENSINGTON BOOKS
www.kensingtonbooks.com

KENSINGTON BOOKS are published by

Kensington Publishing Corp.
850 Third Avenue
New York, NY 10022

All Kensington titles, imprints and distributed lines are available at special quantity discounts for bulk purchases for sales promotion, premiums, fundraising, educational or institutional use.

Special book excerpts or customized printings can also be created to fit specific needs. For details, write or phone the office of the Kensington Special Sales Manager: Kensington Publishing Corp., 850 Third Avenue, New York, NY, 10022. Attn. Special Sales Department. Phone: 1-800-221-2647.

Strapless and the Strapless logo are trademarks of Kensington Publishing Corp.
Kensington and the K logo Reg. U.S. Pat. & TM Off

ISBN 0-7582-0758-1

First Kensington Trade Paperback Printing: April 2005
10 9 8 7 6 5 4 3 2 1

Printed in the United States of America

For Mike.

Acknowledgments

Many people helped me along the way as I worked to write this book. In particular I'd like to thank Sara Jade Alan, Veronique Boisnard, Mike Mitchell, Tom McQuaide, and Perry Daniel.

Podunk, Col. pop 450

Petite 5'1" 100 lbs honey blond hair

Vegetarian, born 1978
  does like milk, cheese, eggs, coffee
BA in Jouralism U of C, Boulder class of 2000

Creative Projects Manager at Pinnacle Media, Boulder
        2000 to

jogger, runs to relax

4 day weekend holidays flies to a city in U.S., Canada or Mexico
likes to drink, sometimes to excess (really likes beer)
likes to dance
can't read maps
despite her hippie parents she will not do drugs and is very fastidious
      about her personal + spatial hygene. Hates clutter.
Took remedial French in High School.
Sartorial klutz
Loves the great Impressionists, Surrealists (Bosch, Dali, etc) + cubists

1

Boulder, Colorado

"It couldn't possibly have been that bad."

"Oh, but it was. I saw his you-know-what within an hour of knowing him, totally against my will."

"He flashed you?"

"Not exactly. We stopped by my apartment after dinner before we went to the club because we'd gone for Italian, and I had garlic breath, and I wanted to brush my teeth before we went dancing, even though I knew within four seconds of meeting him that it could never go anywhere. I don't know *what* Sylvia was thinking setting us up. But to be polite I had to go through the charade of the date anyway, even though I wasn't remotely attracted to him. So I started brushing my teeth, but I wanted to check on him and make sure he was okay, so I came out from the bathroom into the living room, and he was just sitting there on the couch, naked."

"No!"

"Yes. Naked and, ah . . . You know, aroused." I'm stuck in traffic, story of my life, talking on my cell phone, which is paid for by the company I work for, making it one of the very, very few perks of being employed by Pinnacle Media. "I mean I know it's been a while since I've dated anyone, but isn't the whole point of dating and sex to kind of, I don't know, enjoy this stuff *together*? Like getting turned on by the other person's touch, and not by the sound of someone brushing her teeth in the bathroom?"

"So what did you do?"

"Well, I looked at him like the maniac he was, and he realized that I was appalled and said that he'd assumed that when I said I was going to the bathroom to brush my teeth, what I really meant was that I was going to put my diaphragm in."

"I don't . . . Is English his native language? I don't see how anyone could possibly come to that conclusion."

"Right, Tate, that's my point. The guy was a loon. So I reply, quite logically under the circumstances I think, my mouth foaming with toothpaste, 'No, I willy was bruffing my teef.' And this whole situation strikes me as so wildly funny. I mean in the past six months I've dated a bitter divorcé, been hit on by a string of lesbians, and now this. How did my dating life go so tragically wrong? Anyway, I just lost it. I crumpled to the ground in a fit of hysteria. I mean I started laughing so hard I literally couldn't stand, and he looked all put out and confused and out of the corner of my eye, as I was convulsing around like a fish out of water, I see him get dressed, and then *he stepped over* my writhing body and said, '*I don't know where things went wrong between us . . .*'"

"No!" Tate howls with laughter.

"Yes. He said some other stuff, but I was laughing too hard to hear him. I mean, hello, I can tell you *exactly* where you went wrong, buddy."

Tate and I laugh, then she says, "Did you tell Sylvia about how the guy she set you up with is a kook?"

"Hell, yes. I called her up and I was like, 'um, thanks for setting me up with a sexual predator.' And you know what she said? She said, 'I knew it had been a long time for both of you, and I thought you might just enjoy each other's company, even if it never got serious.' I don't think you need to be an English lit major to read the hidden meaning in that sentence. I mean, obviously Sylvia thinks I'm such a sad schlub who is so desperate for sex I'll have a one-night stand with a scrawny, socially inept engineer."

"Jadie, look at it this way: you can put all these experiences into your writing. Maybe you'll write a book one day about all the hilarious dates you've been on."

I groan. "Oh God, please don't tell me I'm going to go on enough bad dates to fill an entire book."

"There's a guy out there for you, I know there is."

"Maybe. I'm just pretty sure he's not in Boulder, Colorado."

"He's out there. I know he is. Somewhere. Look, I gotta go. I'm going to be late for my shift."

"Have fun slinging tofu."

"Oh, you know I always do."

I click the phone off, and now that I have nothing to occupy myself with I can focus completely on how annoyed I am at sacrificing yet another hour of my life to traffic. Why aren't we going anywhere, why?

I can't wait until the day I can work full time as a writer and won't have to commute in highway traffic twice a day any more.

I'm a travel writer, though most people call me a "creative project manager" for a Web design company. Personally I think this shows an appalling lack of imagination. I *have* published travel articles, after all. Several of them, in fact. Granted, all told, in my five years of freelancing I've only made a few hundred bucks on my writing and my travel expenses have come to about ten times more than what I made from my articles, but it's a start. (By the way, in case you're wondering, "creative project manager" is a fancy title for "underpaid doormat who works too hard." Essentially, my job is to manage people who do ac-

tual work. I make sure the copywriters, graphic design-
ers, and programmers are getting their pieces of the puz-
zle done on time. Every now and then I get to brainstorm
ideas for how to design a Web site, and those are the few
moments when I actually like my job, when I get to be
creative and use my brain, letting the ideas come tum-
bling out. But mostly my job feels ethereal and unsub-
stantial. The world of the Internet moves so quickly that
by the time a Web site gets launched, the company we
created the site for is already working on a redesign, and
within months, any work I did on a site disappears. That's
why I like writing for magazines. I do the work, it gets
printed with my byline, and I have the satisfaction of having something tangible to show for my efforts.)

Finally I see what has been holding traffic up—a car
that's pulled over to the side of the road with a flat tire.
Great. Forty extra minutes on my commute so people
can slow down to see the very exciting sight of a car with
a flat tire.

Eventually I make it home, grab the mail, unlock my
door, and dump the mail on my kitchen table, my keys
clattering down beside the stack of bills and catalogs ad-
vertising clothes I wouldn't wear under threat of torture.
I sift through the pile; in it is the latest issue of the alumni
magazine from the journalism school at the University of
Colorado at Boulder, my alma mater. I flip idly through it
until I see a classmate of mine, Brenda Amundson, who
smiles up at me from the magazine's glossy pages in her
fashionable haircut and trendy clothes. As I read the article, my mood sinks.

I know I'm not the first person who has struggled to
make it as a writer, but sometimes, like, oh, say, when I
get my alumni magazine and read that Brenda Amundson,
who is my age—twenty-seven—and has the same degree
I have, is making a trillion zillion dollars a year writing

for a popular sitcom in L.A. while I'm struggling to get a few bucks writing for magazines no one has ever heard of, my self-esteem wilts.

I change into a T-shirt and shorts to go for a run—I need to blow off steam. To warm up, I walk to a park, then I start an easy jog along the path along Boulder Creek. It's 7:30 at night, but the sun is still out and the air is warm.

Boulder has its faults, but it's so gorgeous you forgive them. No matter how many years I've lived here, the scenery never stops being breathtaking. As I run, I take in the quiet beauty of the trees, the creek, the stunning architecture. The University of Colorado at Boulder is an intensely gorgeous campus. Every building is made out of red and pink sandstone rocks and topped with barrel-tiled roofs. Behind them are the Flatirons, the jagged cliffs in the foothills of the Rocky Mountains that draw rock climbers from around the world and help routinely put Boulder on "best places to live" lists in magazines.

I jog for about half an hour, then walk and stretch until I've caught my breath. I sit down on the grass and watch three college students playing Frisbee in one corner of the field. Across the way, two young people with dreadlocks and brightly colored rags for clothes are playing catch with a puppy.

The puppy makes me smile, but I realize as I watch it that I still feel tense. My jaw muscles are sore from clenching them, a bad habit I have when I am stressed, which is most of the time these days it seems.

I need to get away, to relax. I long to hit the road.

I've always loved traveling. Since I was a little kid I always wanted to escape, to find a place I could comfortably call home and just be myself. In the small town where I grew up, life was a daily exercise in not fitting in.

The fact that I was considered weird was mostly my parents' fault. They ran a health food store/new age shop where they tried to sell crystals to align chakras, tarot cards, incense, meditation music, that sort of thing. I'm fairly certain that no one ever bought a single sack of brown rice or bag of seaweed from their grocery store. They got by because of the side businesses they ran in the shop—Mom cut hair and Dad built and repaired furniture. Yes, I know, a health food/new age/hair salon/furniture shop is unusual, but when I was growing up, it was all I knew.

My mom was the kind to bake oatmeal cookies sweetened with apple juice and honey and would rather have me gnaw off my own arm than eat a Ding Dong or another processed-food evil. You can imagine how popular the treats I brought to school for bake sales and holiday parties were. About as popular as me. Which is to say not at all.

I sat through years of school lunches all on my own, eating carob bran muffins and organic apples while every other kid had Ho-Hos and Pop-Tarts and peanut butter fluff sandwiches washed down with Coke or chocolate milk. And as I would eat in solitude, I would dream of getting away. I longed to see the world. I ached to find some place where I could be whoever I wanted to be and wouldn't be the weird kid in town.

I found that place in Boulder, Colorado. Boulder is a place where pot-smoking, dreadlocked eighteen-year-olds claim poverty yet wear Raybans. Boulderites believe themselves to be one with nature, but own some of the most expensive homes in the country and drive CO_2-spewing SUVs without irony. It's a place that manages to be somehow new age and old school. A place where yuppies and hippies collide and where, inexplicably, people think running in marathons is actually fun.

My life is equally mixed up. It feels like a pinball machine—I'm the ball, getting flung around in directions I couldn't foresee and never considered. Like how I ended up working for Pinnacle Media. I thought that after graduation I would become this world-renowned journalist covering coup attempts, international corruption and intrigue, the works. But after I got my degree, I couldn't get a job writing so much as obituaries for some small-town newspaper. Frustratingly, papers like the *New York Times* and *Washington Post* seemed to be doing okay even without my help, and nobody from their respective papers was banging down my door begging me to write for them. They didn't even glance at my resume, just like every other newspaper in America, no matter how small or inconsequential. So I took a job doing Web content at an Internet company during the height of Internet insanity, when every twenty-year-old kid with a computer was declaring himself a CEO and launching an online business determined to get rich quick. The company was living large for a while, but then the economy started to turn. I could tell we were going down, and I felt lucky when I landed the job at Pinnacle.

That feeling lasted, oh, twenty-eight seconds.

I've been looking for a new job since about the day after I started with Pinnacle, but with the economy the way it is, there have been almost no jobs advertised that I'm qualified to fill. My mantra is *someday the economy will get better and I'll be able to find another job. Someday the economy will get better and I'll be able to find another job.* But until then, my situation feels a lot like being trapped.

I travel to get away whenever possible, taking a handful of short trips each year to cities in the United States, Mexico, or Canada. I've been saving up money and vacation time to go on a real trip, something longer than a four-day weekend, but I keep waiting for some flash of insight that will tell me where the best place to go is, some location that will prove a treasure trove of sales to magazines.

Although maybe it doesn't really matter where I go, whether Barbados is the happening spot this year or if Madagascar is the place to be, whether the Faroe Islands are going to be the next big thing or if Malta will be all the rave. After all, the articles I have sold haven't come from the short trips I've taken but from living in the Denver/Boulder area—stuff about little-known hotspots in Colorado and how to travel cheap in Denver. Mostly I write for small local newspapers and magazines. I've gotten a few pieces published in national magazines, but the biggies, the large circulation publications that pay livable wages like United Airlines' *Hemispheres* or Condé Nast *Traveler*, remain elusively, tantalizingly out of reach.

In the past year, depressed about my career, I decided I would try to get another area of my life in shape—my love life. It hasn't exactly gone according to plan.

First, there was the bitter divorcé. I didn't know he was bitter until we went out on our first date. I knew he was divorced; he'd told me. I just didn't know how frightening the depths of his contempt for his ex went.

I met Jeff at the Greenhouse, the restaurant where I used to work when I was in college. My friend Tate still works there, and I was waiting for her to get finished with her shift when Jeff and I got to talking. I was sitting at the table next to him, and as another waitress, Sylvia, brought him his shot of wheat grass, he said something that made me laugh, and he kept on cracking me up with little quips and witty remarks. I don't even remember what we talked about, just that he seemed like a nice guy, and when he asked if he could have my number, I told him he could. I started to write it down, and he said abruptly, "Before you give me your number, there is something you should know."

I immediately thought he was going to say that he was out on bail for murder charges or something.

8

"I'm divorced and have two kids."

I waited a beat. "And?"

"And what? That's it."

"That's your big secret? You're divorced and have kids?"

"Yeah, that's it."

"I think I can handle it."

(Of course that really wasn't his big secret. His real secret was that he was a complete psychopath whose rage toward his ex festered in a frightening and unseemly way.)

The fact that he had kids appealed to me. He told me he saw them—a three-year-old girl and two-year-old boy—every other weekend. I imagined Jeff and me getting married, and I would be able to help raise these kids and watch them grow, but on a convenient part-time basis without any of that painful pregnancy and birthing business.

But then I went out on my one and only date with Jeff and that fantasy was blown to bits.

Things started well enough. Then in the middle of a nice meal after a couple of glasses of wine, I asked him something about his ex. Something like if they'd managed to stay friends or why they broke up, I can't remember exactly. Jeff got this maniacal look in his eyes and said, "That lying, money-grubbing bitch. I hate her. Women—all they want is your money. Lying . . . cheating . . . manipulative bitches. But sometimes you get sick of porn and want the real thing." He laughed about that last thing, as if it were a joke, but it very clearly wasn't. And when I looked at him wide-eyed and open-mouthed, he seemed to come out of his trance and our gazes met. I was blinking in shock, and I think he realized that, like an evil villain going around disguised as a good guy, he'd accidentally let the mask slip off and some serious damage control was in order. He smiled. "Just kidding. It was rough going there for a while, but we're friends again." He saw my incredulity. "No, really. I love women." *Yeah,* to have sex with. "*Sometimes you get sick of porn and want the real thing*" . . . *unbefuckinglievable.*

So that was the end of Jeff.

Now you'll want to know about the lesbians. Their names are Laura and Mai and they live in my apartment building.

We'd always been polite when we'd met in the hallway or at the mailboxes over the years. Then a few months ago, as I held the front door to the building open for them, they asked me what I had going on that night. It was a Friday, yet I had a whopping nothing to do and no place to be. They said they were going dancing at a lesbian bar that night; did I want to go with them? I said sure, it sounded like fun.

Laura and Mai are both big girls and very pretty. Laura looks like Mandy Moore would if Mandy were a size fourteen. And Mai has a build like Oprah—busty and curvy and strong. And they have the cutest style. Their outfits wouldn't be featured in *InStyle* or anything, but I think they have a certain bohemian charm. And can we talk accessories? Clunky, colorful jewelry to die for.

We hit the club a few hours later, dancing our little hearts out. For some reason I didn't think it was strange that they kept buying drinks for me and plying me with alcohol. After all, they knew I was straight, I knew they'd been dating each other forever—what was there to worry about?

It was late when we got back.

"Do you want to come to our place for a nightcap?" Mai asked.

"No. Can't drink no more. Alcohol . . . too much."

"Why don't you come inside and we'll give you some water so you won't have a hangover," Laura said.

I was too drunk to protest—or really even to know what was happening. As I staggered into their apartment,

I noticed that the hide-a-bed had been pulled out. I remember thinking, *I didn't know their couch had a hide-a-bed.*

We sat on the edge of the hide-a-bed, the two of them flanking me on either side. In an instant, Laura was blowing in my ear and Mai was kissing my neck and stroking my breast. It took me a moment to process what was happening. My brain was working in slow motion. It was like I'd gotten stuck in a sand trap, and no matter how much I tried to accelerate, the wheels of my brain just went around and around and never got anywhere. But eventually I realized that my breast was being stroked by a woman. I found this information to be very confusing.

Once I finally noticed what was going on, I seemed to sober up instantly. I sprung up off the couch. "I'm . . . I'm . . . I'm straight!" I yelped.

"There's no reason to be locked into these artificial constructions . . . these meaningless boundaries . . ." Mai began.

"Like boundaries! Boundaries good!" My English skills, despite my degree in journalism, had been reduced to the level of a two-year-old. That's when I began backing up toward the door. In moments I was sprinting backward at Mach-10 speed, a blur of a human at break-the-sound-barrier velocity.

Unfortunately, I hadn't noticed a coffee table between me and the door to freedom.

Another person would have stubbed her leg on it, or perchance been knocked sideways. Me? I was going so fast I became airborne and did a back flip—my head hit the corner of the table on my way down. I knocked myself semi-unconscious.

They say fear evokes two responses: fight or flight. No one ever said that knocking yourself unconscious was an appropriate reaction to an uncomfortable situation. But there you have it. I'd turned myself into the perfect victim. I had no way to defend myself. I was at their mercy.

Fortunately, Laura and Mai weren't rapists. They'd put the moves on me, been rebuffed, and now they were a flurry of concern, hovering over me and wanting to know if I was okay.

In my half-conscious state, I was dimly aware that the two of them were dragging me over to the hide-a-bed and hoisting me onto it—managing to knock my head on the metal frame as they did. I quickly fell into a merciful sleep.

In the morning, I didn't remember where I was or what had happened, I just knew my head was in excruciating pain. In addition to a bruise the size of a plum on the back of my head from the coffee table, I had a searing pain just above my ear from where they'd knocked me against the bed frame. On top of all that, I had a blinding hangover.

I groaned in pain. Moments later I heard the patter of bare feet against the wood floor, and I opened my eyes in an attempt to figure out where I was and what was going on.

It was Mai and Laura, who'd run to check on whether I was all right. They were naked, hovering over me like oversized Florence Nightingales, so that when I opened my eyes all I saw was tit. Four large, ponderous tits, encircling me in a mammary orbit.

I promptly shut my eyes and wondered, *how did my life start to read like a* Penthouse *letter?* Sure, some people—guys, no doubt—might like a life that read like a *Penthouse* letter. I was not one of those people.

Laura and Mai still smile at me when we pass each other in the hall. Once they even asked if I wanted to go dancing with them again. (I replied that if I got one more head injury, I'd need to go to the hospital for sure, so it was probably safer if I didn't go out with them anymore.)

A few weeks later I had yet another tangle with a lesbian—that night also involved alcohol and confusing and misguided tit-groping, though thankfully no head trauma—but if you don't mind, it's still too painful and embarrassing to think about, so I'd rather not tell the story in all its gory detail.

Add on the sexual predator from last night, and you have the sum total of my love life in the last six months. And it was no romance novel before that, I can assure you.

I wonder if there is a place where this whole dating and romance thing is easier. Some country where the men aren't as psychotic as the men in America all seem to be. If so, I'm moving there post haste. I just need to find this magical la-la land. I'll search the globe until I find it. . . .

I smile at the idea, then I wonder how dating *is* different in different parts of the world. I know some places have arranged marriages, but where? How are African wedding ceremonies different from Swedish ones or Chinese ones? Do other countries do blind dates? Double dates? Internet dating? Do Russians sweat how many days to wait to call after a first date like Americans do?

I vow to research the cultural differences of mating and love, and that's when it hits me: *if I'm interested in how romance is different in different parts of the world, maybe other people would be too. Maybe that could be my angle when I pitch stories; maybe it would be unique enough to get me in the door of the major magazines.*

The ideas zip through my head, and I have internal arguments with myself about where and when I should go. One part of me really wants to just take off. For months

I've been fantasizing about how different my life will be if I can just get away for a while so I can rejuvenate my brain by filling it with art and culture and recharge my body by having lavish amounts of salacious sex with a handsome stranger with a sexy accent. But the other part of me knows for a fact that I'll lose my job if I leave. There have already been numerous rounds of layoffs at my company. I'm the lucky one for still having a job. Well, that's what I tell myself anyway. *I'm lucky to have my job, I'm lucky to have my job.* I know a lot of people who have been out of work for months. As a single woman with no more than a couple of months' of survival savings in the bank, I'd be in the poorhouse in no time if I got laid off, so I *am* lucky to have a job. But since the layoffs began, everyone at work has been worried they'll be next and they are resentful, tense, and hostile. Looking for other jobs while at the office is a generally accepted practice. The bitterness factor went through the roof when we survivors were doing our own jobs plus the jobs of the people who'd been let go. These days the opposite problem has hit—there's almost no work to go around, and somehow that's even worse, at least for me. The strain of trying to pretend to look busy is much worse than the strain of actually being busy. For one thing, I'm constantly bored, and for another thing, I live in constant terror that someone is going to figure out I don't have anything to do and that they could easily get along without me and they're going to fire my ass.

But the thing of it is, I hate my job, and there is a part of me that would love to get fired despite the economic strain. I'd finally have the time I need to pursue my real dreams and goals. Anyway, I've been wracking up vacation time for months—I should take it before the company goes under and I lose it all.

But taking a trip would be so impractical. . . .

But is "practical" the kind of person I want to be? No! I want to be adventurous. I want to take risks and follow my dreams.

I jump up and run home. There I strip out of my sweaty clothes, take a quick shower, throw some fresh clothes on, and sprint the four blocks from my apartment to the Greenhouse, where Tate is working tonight.

Tate has just finished taking an order from a table and is heading to the kitchen to give it to the cooks.

The Greenhouse specializes in food for diners who have wheat allergies, are lactose intolerant, and so on. Vegetarian, vegan, whatever your dietary oddity, the Greenhouse is here to serve. The Greenhouse does pretty well, what with it being located in Boulder, one of the most health-conscious cities in the universe. Boulder attracts skiers, hikers, mountain climbers, and marathon runners up the yin yang. A Boulderite is as likely to eat red meat as to stir-fry a hubcap for dinner.

The Greenhouse is brightly painted. One wall is purple, one red, one deep blue. The ceiling is pale green, and the work of local artists decorates the walls.

When I worked here during college, I was the only member of the waitstaff without multiple body piercings or a single tattoo. Tate has several of both. Her belly button and nose are pierced and her ears are studded with earrings. She has a tattoo of a thin blue and white ring encircling her upper right arm that looks like a wave, a rose on her ankle, and the Chinese symbol for harmony on her breast. (Only a special few have seen this one, and one drunken night she flashed me and I became one of them. It was a shining moment in an otherwise disappointing life.) Today she is wearing her long black hair in a loose bun that is held together by what looks like decorative chopsticks. She's petite, but so thin her limbs seem long and she looks taller than she is, with the graceful, lithe muscles of a ballerina. It would be fair to call Tate's look exotic. My looks, with my honey-blond hair and dimples, would be best described as wholesome-Iowa-farm-girl.

I follow her into the kitchen.

"Tate, you're a genius."

"What are you talking about? Lance, leave the onions out of this burrito."

"Just write it down," Lance booms.

"I did. I just don't want a repeat of last time. I lost that tip because of you."

Lance, the cook, just grunts.

"Your idea for the book," I continue. I follow her over to the refrigerator, where she pulls out a couple of cans of organic soda. "What I'll do is write a book about romance and dating around the globe. I'll interview women all over the world and find out their most hilarious dates ever. I'll find out about differences in dating and marriage in different cultures—the works. I'll be able to sell tons of articles, based on my research, to bridal magazines and women's rags. You know—stuff like, 'Looking to make your wedding original? Borrow from traditional Chinese or Turkish or Moroccan customs to make your wedding an international success.' Or for *Cosmo* I can write about different sexual rituals around the world, or for *Glamour* I can write something like, 'You think the dating scene in America is grim? At least you don't have to do like the Muka-Muka do—they have to eat worms and beat each other up to see if they're compatible.' "

"Who the hell are the Muka-Muka?"

"Well, that's just to illustrate. I don't know the worst mating rituals in the world yet—that's why I need to write a book about it. I'll be like the John Gray of international relations between men and women. I'll be like an anthropologist studiously researching the most important issue known to humankind: love."

"And along the way, as you're doing all this important academic research, you might just happen to stumble on Mr. Right."

Damn. Sometimes it's a problem that this girl knows me so well. "Well, you know, if it just so happens that way . . . But you have to come with me. You have money saved."

She pushes the kitchen door open with her butt and delivers the sodas to her table. She drops off a bill at another, then clears off the plates at yet another. I hover at the doorway of the kitchen, waiting for her.

"How much do you have saved?" I ask her as soon as she gets back.

"Order up!" Lance says.

Tate checks the order and starts balancing the plates on her arms. "I'm not sure exactly. Maybe five thousand."

Five grand! And she makes a lot less money than I do. Granted, she doesn't need a car, she lives with four roommates, and she doesn't need to spend a dime on her wardrobe for work, but still, I'm impressed.

"What are you going to do with it? What could be better than traveling the world with your friend? Come on, Tate, we need some adventure. We need to shake things up a bit."

"Where were you thinking about going?"

"I don't know. I'd like to see the whole world, but I don't have nearly enough vacation time saved up for that. How about Europe—the countries are small so we knock out a bunch at once. Paris . . . Italy . . . Germany . . ."

"But we don't speak those languages."

"So? It'll be an adventure. You're not scared, are you?" Okay, I admit I'm being manipulative. I know Tate well enough to know that the best way to get her to do something is to accuse her of being scared to do it.

"Of course I'm not scared!" She stomps out of the kitchen and delivers the order. When she returns, she pulls me aside conspiratorially. "What about our jobs?"

"I'll work it out with my boss, ask if they can hire a temp for a while or something. And Jack will understand. His waiters are always taking off on road trips for weeks at a time."

"That's true."

"So you're thinking about it?"

"When are you thinking of going?"

"As soon as possible."

"You'll plan everything?"

"Of course. Come on, it'll be the adventure of a lifetime. And maybe you'll find your soul mate. Another free spirit just like you."

She bites her lip. "It might be fun."

"It'll be a blast."

"Do you really think we could do this?"

"Of course we can."

She nods. "This is crazy."

"You love crazy."

She's still nodding. "Tell me when I should show up at the airport."

"Yes!" I give her an enormous hug. "It's going to be the experience of a lifetime," I assure her.

It's a big promise, but there is no doubt in my mind that it's a promise I can keep.

2

London, England

Just thinking about finally getting to travel makes me feel happier. I lie in bed that night smiling. I can't wait to see the art and architecture I learned about in college up close and in person. I imagine having important political discussions with strangers from around the globe. I fantasize about a whirlwind romance with someone who will ask me to move to Europe to be with him. I'll be able to triumphantly report to my alumni magazine that I'm leading a thrilling life filled with international intrigue and excitement. I will develop a worldliness beyond my years.

When I go into work the next day, my excitement fades. My office has the same effect on me that the Dementors had on Harry Potter—I start to get depressed and begin to lose my will to live. I think I could like my job if it weren't for my manager. Tina and I have opposing ideas on the best way to accomplish tasks. I'm an everybody-plays-an-important-part-on-the-team kind of person while Tina is all about hierarchy. She's the boss, and she's never going to let you forget it. Tina is insecure and so to reassure herself that she's more important than you, she'll seize every opportunity to remind you you're a grunt. Sometimes I think she stays up at night plotting menial tasks for her staff to do. It's all very exhausting and soul-crushing.

Tina is thirty-two and pretty in a sharp and scary way.

She's thin and always impeccably dressed. She has black eyes and black hair, and if you piss her off she can glare at you in a way that will make your heart sink and your toes curl in fright.

I knock on her door.

"What?"

"Hi, Tina. Could I talk to you for a second?"

"I'm very busy."

"Uh, is there maybe another time you'd have to talk?"

She sighs. "Come in. Let's get this over with. What is it?"

She taps her glinty red fingernails against the top of her desk.

"Thanks. Well, Tina, as you know, we haven't had much work lately, and I have four weeks of vacation saved up, and I thought since the workload is so light right now, this would be the perfect time for me to use up my vacation time."

"You've got to be kidding me. You want to take four weeks off? Who would take care of your work?"

"Well, that's the thing. I haven't really had any work lately. But if something came up, I thought you could do some contract work with Burt." Burt used to have my job. When the work started slowing down, there was no need for two of us and he got the ax. "I still e-mail him every now and then and he hasn't gotten a job, so I'm sure he'd be very grateful for any work at all."

"I don't think so."

"Maybe you could think about it. The thing is, we want to go to Europe, my friend and I, and tickets to Europe are very expensive and I'm not sure when I could go back."

"You're putting me in a difficult situation. I don't have time to do your job as well as my own."

"I know that, Tina, I just thought—"

"I'll think about it, but I'm not making any promises."

"Thank you, Tina, I really appreciate it."

I slink back to my cube feeling punished. I begin my

day with my daily ritual of looking through the classified job listings on-line, willing for there to be a job I'm qualified for. As usual, there isn't, so then I begin looking up information on traveling through Europe. I literally have no work to do. When I have nothing to do but pretend to look busy, eight hours is a long, long time. So I spend my day fantasizing about Europe. Imagining adventures in exotic foreign lands is the only way I can survive the dreary reality of my life.

Three days go by before I work up the courage to ask Tina if she's had a chance to think about letting me take my time off. She barks at me that she's busy and doesn't have time to talk to me. All through the long days in which I have no work to do but am trapped at my desk pretending like I do, I pray for Tina to come up to me and tell me she's agreed to let me go. I know she's making me sweat it out just because she's the boss and therefore she can.

After several more days, I ask Tina again. She sighs dramatically and shoots me her trademark glare.

"You're a talented employee," she says. "Four weeks is a long time. But you're right, there hasn't been much work for you to do lately. Hopefully the sales group will close some deals shortly, but if you want to take this trip, I guess now's the time to do it."

"I can go? Thank you, Tina! Thank you."

Tate and I pack nothing besides what we can fit in our backpacks—a few T-shirts, a sweater, another pair of shorts, four pairs of underwear, a pair of jeans, a skirt for going to the chapels in Italy, a comb, another bra, and a few pairs of socks. I also have a notebook for capturing my findings on romance and love as well as a journal in which I'll detail every part of every day of our trip.

I have high hopes that Europe will serve as my muse

and get me writing again. I haven't been writing regularly for a while now. My excuse used to be that I worked long hours at Pinnacle and most nights after getting home from work I'd be too exhausted to do anything but mindlessly watch TV until I passed out drooling on the couch. Lately I haven't had any excuse, I just haven't been doing it, which makes no sense because I've wanted to be a writer since I was a little kid. As my school was small and there weren't many kids my age, I didn't have many friends to fill long summer days or weekend nights. So I wrote stories of faraway places to keep me entertained. I kept right on writing through high school. Those stories, they got me through all those lonely nights.

But when I stopped writing just for me and started writing to make money and get published, the looming threat of rejection took away much of what made writing fun.

I thought that after I got a few things published it would get easier, but I still get armfuls of rejection letters for every one article I manage to sell. And by "sell" I mean basically give away for free or at a monetary loss.

I'm waiting for the day when it all gets easier and I don't constantly have to struggle. I mean it. Any day now would be just fine.

Tate and I have a 5:30 P.M. flight. The plan is to sleep on the overnight flight and get to London around midday London time.

Our trip starts with blundering confusion before we even take off. Tate and I get shifted to a different flight—there is some conflict with connecting flights—and on the new flight we're not sitting next to each other. The ticket person tells us there is another single flyer next to me exactly two rows behind where Tate's seat is, and we can probably get that person to switch with Tate.

It turns out the person is a young woman who doesn't speak English. When I try to explain the situation, she just keeps shaking her head and saying "No English. No English." But for some reason I keep talking in English, enunciating wildly and using crazy hand gestures to communicate you-you, here-here, like an air traffic controller. Without saying anything, she does move. "Thank you, thank you," I keep nodding and smiling and bowing like some kind of Chinese dignitary.

I think we're off to a good start.

Tate and I spend the first few hours talking about the things we usually talk about: people we both know, usually through some connection to the Greenhouse. Our friends are our family, and I mean that quite literally, particularly for Tate.

Tate is an orphan. Her mother died when she was just a little girl and her father died when she was thirteen. I'm not technically an orphan like Tate, but after leaving my hometown and my parents to come to college, I felt like one.

Home for me is a miniscule town in southern Colorado. Population 450. It goes without saying that nothing ever happened there. There was one movie theater a couple of towns over that got a movie (note the singular) a year or so after the rest of the world had seen it and that would be the only movie shown for months and months until they finally got another year-old film. But because there was nothing else to do, I'd see the same movies over and over and over again. I can recite the lines to more bad films than I care to admit. And that covers my entire social life from fetus to age eighteen.

When you live in a town that small and then are thrust into a city of more than 90,000, it's disorienting. Suddenly there was so much to do I couldn't keep up. Tate took me under her wing, showed me the things Boulder had to offer, and kept it from being terrifying and overwhelming for me. In me, Tate finally had a friend who was going somewhere, getting a college degree and not frying her brain with illegal substances. I had goals and plans and dreams. Funny though, the part about how I'm still no closer to accomplishing those dreams five years after graduation. At least I pay my bills on time, and in Tate's circle of friends that makes me a Type A overachiever.

Our friendship was cemented one time at work when I'd completely messed up this woman's order—my mind was someplace else, it was completely my fault—but the woman yelled at me in a way that was so unnecessarily mean—lots of yelling about what an idiot I was—that I sprinted to the bathroom and burst into tears. Her words hurt so much because sometimes I worry that I am, in fact, a talentless, worthless idiot, and she was confirming my worst fears. (There are just some days when it's so much easier to believe a bunch of horrible things about yourself than to imagine you have any redeeming qualities whatsoever.) Tate came into the bathroom stall to comfort me, telling me the woman was repressed and un-fulfilled and probably hadn't had an orgasm even once in her life and she was taking her anger and frustration inappropriately out on me. I had to smile. The mistake had completely been mine. It was true that the woman hadn't needed to freak out like she did, but I thought it was hilarious that Tate brought the woman's alleged frigidity into a conversation about mixed-up dinner orders and incorrect salad dressings. I loved how totally, thoroughly, and completely Tate was there for me, ready to defend me and bolster my spirits. There are days when you really just need to know there is going to be someone on your side, even if you're the one screwing up.

* * *

I manage to catch a few hours of sleep here and there on the flight, but I get nothing even approximating a good night of sleep.

Mixed in with my excitement to get to Europe are lingering stresses about work. Also, I'm strangely nervous about the trip. I've spent the last few weeks reading and planning for it, staying so busy I didn't take the time to stop and reflect on the fact that I've been dreaming of going to Europe all my life, which makes this trip the realization of a life-long dream—and thus, it has a lot to live up to.

Whenever I'd muse to my mother about how much I longed to go to Australia or Europe or South America or somewhere, she would say I could escape a place, but I couldn't escape myself. I see her point, but I don't completely agree with her. When I left Podunk, Colorado, and came to Boulder, I did, over time, escape the person I had once been. Growing up, I had been so shy, I did my best to never utter a word in public. Then I came to college in Boulder and met Tate at the restaurant and I started to become more outgoing. It didn't happen all at once. At first, I was so guarded with people, so ready for them to make a sarcastic comment or biting remark—I survived many years of being teased about my parents and my uncool clothes—but over time I came to realize that there were a lot of down-to-earth, funny, smart, kind people who had dreams and ambitions just like mine. Over the course of my freshman year in college, I came out of my cocoon and became part of an extensive network of friends. I was still a book-reading fanatic happy to be by myself, but I began spending a lot more time socializing than I had when I was growing up, frittering away hour after hour just hanging out with people, talking about everything and nothing. I'd always thought I was intractably shy; it was fascinating to watch myself become this talkative person. It's how I learned that *where* you are can absolutely play a part in *who* you are.

At last our plane lands. The first task at hand is to figure out how to catch the tube (subway) station to our hotel. All I can say is: thank God for Tate. I'm pitiful with directions and we'd be wandering the city for hours if it weren't for Tate's ability to figure out a map and negotiate the tube system. (Maps may be ancient runes or tea leaves clinging to the bottom of a cup for all they help me divine where I am and how to get to where I want to be.) In our friendship, I may have gotten the book smarts, but Tate got the street smarts for sure.

The only down side to London is that we nearly get killed the moment we step out of the tube station and onto the road because the cars are coming at us from the wrong direction. I literally almost step into a double-decker bus within minutes of setting foot into the city. My heart nearly catapults out of my chest it's throbbing so extravagantly, and I come to this epiphany: it's very tricky trying to look around and absorb all the views that a foreign city has to offer while simultaneously trying to avoid becoming road kill.

For the entire walk to our hotel near Hyde Park, I feel apprehensive and angry at London for trying to deliberately smoosh me into the asphalt, like the city was personally out to get me or something. Unreasonable or not, it's how I feel.

Our hotel room is microscopic and ludicrously expensive. It's just big enough for two narrow single beds and a tiny dresser. There is just enough room between the beds to walk in sideways with our guts sucked in, and when I try to get to my bed to dump my stuff on it, I wallop my thigh so hard on the dresser that I begin this hopping and yelping song-and-dance routine and then manage to stub my toe on the bed frame. When it's my turn to shower, it's so tiny that I can barely fit into it. When I accidentally drop the soap, I have to step *out* of the shower to be able to bend down and pick it up. I'm a petite person, and the shower can barely contain me. How a brawny male would fare with this bread-box-size contraption is beyond me.

Despite being bruised and having nearly been killed and being delirious from sleep deprivation, once we head out to really check out the city, my excitement returns.

We are in England! Land of tiny munchkin cars, red phone booths, guards in front of Buckingham Palace wearing furry upside-down garbage cans on their heads, and narrow streets that would be side streets back home but are passed off as main thoroughfares here.

After walking around for a bit, we head to the tube station to catch a train to Covent Garden. We only get a few stops when the train stops and everyone gets off except Tate and me, two Chinese girls speaking Chinese and looking at a guidebook, and a German mother and father with their teenage son.

I look up from the guidebook I've been studying and ask Tate what's going on.

"I don't know. I heard a guy over the intercom say, 'I'm sorry . . .' but then I couldn't make out the rest of what he said. He just sort of faded into this inaudible mumble."

We sit there for several minutes, staring across the way, blinking and expectant, at the Germans and the Chinese girls.

It pains me to point this out, but here Tate and I are, lost and confused, and, unlike the Germans and the Chinese girls, *we speak English*. It is, in fact, our native tongue. How we will fare in countries in which English is not the primary language, I have no idea.

Finally we all clamber off the train because there is nothing else we can do. We stand with the milling crowds on the platform, waiting for divine providence to deliver us to where we want to go. There are no signs pointing us in the right direction, at least not here where we're standing, and just as I'm wondering if we need to go someplace else to get information, Tate grabs my arm and pulls me onto a train on another track.

"I heard that woman say this train goes to Kings Cross. We can switch trains there and catch the one to Covent Garden," she explains.

We go back to all the places we just came from, and it takes about a million years, and a tube station, pungent with the odors of urine and body odor, is not a place you want to spend one extra second in, but at last we get to where we want to go.

We follow the signs to Trafalgar Square, snap a few pictures, and look around. We've spent exactly eleven seconds here, and it appears that's all the time we need. Somehow the guidebook made it sound like a more exciting place.

Next we walk down to Westminster Abbey and Big Ben and admire the sun glinting off the Thames and take the requisite photos eight trillion other people have taken.

Every place we go is teeming with people, and I have to say I feel the same stressed-outness I feel when I'm in New York City. In Boulder, pedestrians rule, always getting the right of way over cars. In New York City and London, anywhere you walk on your own two little feet you do so at your peril. The cities are giant Frogger games and we're the expendable frogs. I don't think drivers in big cities necessarily *want* to kill you, I just think they have places to be and don't give a crap if you happen to get in the way of them and their destination. Even though my I-almost-became-a-pancake-once-already-today terror is still with me, I nearly get squashed two more times because the streets confuse the bejeesus out of me.

"Are you almost ready for dinner?" Tate asks.

"I am kind of hungry, but that doesn't make any sense. It's only ten in the morning back home. It can't be time for dinner yet."

"It's dinner time in London," Tate notes. "An early dinner, but still."

Our bodies are all off kilter since we were more or less served breakfast at 4:00 A.M. Denver time. When the flight attendant served me my muffin this morning, I kept thinking, why am I eating a muffin at this Godforsaken hour? But Tate is right, we're in Europe now, and it's close enough to dinner time.

We walk through SoHo, which is all neon lights and advertisements for sex clubs, and stop at an Indian restaurant for dinner because we know it will be easy for us to find vegetarian food.

I've always been a vegetarian—it's how my parents raised me. My parents are unapologetic hippies and they believed eating animals was bad for your chakra and worse for your karma, and by the time I was old enough to decide what to eat for myself, it was too late, I couldn't quite bring myself to try a hamburger. Tate is veggie because she's one of those people who act tough but are secretly softies who bawl their eyes out whenever they see a dead animal on the side of the road and can't even bring themselves to kill a spider that has taken up residence in their house. Ever since Tate realized there was a correlation between the cows in the pastures and the steak on her plate, she wanted nothing to do with meat eating ever again.

The restaurant is crowded, with tables so close together that if you turn too quickly you elbow your neighbor in the ribs.

As we wait for our food to be served I ask Tate what

she wants to do tomorrow. I list about a dozen possible things to see or do, and we form a rough plan. By the time our food arrives, Tate and I have run out of stuff to talk about. We had a twelve-hour flight with nothing else to do but talk and we spent the day walking around and chatting, and for the moment, we have nothing else to say. It's not that Tate and I can't comfortably coexist through silences, but when we're trapped facing each other at a table with nothing but the sound of chewing being exchanged, it's a little awkward. I look over at the table to our right, where there are three stylish women, two Indian and one Caucasian. Looking around the room, I notice that every table has a diverse group of people. There is an Israeli sitting with an African and an Asian at one table, a white guy with a black guy in dreadlocks at another, and what seems like every conceivable combination of ethnicities filling out the rest of the tables. At home, I never see this. Boulder is very white.

Maybe I should tell these women about how I'm researching men, romance, and dating around the world and see if they'll offer their insights. I cast a brief look at the remains of my vegetable curry congealing in oily puddles on my plate and then muster my courage to introduce myself, tell them what I'm trying to learn about, and ask them if they'll help.

"I'll try to help," one of the Indian women says. "My name is Vani. This is Gita and this is Lisa."

"Hello," Gita says. Lisa nods and smiles.

Vani is very pretty, with clothes that perfectly fit her slender frame. Her dark hair is thick and falls in a tumble of waves on her shoulders. She has a rather large nose and lips painted red that contrast against her dark skin. The other Indian woman, Gita, has lighter skin, thick red lips, and dark hair in two thin braids that curl around her neck. Lisa is a blonde with large brown eyes.

I open my notebook and ready my pen, and then I

wonder what the hell to do next. "Well, ah, I guess to start, tell me what dating is like in London these days."

"It's a bloody nightmare. This one was smart," Lisa says, gesturing to Vani, "she had her parents set her up."

"You mean, like an arranged marriage?"

Vani nods.

I have to say I'm taken aback by this. She seems so hip and modern, and my prejudice says that arranged marriages are a medieval custom from a time when women didn't get opportunities and weren't allowed to make decisions on their own.

"Did you have to have an arranged marriage?"

"No. I wanted one. After college I asked my parents to find me a suitable husband. We've been married nine years. We're very happy together."

I'm doing my best not to look aghast, to take this little bit of news without judgment. I suppose I thought arranged marriages were happening someplace in the world, I just didn't realize they were going on in a bustling metropolis like London.

"So how did it work? Did you meet him at your wedding or did you meet him ahead of time? Did you have veto power if you didn't like the guy?"

"We met a few times before we decided. I could have said no. The first time we met, both our families were there, but a few times after that we caught a movie together or got dinner just by ourselves."

"So you met and you both liked each other. How long after that was it before you got married?" I ask.

"A few weeks later. We exchanged rings at a big party, like an engagement party, and then four weeks later, there I was getting married in front of three hundred people."

"So what was it like, the wedding?"

"Indian weddings last several days. There are many ceremonies, and lots of drinking, dancing, and partying."

"And outfits!" Gita adds.

"Yes, I changed into many different saris over the course of the wedding," Vani says with a laugh. "Two days before the ceremony, there is what's called the 'making of the groom.' Musicians play music, the groom is washed, and his face is painted—a black dot on the groom's right cheek is supposed to scare away bad spirits. The day before the ceremony, there is the making of the bride. Vegetable dye is painted in a decorative pattern on her hands, lower arms, and palms as well as the backsides of her feet. It sort of looks like a tattoo."

"Why? Does it represent something?"

Vani scrunches her face in thought. "I'm sure it meant something at one time, but now, I think it's just done out of tradition."

"I think it means good luck," Gita says.

"Does it? Well all right then." Vani goes on to describe the actual day of the ceremony, an all-day event starting early in the morning and going until late at night, with hundreds of people, lots of music, and endless numbers of ceremonies and rituals. Even as she explains it to me, I just feel like I have more questions. There is so much about the world I simply have no clue about.

"How could you possibly plan a several-days-long wedding for three hundred people in four weeks?"

"Everyone helps," she says simply with a shrug. Clearly there is no room for arguing about where to hold the wedding or what food to serve. Just a SWAT team of family and friends coming together to make it all work, and so much tradition to follow there is no room for disagreement.

"What are non-Indian British weddings like?" I ask.

"They're a lot like in the United States," Lisa says. I give her a curious look and she explains, "I lived in Chicago for about three years."

"There aren't any differences?"

32

She thinks a moment. "I don't think the ceremonial parts are really different. The main difference would be the reception. In America, it's over just like that," she says with a snap of her fingers. "You're in by seven, out by eleven. Here, you party and drink and talk all night long," she pauses, looking thoughtful. "Also, I would say that in America, weddings are more about showing off your wealth. Here, there are some people who have weddings like that, but mostly weddings are an excuse to get together with friends and party. It's not important how much money you spend or how lavish the ceremony is.".

The five of us keep talking for at least another hour, and I feel content, pleased to be talking and laughing with people from halfway around the world who are at once completely different from me and also a lot alike.

Eventually we say good night, and Tate and I return to our hotel and catch up on our sleep. It's probably a good thing we got so little sleep on the plane because even though it's only 4:00 P.M. in Denver, we fall straight to sleep. I wake up a few hours later and spend a great deal of time lying in the dark despairing that I won't be able to fall back asleep, but eventually I do, and when I wake up in the morning, I feel well rested.

We head to the Tower of London first thing after breakfast. A beefeater (the guard) gives us a tour. He seems very excited to let us know about all the deaths, decapitations, and torture that used to take place here.

After the beefeater's tour we go check out the crown jewels. Even though we're early, the lines to see the jewels are still preposterous, but I don't care, because it's interesting watching the other people in line, and listening to the odd cacophony of dozens of different languages being spoken all around us.

We see the world's largest cut diamond, which is 530 carats, in the Sovereign's Sceptre. I know I should be dazzled by this and all the jeweled crowns, but it all looks like costume jewelry to me. I do think it's cool, however, when a piece of jewelry or a gold salt shaker or goblet isn't there and in its place is a sign, "in use." I love that somewhere a royal person of some sort is salting her food with salt from a gold salt shaker.

After the Tower of London we head to the British Museum, which has the blessed distinction of being free. We take a picture of the Rosetta Stone, stroll around through the Greek and Egyptian artifacts, and after a paltry hour there, our feeling is, "Yeah, yeah, yeah, the art and culture of the dawn of civilization, blah blah blah, I'm ready for a beer."

We have a delicious dinner at Wagamama's, slurping our noodles and murmuring appreciatively over the oversized wooden spoons they've given us to eat our meals with. After dinner we walk around looking for a pub to get a beer at and quickly find a crowded bar with music thumping through the air. We sit at a small table and order Fullers.

"So, what do you think of London so far?" I ask Tate.

"It's okay. It feels a lot like New York, actually."

"I was thinking that same thing! I mean all the movie posters, they're all for American movies. And all the musicals at the theaters are for musicals we can see back home! And it's so expensive here. When I went to Canada, every time I paid for something, I knew it was about forty percent cheaper than what it said it was. Here, we basically have to double the cost of everything, and it's not like anything was cheap to begin with."

We talk a little more about London, but eventually we run out of conversation again. I can't think of single thing to say; I wrack my brain for a conversation topic and I look enviously at the two women sitting next to us who are speaking rapidly in Russian, wishing Tate and I had as much to talk about. I watch as one of the women gets up and walks across the bar. Then I notice that her scarf has fallen off her chair, so I lean down and pick it up and put it back on the chair back.

"Thank you," the woman who's still seated there says in flawless English.

"No problem. Are you guys visiting London?"

"I live here. I've been here for five months. I lived in Australia for ten years before that."

Her friend returns just then and seems irritated that she is talking to us, but I don't care. I'm here as an investigative reporter and I want to gain insight from Russian expats on the state of dating in Britain.

I ask the cranky friend about British men and she rolls her eyes. "British men never hold the door open for you, they don't help you put your coat on, they don't pay for dinner. They never say they'll call because it's like they're scared you'll sue them for breach of promise if they don't call exactly when they say they will."

"So have you sworn off Brits entirely?"

"I get my romance when I travel to Italy. I try to take a trip there each summer."

"Yeah, what's so great about Italian men?"

"They're more romantic. They say the most beautiful things. They're lies, but I don't care. British men, Australian men, American men—they're all too reserved."

I, for one, would rather put my own coat on and open the door myself and be with an honest guy than a guy who tells me romantic lies to get me into bed, but I'm intrigued to find a woman who prefers compliments to commitments.

I ask the other woman her thoughts. She says she's engaged to an Australian who is moving here in a couple months to be with her. As she talks, her friend is text messaging like crazy on her phone, her thumbs flying over the tiny keypad.

I continue asking the two of them questions for a few minutes. The woman who likes Italian lies gets immediately bored when she's not the object of the conversation and she goes back to text messaging whenever I ask her friend a question. Then Italian lies woman abruptly grabs her friend and announces that she just got the message from so and so about where some people are getting together, and she practically drags her friend out the door before they've even finished their drinks, so in a hurry is she. The engaged friend gives a polite nod good-bye to us, but the Italian lies woman acts like we don't exist.

I'm disappointed that they're leaving before I can learn anything about Australian or Russian wedding traditions. I have a sneaking suspicion the two women would still be talking to us if Tate and I were cute guys and not young women. And I have to say I hate when women treat each other like that.

Within seconds of their departure, two guys snap up their table. The cuter, darker-haired guy says, "Hello."

"Hey," Tate says.

"Hello." I nod and offer a smile.

"Americans! What brings you to the U.K.?"

"We're traveling all over, seeing the world," Tate says.

"Traveling all over! Seeing the world!" he says in a jokey tone, an expression of mock horror on his face. "Why would you go to all the trouble and expense? You could just watch a video. Virtual tourism."

"This is the age of the Internet, for God's sake. You don't have to even leave your living room these days," the blond guy adds.

The guys are cute, though they aren't really my type. The blond guy is too tall, with a light wispy down of hair encircling his head. I can still see far too much of the little boy he once was to have any romantic designs on him. The darker-haired guy is definitely the one with sex appeal of the two, though his skin looks like he's smoked a few too many cigarettes and logged a few too many hours in a pub. He's got that kind of smile that suggests everything he says—whether it's about football, fish and chips, the weather—is really about sex.

"If we'd just watched a video at home we wouldn't be talking to you fine gentlemen, would we now?" I say. "Anyway, I'm a travel writer, so I need to do firsthand research and come up with my own opinions and impressions. It seems like most travel writers are older guys. The world needs a young woman's perspective on things."

"A writer," the dark-haired one says. "Are you famous? Should we know your name?"

"I'm not famous, but you should know my name. I'm Jadie and this is Tate."

"J.D., Tate, it is a pleasure to meet you. Right then, my name is Mark and this is David. So, J.D., tell me, what does J.D. stand for?"

"No, it's Jadie like J-A-D-I-E," I say.

"Jadie? That's an interesting name."

"My parents . . . what can I say, they're original. If you knew them . . . I lucked out with Jadie, that's all I'm saying." I stop talking and we spend about a microsecond just staring at each other. There are times when I simply can't bear silence, and this is one of them, so I continue on. "Having an unusual name makes me fit right in to Boulder, Colorado, which is where we're from. I went to this party one time, and the first thing I heard was one mother asking another mother, 'Why is Seth crying?' The first mom said, 'Mercury won't let him clean his room.' I thought she was saying that, you know, Mercury was in retrograde so the signs of the zodiac were hindering him getting his toys in order or something, but it turns out that Mercury was the name of this other little kid who kept bothering Seth. Then I met the rest of the kids at the party. Their names were Rain, Dakota, and Phoenix. One out of the five kids there had a regular name, the rest were all, well, very Boulder."

"Boulder, huh? I've been through there many times on my way to Aspen," Mark says. "It's a beautiful place." We all nod at each other for a few seconds, agreeing with him. Then Mark points to the wave-line tattoo Tate has encircling her arm. "What if you decide you don't like this anymore someday? It's not like a hair color you can wash out or a piece of jewelry you can take off, is it then?" he says with that teasing smile of his. "What if you get bored with it?"

"Well then, I guess I'm screwed," she says, smiling. I can't decide if she's attracted to him. She usually goes for scruffier-looking guys who look like wounded birds in need of a good hearty meal and a warm place to sleep. She likes patchouli-smelling, potsmoking underachievers with the attention span of a narcoleptic kitten. It's been even longer since Tate has had a boyfriend than it's been since I've had one, so I'm all for Tate finding a little romance on this trip.

Tate doesn't obsess about finding a guy like I do, or at least she doesn't talk about it. She just says she and a guy might "hook up." Hooking up is a nonbinding deal, the acknowledgement of mutual attraction without promises about tomorrow, something that lasts only as long as everything is always fun and feels good.

The only serious boyfriend I've known Tate to have was one of those guys you know from the second you meet them are no good for your friend, but since your friend is insane over him, there's nothing you can say or do.

Tate and I were both twenty at the time. I was a junior in college. Tate and I were roommates my sophomore and junior year, an experiment we decided to end before we ended up hating each other. In almost every way, Tate is the easiest person on the planet to live with. Me? I'm another story. I'd get grouchy or tired and when we lived together I'd occasionally take my mood out on Tate, who has some kind of force field that keeps negativity from bothering her.

What made the living arrangement untenable was that the easygoing quality that made her so nice to be around also applied to her feelings toward dishes and junk and dirt in general. The house could be a putrid cesspool, and Tate wouldn't notice or care. Nagging her to do her dishes did no good, so I would just quietly seethe as I constantly cleaned up after her. When we finally got our own places, I didn't care about the pigsty Tate lived in, and our friendship was magically restored.

But Eric entered the picture before Tate and I figured out that while we were meant to be friends, we weren't meant to be roommates.

Eric was a friend of one of the waiters at the Greenhouse. He had long brown hair he pulled back into a ponytail, a strong chin, thick lips, and a powerful build.

The first time I met him, it was eight o'clock in the morning. I'd been up late the night before studying, and I hadn't gotten nearly enough sleep, but through a Herculean effort, I was trying to get my ass out the door to make my nine o'clock class. Every day I kicked myself for signing up for a class that early. Between studying, working, and partying, a 9:00 A.M. class to me was like sunshine to a vampire.

I staggered downstairs, thinking only of coffee. The world would be righted and all would be well if I could just get my hands on some coffee.

And there he was, sitting on my couch drinking beer. Tate was asleep beside him.

"Excuse me, but who are you?" I asked.

Tate woke, blinking as her eyes adjusted to the light. "Hi."

"Tate?" I said in a you'd-better-get-over-here-and-tell-me-what's-going-on tone.

She stood and padded over to me. I proceeded to make coffee, forcefully spooning the coffee grinds into the filter, crunch crunch crunch.

"We hooked up last night," she said quietly. "He's a friend of Angel's. He's going to be in Boulder for a while."

"Fine, but why is he drinking beer on my couch at eight o'clock in the morning?"

"We had some dinner and drank some beer at Angel's last night, and then Eric had to go to work. He works the night shift at the 7-11. I kept him company while he worked at the store. We just talked and talked. Even though we were having a lot of fun, he was pretty tired and he needed to take some speed so he could stay up all night. He needs a few beers so he can come down and get some sleep. He's got a kind soul, don't you think?"

Naturally, I wanted to throttle her. He *had* to take some speed? He *needs* a few beers to come down? Girlfriend, run! Run in the opposite direction as fast as you can! What are you thinking?

But Tate doesn't have my squeamishness when it comes to drugs. She believes drugs can be used in a mystical spiritual way, like Indians taking peyote to commune with the Earth and the gods in an altered state. When I think of drugs, I think about crack whores, broken dreams, AIDS, jail time, degradation, and nearly lifeless bodies passed out in condemned buildings with broken windows and stained ceilings just like any good American raised on PBS specials. I knew my arguments against Eric would do nothing but make Tate pissed at me. So I said, "Well, he's cute."

"Isn't he?"

I could see she really liked him. She wasn't one to casually fall for just any guy.

Over the next six months, Tate and Eric were inseparable. After getting to know him better, I did have to admit he had more going for him than his looks. He had a good sense of humor and he knew how to tell an entertaining story. Plus, he was an exceptional guitar player. He'd play at barbeques and parties, low-profile stuff, and I'd watch Tate watch him, her eyes so filled with love. I ached to have someone look at me like that. I wanted there to be a person in the world who looked at me with such loving, such longing.

During the time Tate dated Eric, she opened up emotionally in a way she normally didn't do. She was happier than I'd ever known her to be, and so I was happy for her. Then, one day I got home from working at the Greenhouse, sweaty and food-stained and tired, and found Tate weeping in a crumpled heap on the couch.

"Tate sweetie, what is it? What's wrong?"

She lifted a tear-stained sheaf of paper ripped from a notebook, its edges frayed.

Tate,
   It's been fun. The mountains call. See you around sometime.

                              Later, Eric

"That bastard!" I was furious. Tate loved him, and this was how he treated her? *It's been fun?* "I can't believe you gave him a place to stay for six months and he just leaves with this pathetic note, not even a real good-bye."

For the next several weeks Tate was depressed (though she wouldn't use that word, she'd say "bummed out") and even when the depression lifted, she was different than she'd been before Eric had come into her life. She was more guarded, more cautious.

She has never, not once in seven years since then, gotten serious about another guy. She'll flirt with guys, "hook up" with them, date casually, but she's careful now not to love too much.

Tate and I spend the next couple of hours drinking beer and talking and flirting with Mark and David and generally having a great time. Eventually Tate and I tell them we have to get going.

"How do we get to the nearest tube station?" I ask them.

"Do you know where the Virgin Records is?"

"No."

"Do you know where the Hard Rock Café is?"

"No."

"You do know you're in London?"

"Yes, and that's about all we know."

They give us directions to the nearest tube station, and as Tate and I walk there in the cool night air, I feel happy. Hopeful. I haven't met the guy of my dreams yet, but Europe is, after all, a pretty big place.

3

Paris, France

After another day of sightseeing in London—we visit Buckingham Palace, which is all incredibly ornate ceilings, dour paintings of lords and ladies, furniture with gold trim, and preposterously large chandeliers—we take a three-hour high-speed train ride to Paris in the evening and find a room in the Marais area, not far from Notre Dame.

Our room is off in this tiny little hallway with only one other room. The small hallway is completely dark—we have to switch the light on ourselves, and it goes off automatically before we can figure out how to work the lock to actually get in the room. We turn the light on again, struggle with the lock some more, and finally manage to let ourselves in.

The room itself isn't fancy, but it's clean. We get a good night of sleep and in the morning we take turns showering.

I'm done first and I'm halfheartedly flipping through our guidebook when Tate emerges from the bathroom wrapped in a white towel, her long wet hair flowing around her as she combs it out. Tate's beauty regimen consists of brushing her teeth, showering regularly, and washing her face. That's it. No special hair conditioners, no skin moisturizers, no make-up. She'll wash with whatever soap or shampoo is lying around, she'll comb her long hair out and let it dry naturally, wearing it loose or pinning it back in some kind of ponytail or bun. Her long dark lashes don't need mascara, and her lips are naturally a soft rose color.

It's disgusting.

We have a simple breakfast of café au laits, croissants, and fromage blanc (a cross between sour cream and yogurt). We buy a couple of bottles of water, which we put into our day bags along with our camera and guidebook, then we head over to Notre Dame and take a few million pictures. Then we walk through the Latin Quarter, which has millions of cafés and restaurants serving cuisines from around the world.

I love how beautiful everything is—all the balconies adorned with flowers, carvings on buildings everywhere we look, the narrow, winding streets. Every step we take, every fountain, every street sign, seems picture-worthy, and we are photo-snapping machines.

After we regain our strength by resting at a café and drinking espressos, I tell Tate I'd like to head out to the Champs-Elysées and the Arc de Triomphe. She's up for it, so we head that way. As we walk, we come upon an enormous building. We wonder aloud what it could be and then turn the corner and see the sign that says this is the Louvre. We walk into a courtyard, and my jaw drops. The outside of the building is adorned with sculptures, façades, and elaborate decorations. We walk into the main courtyard area, the one with the famous glass pyramids, and I'm just staggered.

"This place just goes on and on!" Tate says.

"We're going to have to come back here tomorrow with some seriously rested feet to get through the inside of the museum."

Eventually nature demands that we put our awe on

hold and find a bathroom right quick. We walk all through the public areas of the Louvre to find one. They are very secretive about where they keep their bathrooms, but we finally find it, only to discover it costs 50 Euro cents to use it, and we don't have any change whatsoever. It burns my butt that I have to pay for bottled water and then pay for the privilege to pee it out.

"Well, crap. Should we get some lunch and hope we get some change back?" Tate says.

"Sure. I guess. We'll just eat quick and I'll keep my legs crossed."

We hasten to the food court, which offers much swankier food than food courts at malls in the states. We go to a Mediterranean place and get falafel sandwiches. After we eat we hustle back to the bathroom. It's crazy how much time is spent when you're on the road trying to do things that take no effort whatsoever back home—eating, drinking unpolluted water, finding a bathroom you can actually use.

We leave the museum and walk through the expansive Tuileries Gardens, which are jam packed full of statues and fountains and flowers. These Parisians, they don't skimp on art and beauty.

Next we walk down the Champs-Elysées, the avenue linking the Arc de Triomphe to the Place de la Concorde that's lined with stylish shops, cafés, showrooms, and, unfortunately but predictably, fast food joints.

There are a ton of hip, good-looking young Frenchmen as far as the eye can see. Naturally, they pay no attention to us whatsoever. As we're walking, a middle-aged man says, "*C'est un beau jour, n'est-ce pas?*" *It's a nice day, isn't it?*

"*Oui, très joli,*" I say. It takes me far too much effort to get this remedial phrase from the recesses of my brain from my years of high school French.

I thought I was saying, "yes, it's very pretty," but apparently I was saying, "Please follow me and grope me to your heart's desire," because at once he's all over me, touching me, walking close behind. Tate and I walk faster. He keeps telling me how pretty I am, and saying other things I don't understand.

"*Au revoir, au revoir*. We have to go," I say, but this in no way detours him.

"Leave us alone!" Tate yells in her best daytime talk show don't-you-be-getting-in-my-face tone, but it's no good. He keeps trying to put his hand on my arm and just when I dodge one stroke, there is another one of his hands to elude. Finally I yank Tate into one of the hip clothing stores and we race back to the changing room. After a few minutes, I peek an eyeball out over the dressing room door. I don't see a lecherous Frenchman, just a highly irritated French woman, who is as skinny as a sharpened pencil, teetering on high heels. She says something angrily to me I don't understand, something like, "*Le blah blah blah.*" I smile cheerily at her. "*Bonjour, bonjour! Merci, merci!*" I call stupidly as Tate and I bolt out of the store.

We continue ambling down the Champs-Elysées and I observe this: all of the women in France are well dressed, and it reminds me of being back at the office with my coworkers who are always wearing expensive clothes that they can put together with just the right accessories, while I am a walking Fashion Don't.

I try to not be totally fashion inept; I've even tried to read fashion magazines, but it's useless. Season after season, it all looks the same to me.

I lucked out when it came to fashion in high school. It was the era of slacker fashion—a lot of mismatching of clothes bought strategically from thrift stores. That was a look I could manage. It was the days of T-shirts over long-sleeved cotton shirts. Jean jackets and flannels paired with Converse shoes. The jean jackets and flannel look was a boundary-crossing ensemble worn by nonconformists and school-activity enthusiasts alike (but only by the latter when they were getting down to the dirty jobs like building floats for homecoming). For the sports crowd, which I most assuredly was not, it was definitely Umbros—even off the field. For the student council type it was Guess jeans and body suits and even vests. (!) Sometimes being unfashionable has its advantages, though—there are no pictures in existence of me sporting the junior high look of stone-washed peg-leg jeans or stretch pants with double layered/colored socks, for example, thank the good Lord.

But at work, my coworkers wear uncomfortable shoes that actually match their outfits. I try to do the same (albeit with comfortable shoes), and yet I fail miserably every time. I try to keep things simple: there is a lot of I-want-to-be-a-writer-and-not-a-corporate-slut mourning garb black in my wardrobe, and you'd think it'd be so easy to match black pants to black socks to black shoes, right? But somehow I can never quite get the black on my pants to be the same black as my socks or the black on my shoes. It is profoundly pathetic, and yet this is my sad reality.

I thought I could escape feeling like a dweeb by coming to Europe, but it turns out I'm still a dweeb here and all the sleekly dressed Europeans know it.

After visiting the Arc de Triomphe we return to our hotel by subway and rest our feet for a little while, then set out to find ourselves some dinner. We return to the Latin Quarter, and now it no longer seems as quaint as it did this morning. It seems touristy and like every place is trying to screw us out of money. We finally stop at one place just because, even after resting, our feet and legs are weary with travel, and there is something on the menu we can eat—salad with toasted goat cheese.

We sit at a table outside and watch a cat curled up on a truck parked nearby. Our waiter seems extravagantly bored. We order a bottle of wine and as he opens it, he casually tosses the wrapper underneath the car parked on the road just in front of us. With the cork he makes like he's going to throw it at the cat before flinging it, too, on the street in front of us. His attitude is off-putting, but the guidebooks have said you just leave a couple of coins for waiters in France—no more than fifty Euro cents or a single Euro for most meals—since a twenty percent "value added tax" is added to every bill (it would add value if the waitstaff weren't surly, is what I think). The food is just okay and I'm mad at us for wasting one of our dinners in Paris at a place with touristy, so-so food. When we're done eating, I'm more than ready to get going, but our waiter has apparently disappeared off the face of the earth. After several minutes of Tate and I staring at each other in silence, Tate eyes the candle on our table and says, "Maybe if we set the napkins on fire he'll come."

"If that doesn't work, we can set the tablecloth on fire, get a real bonfire going."

We spend several minutes devising ways to get the waiter to notice us, until at last he comes by of his own accord. We practically leap on him, begging for the check, which he finally, finally brings.

Tate and I walk along the Seine and decide on impulse to take a moonlight cruise to see the City of Lights all lit up.

We float down the Seine and see the spiky fingers of Notre Dame's flying buttresses illuminated against the black night. The Eiffel Tower puts on a flashing light show, the white-yellow lights spinning and flashing like batons being twirled in a parade.

As we cruise along, I tear up. I love Tate more than anybody, but I'd really like to share this night with a guy. I want to hold his hand and exchange kisses that express longing that will be fulfilled later behind closed doors.

My dating history wasn't always so bleak, but it started out that way. I didn't date at all in high school because I was Weird Girl. I'm not sure if every last guy at my high school thought I was too weird to date, but I never gave them the chance. I tried to never speak in class, and if I had to be alone in the cafeteria for some reason I brought a book to ward off threats of socializing.

In college, after I finally got over my crippling fear of talking to people, I fell in love with Will. At least, I thought I loved him. Maybe I just wanted to be in love. Or maybe it was just that the sex was so good it made me delirious with gratitude.

We met when we were waiting outside our professor's office for help for an upcoming test. The class was called something like Math for Complete Idiots. Even though it was the easiest math class you could take to fulfill the one math credit you needed to graduate, it was still too hard for me. It turned out Will was an English major, and the two of us commiserated over being right-brained people forced to take a left-brain kind of class.

After we spoke with our professor, Will asked if I wanted to get a cup of coffee with him and I said I did. We talked for six hours straight. We saw each other every day after that. After three weeks, we lost our virginities together in an awkward, mechanical, and very brief coupling. But we set off to learn how to have good sex, with lots and lots of practice. (It's frankly a wonder we managed to continue getting decent grades and didn't end up getting kicked out of school, so determined were we to explore this new world.)

We dated on and off for three years. We'd have these fiery, accusatory break-ups and amazing get-back-together sex, and what finally ended things between us was that during one of our time-outs from each other, he found another girl. Sometimes I wondered if things could have worked out between us if we'd been older when we met. But then, a couple of years back, I ran into him at the grocery store and he invited me out for drinks. It was fun to catch up with him, but as we talked, he griped about everything under the sun. I remembered that he'd always been a complainer, always seeing the dark side of any situation. Will had a lot going for him, but Mr. Right he wasn't.

Then came sexy, muscular, bad boy Tony. Tony had just moved to Colorado from New York and he had no friends in the area. We met the day he moved in next door to me. I saw him struggling to get a table up the stairs and asked him if he needed help unloading his things. He eagerly accepted my offer of assistance. He didn't have much furniture, so we got his stuff upstairs in no time. All the while we talked and laughed and when we were done moving his stuff upstairs, I volunteered to help him unpack. We ended up spending the rest of the day together. We went grocery shopping for food and he made spaghetti for dinner, and just doing all these mundane things seemed like fun because I was with him. It was a great first date.

By our second date, however, I was beginning to discover a neediness in Tony that was draining. Because Tony had no other friends in the area, he wanted me to keep him constantly entertained. He e-mailed me and called me at work all the time, and when I told him that he needed to cut down on the interruptions because I actually had work to do, he got petulant and moody.

Worst of all, because we lived next door to each other, there was never any escaping him. He could hear me unlocking the door to my apartment, so he knew the second I came home from work and would come running over and knock on my door. I couldn't exactly pretend I wasn't home. I would tell him that I needed a night to myself to read or write, and he would say that we should go to a café so we could read or write *together*. He didn't always wear me down, sometimes I managed to stand up for myself, but he was such a persuasive salesman that I found myself getting sucked into doing things his way too much of the time.

I finally broke up with Tony after a month—it's not a very long period of time, technically, but it felt like an eternity. Getting out of that relationship was like hitting the surface of a pool after I'd been under for too long—I could breathe again. In hindsight, I felt like an idiot for being in such a relationship, even if it didn't last long. Like, *oh, relationships aren't supposed to be exhausting? Each partner is supposed to support the other rather than one person constantly bending to the will of the other?* Obvious stuff, but sometimes, when you're struggling to convince yourself you should stay in a bad relationship, you can forget that.

Fortunately, Tony moved back to New York three months later, before either of us started dating anyone new, sparing us from the highly awkward situation of having to listen to each other having sex with other people through the adjoining apartment walls. In fact, I only ran into him a couple of times during all those weeks; I'm pretty sure he was hiding from me, and I couldn't have been happier about it.

Then there was Zach, a.k.a. the guy I thought I was going to marry, the last guy I've had sex with. (And that was a year ago! Oh the inhumanity!) We dated for two years. The beginning was great, as beginnings usually are.

We met at work. From the second day he worked there he would come to my desk and flirt with me. He had blue eyes and black hair and I was immediately attracted to him.

As we chatted throughout our workdays, he let it slip that he was a good cook. He said he wanted to prove it to me, and he asked me over to his place for a home-cooked meal.

That was our first date, and we were with each other constantly. Literally constantly because we worked together until Zach found a higher-paying job elsewhere.

I don't know where exactly things started going wrong. We started having little fights here and there. Things started to get worse and worse until eventually I found myself irritated by the way he talked, breathed, chewed, slept, and greeted me when he got home from work at the end of the day. When absolutely everything your significant other does has a nails-down-a-chalkboard quality to it, you know it's time to GET OUT. The breakup came when it came time to renew our lease. He looked at me and asked if I wanted to sign a new lease. "What do you think?" I asked. "I think no." And that was it. It scared me that I had thought I had wanted to marry someone I ultimately didn't even miss very much. I mean I cried and I was depressed, but it was because I felt like a failure for getting into yet another stupid relationship and I was doing that whole angst-filled what's-wrong-with-me? lament, not because I was upset about losing him.

Naturally, between the more serious relationships were the many first dates I thought were promising but then I never saw or heard from the guy again, despite promises he'd call. Worse was when the first dates became second, then third, then fourth dates, and then abruptly, without explanation, the phone calls stopped coming.

I also had a short-lived fling with this new agey guy

who called himself Native American even though he was only one-thirty-second Cherokee. I remember coming home to his apartment where he'd left his radio on all day while he was at work. He didn't have any pets so I asked him if he'd left it on accidentally. He said he left it on for his spirit who followed him around. (My question: if it followed him around, what was it doing at home all day?) The problem with Preston, besides his ridiculous name, was that he had erection issues that wouldn't acknowledge but had plenty of creative excuses for ("I just think we should get to know more about each other before we sleep together." Dude, I'm lying here naked, legs splayed, and you're wearing a condom. You know more about me than nearly everyone I've met in my entire life.) He'd be hard, things would be going fine, and then as soon as he'd be about to come inside me his penis turtled. It was like the sun hiding beneath the clouds when I was trying to get a suntan.

Eventually I broke it off with him—and I had plenty of creative excuses for why we needed to call it quits.

In the morning, we get veggie crêpes with cheese from a sidewalk crêpery stand and munch them contentedly outside Centre Pompidou. I suspect we won't have time on this trip to actually go inside the modern art museum—it's closed right now—so I content myself with snapping a few pictures of its famous exterior, with the boldly colored exposed ducting and glass elevators snaking down along the outside. Then we head over to the Louvre.

I am thrilled to be in the greatest art museum in the world, and more thrilled to see some of my favorite art of all time, like the statue of Nike of Samothrace—I will never get over how much movement and energy can seem to emanate from what is essentially nothing more than a slab of rock. We see Michelangelo's slaves, and about four hundred thousand religious paintings—more Madonna and Child paintings than you can shake a stick at. One problem is that all the descriptions about the paintings are in French, and my French skills aren't nearly strong enough to read them. I know for a fact a lot more people speak English than French, and I think this insistence on having all the signs exclusively in French is *très* rude.

Suddenly, the leisurely pace Tate and I have been admiring the art at is thwarted by a mob of people who nearly trample us like the bulls of Pamplona in their determined haste, and we are essentially carried down the corridor on a wave of tourists.

Tate looks at me, eyebrows furrowed with confusion.

"I think we're getting close to the Mona Lisa," I say. And sure enough, eventually we're spit out of the hallway into a crowd of people jockeying around the small painting. We squint over their heads to try and get a view. All the polite hushed tones that people had been using while admiring the Madonna and Child paintings are gone. Now people are elbowing each other, mumbling loudly, snapping pictures, and stepping on other tourists' feet in an effort to get a closer view.

"I don't really get the fuss," Tate says in a whisper.

"I don't really either," I confess in a similarly muted tone. We stare at the painting for a couple of minutes, hoping to divine what precisely the big deal is and feeling stupid for not knowing already.

We tour the museum for another hour, until my attitude becomes, "Rubens? Vermeer? Raphael? Who cares?" All these great works of art are blurring together in my head and I can no longer tell Boticelli from Bozo the Clown.

So we leave the museum after a fairly pathetically short period of time and grab some lunch at a sidewalk café that gives me a great vantage point from which to boy-watch. Every French guy under the age of thirty-five seems to be slim. In the United States, you have your pump-iron-at-the-gym brawny guys, your big guys, your little guys, and everything in between. In France, your choices are slender, slender, or slender. I usually don't like dating guys who are skinnier than I am, but the French boys have such style, I could definitely see myself making an exception. It's not that they're all decked out in designer fashion, but the way they put a sweater and jeans together and top it with expertly tousled hair is *très* yummy.

Our waiter today is much nicer than our waiter the night before, and we don't even have to set napkins or tablecloths on fire to get our check.

"What now?" I ask Tate, when our stomachs are sated and the last crumbs from our plates have been cleared.

"Can we do something that doesn't involve walking? Maybe we could be teleported somewhere."

"We could take the subway to the Eiffel Tower. Only minimal walking will be involved."

"Okay. But I may be demanding a piggyback ride through Paris to get back to our hotel if any more than a few steps are necessary to get anywhere."

When we get to the Eiffel Tower, we snap about a thousand pictures of ourselves with the Tower in the background, but we skip the ride up in the interest of saving a few bucks.

After sitting in the park around the Eiffel Tower for a while, I convince Tate to walk around this side of town, and we find *rue Cler*, a street that is closed to cars and has dozens of fruit and vegetable vendors, *fromageries* (cheese shops), and bakeries. I imagine myself living here, working as a writer, and buying fresh bread, cheese, milk, and produce every day rather than stocking up on frozen and canned foods once a week. Each night I'd eat meals that were so fresh the taste would dance on my tongue and dinner would be an event rather than a chore of scarfing down tasteless fast food while watching reruns on TV. In France I'd live a life where I'd carefully choose the food I bought rather than glancing at something and throwing it in my cart, going through life in a perpetual mad dash, like a game show player who gets a shopping spree with only three minutes to fill her cart before the buzzer rings, game over.

The next day we visit the catacombs. To get to them, we need to take a spiral staircase down sixty feet. In the late eighteenth century, Paris's cemeteries were overflowing. To avoid spreading disease from an excess of dead bodies unleashed on the city, authorities exhumed the bones of the buried and relocated them in the tunnels of quarries that were no longer in use. For a mile, there is nothing more than stacks and stacks of bones of the dead, along with signs encouraging us to reflect on our mortality. One of the signs says to consider that you may not be around to go to bed tonight, and if you do, you may not make it until morning. *I have to make it until morning*, I think to the sign, to the stack of people who have been reduced to bones and are now nothing more than a tourist attraction. *There are so many places I need to see, so many things I have to do.*

These thoughts are depressing me, but I'm abruptly irritated by the droning voice of a guide with a tour group ahead of us who makes me unable to follow my thoughts, negative though they may be. It's probably best if I don't stress myself out with thoughts of dying before morning comes, but I'm annoyed that I can't tune out this guy's voice. A little kid who is part of the tour group looks bored, and he puts his foot up on the wall as if he's going to shimmy up it like Spiderman. The soft rock crumbles under his feet and I imagine a cave-in, all of us trapped beneath the earth with the skeletons of five million people. I'm about to leap across the room and pull the kid back when his father finally notices his shenanigans and reigns him in. My heart is actually racing from my imaginary rescue—saving the world from a five-year-old and a bunch of dead people. It is clear that within me lives the soul of a true hero.

In the afternoon we tour the Musée d'Orsay. The museum is an Impressionism-lovers' fantasy come true. Lining its walls are the works of Manet, Monet, Renoir, Degas, Van Gogh, Cézanne, and Seurat, and not a rinky-dink one or two paintings from each of them that you get at many museums, but a solid body of work, including many pieces I've never seen. I love that I'm in Paris, the place where these very artists created a movement that rocked the art world.

I'm busy discovering a painting by Monet I've never seen before when Tate comes up to me and says, "Watch out for the guy in red. He stinks so bad he'll make your eyes water."

I assure her I will take precautions to avoid Stinky Man, and I point to the painting and tell her about how Monet's love of water not only influenced his style and subject matter—the liquid meadows and wave-like pulses—but even his brush strokes were watery. Then we come to a Van Gogh and I tell her about how Van Gogh was a preacher in a mining town before living off his brother for ten years, struggling as an artist and only selling one or two paintings in his lifetime, and she says, "Enough already. I get it: you went to college. I didn't. All right already."

I'm hurt by this, and frankly surprised. "Tate, I didn't mean to be showing off. Was that how I came off?"

She shrugs.

"I was just sharing stuff I thought was interesting. I'm sorry if I offended you."

"I'm not offended. I just think . . . how you're talking, it's kind of . . ."

"Pretentious?" As soon as the word is out of my mouth I want to dive after it, throw it back into my mouth, and gobble it up. Of course I'd have to go and tell her what vocabulary word she was looking for at the exact moment she was telling me to cool it with my fancy book learning.

"I just want to enjoy the paintings, okay?"

"Okay," I say, but I'm bummed. For me, part of enjoying the pictures is talking about what I see in them and hearing what other people see in them and how it affects them. If somebody knows what the artist was doing and thinking and experiencing when he painted it, I like to hear about it. For the rest of our tour through the museum, I feel stifled and irritated by the educational divide between Tate and me.

Tate is easily smart enough to have gone to college. Maybe not an Ivy League school, but a state school or community college for sure. She just never had the drive or desire to go. She never talks about dreaming of a different life. She doesn't love waitressing, but she doesn't hate it, and she never talks about wanting a different career. In some ways I wish I were more like her—happy with my lot in life and not constantly wishing for something different, something more. I haven't yet learned how to have goals and aspirations while simultaneously being happy with where I am now. I suspect this is a lesson I'll be learning over and over throughout my life.

The next day, we take a quick train ride from Paris to Versailles. Versailles is unfathomable in its enormity. The pamphlet we pick up at the start of the tour says that at one time the land Versailles occupied was bigger than the current size of Paris—7,800 hectares. Now it's down to a mere 700 hectares, which is still humongous beyond belief. We walk through several rooms of paintings of people I don't know and have never heard of. There is so much art—room after room is covered in statues and carvings and there are paintings on every ceiling and hanging ponderously from every wall—it's overwhelming. It's an art onslaught. Buckingham Palace is puny in comparison to this place.

We walk through the gardens, then come to a little village of adorable thatch-roofed houses that was constructed on the property for Louis XV and that Marie Antoinette used to escape the hubbub of the palace. We walk and walk and come to Grand Trianon, a smaller palace Louis XIV had built so *he* could get away from the main palace. After Versailles, it, too, seems small, although logically I know it's huge compared to a normal person's house.

We wander through the gardens for a while more, and then the pain in my back that had been a dull ache becomes piercing and shrill, my feet begin to throb, and I become tired and grumpy and want nothing more than to rest, eat, and drink.

On the train back to Paris, our brains hurt from information and sensory overload. When we arrive in the city, it's all we can do to stagger to a café and order café au laits.

I write in my journal while Tate people-watches. I've been a journaler since I was nine. I often go back and read my diaries from when I was in high school or college because those journals are hilarious. I never read my adult journals, though, except for the travel diaries. Since graduating college, my journals are filled with more or less endless rants about how much I hate my job and how so and so did this at work today and it really pissed me off, etc. I write in my journal when I travel because I want to remember every second of the trip and relive it again and again. I write in my journal after a sucky day at work because I just need to get the negative feelings off my chest. I don't want to relive that, just purge it.

I've written several pages when a gorgeous French couple enters, arguing about something. They steal my attention completely. He's wearing a weathered brown leather jacket over a white t-shirt and jeans. She's more dressed up in a brown leather skirt, brown nylons, and brown leather boots that are the exact shade of her skirt (I can never exactly match my accessories to my clothes. How do some women do it? How?!) and a gold blouse. Her straight blond hair is cut short, cradling her chin like a person cupping her face with both hands. She has small dimples and a tiny nose; her expression is petulant. She's not classically pretty, but the way she moves, the way she flicks her wrist ever so slightly when she's finished making a point, making her gold bracelet glimmer in the sunlight—I can't take my eyes off her except for brief moments when I watch her boyfriend. Despite my taking French in high school, I can only pick up odd phrases from their conversation here and there. *"Non non!"* (*no no!*—years of French classes to translate that—years well spent, clearly), *"Je suis désolée mais . . ."* (*I am sorry but . . .*), *"Je mettrai vôtre singe dans une boîte."* (*I will put your monkey in a box*—surely that can't be right?) Then, all at once, their squabbling subsides. One of her dimples reveals itself, then the other, then he's smiling too, and they are clearly teasing each other. He scooches his metal chair around the small round table so he's right next to her. In moments, he plunges his tongue into her mouth and at once a tumultuous storm of emotion rages through me, and I'm not even sure exactly what it is I'm feeling, though jealousy is definitely part of the mix. They are so obviously in love. Every glance, every smile, every word they express is imbued with special meaning, extra weight and heft.

I always wanted to have a café au lait in a sidewalk café in Paris. At this moment, I am making that fantasy come true. But now I'd like to add an addendum to that dream: I'd like to have a café au lait at an outdoor café in Paris and between sips of coffee I'd like to make out with a romantic Frenchman in a lavish public display of affection.

A girl can dream.

Tate and I actually manage to find a vegetarian restaurant near our hotel, and after a delicious dinner we hit a club to hear live music. Being the nerds we are, Tate and I get there unfashionably early and have a few drinks and talk until the place finally starts filling up. More and more people pack the place as the band plays its first few songs. The busier the bar gets, the smokier it gets. I have sensitive eyes that start to tear, and for a moment, I miss Boulder, where smoking isn't allowed in public places.

Two women approach us and say something in French. They've mistaken us for being French! We've passed as Europeans!

"I'm sorry, we don't speak French. *Non parlez Français,*" I shout to be heard over the din.

"*Ah bon.* Can we share zees table with you?"

"*Oui, oui,*" I say, making room.

It's too loud to talk to anyone as the band jams, but when the band takes a break, I introduce Tate and myself to the women, who tell us their names are Adèle and Heloise.

"You are American?" Adèle asks.

"We're from Colorado," Tate says, nodding.

"No way! I leeve in Colorado!"

"Really? Where?" I say.

"In Denver. I leeve there two years now." She has a gorgeous accent, but her English is wonderful.

"We're from Boulder. That's so crazy. I can't believe you live in Colorado. Are you just back in France for a vacation?"

"*Oui.* I went to Marseilles where I grew up to visit my family, and then I take the train to Paris, where I moved when I was seventeen. I leeved here until I moved to America."

I love how she pronounces "family," like "fam-i-*lee*," the "lee" lilting up into the air excitedly. Everything about her is animated and expressive.

"So why did you move to Denver?" I ask.

"Love," she says with a laugh. "There was a boy I knew when I was growing up that I had not seen him for twenty years—he moved to the United States when he was a teenager. Then, two years ago, he came home for a wedding. We fell in love that night."

I ask her to tell me more about that night. If I can't have romance, I'll sustain myself on stories of people who do.

"It was the most romantic night of my life. We danced in the moonlight, we drank champagne. The food was wonderful, the music was wonderful, everything was wonderful. We spent that night and the next day together, but then he had to return to America. A few weeks later I had my vacation, so I went to the States to see him. On my third day there he asked me if I wanted to move to the United States and I said yes. In a few months I left my job in Paris and moved to Colorado. Two months after that we got engaged and two months after that we got married."

"That's so romantic!" Tate says.

And it is. To fall in love in one night, to be so sure of that love that you'd leave not only your job but your country after only a handful of days together . . . I long for a love like that.

I congratulate Adèle on her marriage and ask her about her wedding and how weddings in France are different from weddings in America.

"I got married in America. In France, you do not have a maid of honor and several bridesmaids, you have one or two people who are witnesses. I asked a woman I had met in America if she would be our witness. She did not understand this. She was confused, I was confused. Then my husband told me that in America you have a bridesmaid, not a witness. Okay. But still there was confusion. The woman made a very big deal about what color dress she should wear. I said, 'wear whatever dress you like. I don't care.' But no, she kept asking about it, telling me I had to pick. In America, I learned, the bride picks for the bridesmaids, but in France, they can wear whatever they want. Finally my bridesmaid chose a dress for herself, but uh, such work, so much confusion."

"How about engagements, are they different?"

Adèle laughs. "In America, all the women want to know 'how did he propose?', 'what does the ring look like?' In France, we'd just ask when they are getting married. I mean we would look at the engagement ring, but not *jump* on the woman first thing," she demonstrates by grabbing Tate's arm and looking at her hand as if there were a ring there.

"What are some differences you've noticed between French and American men?"

"I have only dated French men. But from my friends in the States, I have learned things. I was shocked to hear about 'blind dates.' I had never heard of that before. In France, if you think two people might be right for each other, you throw a party or all go out together in a big group. Then, they meet, and if they like each other, they decide to go out together, maybe in a group, maybe alone, but you would never just put two people who had never met alone on a date. The other big difference is all these rules you have in America. I had never heard of someone waiting a certain number of days before calling someone. My girlfriend in the States would say, 'Oh no, I cannot call him, it is too soon.' Or, 'No, I cannot call him; he has to call me first.' And American men, it is the same thing, they seem so scared about calling. My husband said he had a much easier time dating French women because there were not all these rules."

"How about rules on when to sleep with someone? What I mean by that is, is there some kind of magic number of dates you go on before you sleep together?"

Adèle looks at me like I'm nuts. "No. There are no rules. Nobody cares. I slept with my husband on a first date."

"Unless you sleep with lots of guys," Heloise chimes in. "Then maybe people would think it is not so good."

Adèle nods, conceding agreement. "Maybe you are right."

"Except in Southern France in the summer. It's very well known that people party and go home with someone whose name they forget the next day," Heloise continues.

"How about you, Heloise, any wedding in the near future for you?"

"No. I need a boyfriend first."

"How is dating going? Tell me about your worst date."

"What do you mean, worst date?"

"Well, have you ever had one of those dates where you just stare at each other and can't think of anything to say for hours and the night just drags on endlessly?"

"No," she says, as if the concept is completely foreign to her. "I never had a bad date. Because we meet people in groups with friends, we already know if we have things to talk about before we go out."

"Wow, no bad dates? That's amazing," I say, moving on to my next question after making a note of this in my notebook. "What about having kids? Is there any taboo on having kids out of wedlock?" Heloise and Adèle look blankly at me, and I realize I'm using vocabulary they aren't familiar with. "In the States, sometimes it's looked down on if a woman has a child if she's not married. Is it like that here?"

Heloise and Adèle look at each other. "Not in Paris," Heloise says.

"No, not in Paris. It is not a big deal. Maybe in smaller towns in France. I have only ever lived in big towns."

"I have lived in Paris all my life," Heloise seconds.

We talk for a few more minutes. When they have no more insights on the topic of Parisian romance, I ask Adèle how she likes Colorado.

"I love it. It is so laid back. Paris, the city around you, like New York, it creates a stress. Driving, it is like this," she pretends to grip a steering wheel, making a gritted-teeth-in-terror facial expression. "I realized after a few months in Colorado I had lost that stress. Also, I had to buy new clothes when I moved. All my dressy shoes and clothes from Paris are in plastic bags in my closet now. I had to buy shorts and more casual clothes. Now I think about getting stuck on a road in the winter wearing my little Paris shoes," she waves her hand dismissively. "I am glad I do not have to do that anymore."

"The driving, it is crazy here," Heloise says. "You should stand on the Arc de Triomphe and watch the cars. Uh!"

"Yeah, having twelve roads converge at once, that wasn't the best planning," I say.

"Yeah. Who planned that?" Tate asks.

"Europe was built a long time ago, well before cars," I

point out. "America is very young. It was a country built up specifically for cars and highways."

"This is true," Adèle says.

"You might not miss the driving, Adèle, but don't you miss the public transportation?" I continue. "Public transportation is pathetic in Colorado. When I go to cities with good subway systems that can get you anywhere so easily . . . I'm so jealous."

"I do miss being able to walk everywhere. The subway in Paris, it is good when the workers are not on strike."

"What do you mean?" Tate asks.

"Strikes, always the strikes. Not that long ago the waste management people went on strike, there was garbage everywhere, filling the streets. And in, when was it, 1995? All public transportation shut down for three, maybe four months. Can you imagine Paris with no public transportation for three months? I had to walk three hours every day. The streets were jammed with cars that would not move at all for hours."

It occurs to me that if I ever bothered to read the *New York Times* international section all of this wouldn't be a complete surprise to me, but the truth is, I glance at the headlines on the front page of the *Denver Post*, read the weather and the comics, and declare myself a well-informed citizen. I resolve to turn over a new, more globally aware chapter in my life when I get home.

"Why are they always going on strike?" I ask.

"Money. They always want more money. They work for the government and cannot get fired. They have it all. The government pays for their retirement, six weeks of vacation each year, and still they want more."

The band returns to the stage, and the crowd that had shuttled off to the bar or the bathroom or the sidelines returns again to the dance floor. Tate and I stay for another hour or so, until the smoke is bothering my eyes so much I can no longer stand it. I shout my thanks to Heloise and Adèle for their help. I insist on buying them drinks to thank them for sharing their insights. They protest that they had fun talking with us, but after much struggling, I convince them to at least let me pay for a round. Then Adèle and I exchange phone numbers and e-mail addresses and promise to get in touch when we're back in Colorado.

The next morning Tate and I stop at an Internet café to check our e-mail. I send off e-mails to family and friends back home, giving them a few highlights of the trip and letting them know we're alive and having fun. I have half an hour of time paid up when I'm done. I think about sending out some queries to the magazines I know accept electronic queries. There is one editor at a magazine called *Making Tracks* who has been kind enough to send rejection letters that say, "This isn't right for us, but keep sending us your ideas." That may not sound like much, but when you're used to getting stacks of form letters that say basically, "This idea was so bad we're not even going to take the time to reject it personally," having someone offer even the slightest bit of interest in something of yours takes on a fair amount of significance. I type Abby's e-mail address in the "To" line and then when I get to the "Subject" line I get stuck. I usually write a teaser in the subject line about what the query is about, something like "What to do in Denver after dark," or "Things to do in Denver when you're on a budget." But I have no idea what kind of article I want to write.

Maybe I just need to finish doing my research—talk to more people, see more of Europe, collect my thoughts and impressions like postage stamps that can then be carefully and thoughtfully arranged. Maybe I'm just too jumbled from traveling and being on the road. I'm writing for at least an hour in my journal every day, so it's not like I'm not writing . . .

Right?

I'll query her when I get home, I really will.

I decide to use the time I have left looking up random checks on the Internet for statistics. I learn, for example, that the out-of-wedlock rate of first-born kids is fifty-seven percent in France, compared to about thirty-three percent in America. I also look at divorce rates and learn that Italy wins the day with only twelve percent of marriages ending in divorce. Only twelve percent! Compared to fifty-five percent in America and England and a staggering sixty-four percent in Sweden. I write this all down in my notebook with a note to myself: *Why is this? Must investigate.*

The next day Tate and I head out to Fontainebleau, a forest thirty miles southeast of Paris, for a day of hiking. When we get off the train, we suddenly feel lost. We try to ask a man where the hiking paths are around here, but even using a combination of wild hand gesturing and pitiful French (mine, not his) we're unable to understand each other. Tate and I decide to just take our chances and start walking and hope like hell we don't get lost and die a slow and painful death from starvation.

At least we have all the important provisions in our backpacks: lots of water, bread, cheese, and fruit, so we shouldn't die of malnutrition or dehydration for at least a few days.

There are paths everywhere through the woods, and every step brings another picturesque view. There are the most unusual sandstone rock formations that just spring up from the ground. We march happily through the trees and ferns, taking in views of verdant valleys.

It's a nice, calming retreat from bustling Paris, and we enjoy several hours of meandering happily around before taking the bus back to Paris and getting on the overnight train to Italy.

4

Cinque Terre, Italy

On the Eurail, we share a four-person car for the night with two smiley, burly young men who speak no English and jabber enthusiastically with each other in a language I can't quite place—Ukrainian is my closest guess. Tate looks out the window, lost in thought. I write in my journal for hours. At some point I notice Tate is asleep and look at my watch: 10:03 P.M. I'm jealous of how she can just lay her head down and sleep anywhere, any time. At some point a little later on, the guys lower their chairs to a horizontal position. A watch check reveals it's 11:48 P.M. I'm tired, but I'm too wired to sleep. I keep reflecting on things we've seen so far, and I can't stop daydreaming. I have this persistent fantasy I can't shake. I keep imagining that I fall in love with a gorgeous stranger, maybe he's French, or Italian, and he speaks English but with a sexy accent. We have an amazing time together and then it's revealed that he has a pile of money and he wants to whisk me away to his villa where he's happy to support me for as long as it takes for me to make it as a writer. I know this is a cliché and totally anti-feminist fantasy, but it seems a way for me to get everything I want: love, romance, success as a writer, and the ability to not have to worry about money anymore. I so, so long to travel and see the world without worrying about how I'm going to pay for it.

* * *

I finally manage to get a few hours of sleep here and there, and in the morning, we arrive in Genoa and catch a bus to Cinque Terre, five cliff-side villages suspended between earth and sea. We spend our first day there lolling on the beach, recovering from our trip thus far. It's the first time since we've been in Europe that I let go of my American go! go! go! accomplish! accomplish! accomplish! sense of time for a while and just relax.

The next day we hike in Riomaggiore along a winding trail lined with olive groves, bamboo, vineyards, and wild herb patches. The views of ocean cliffs with 1,500-foot shear dropoffs put a smile on my face that doesn't go away. At one point we stumble on an old castle decorating the skyline. I love that we're in a place where we can just walk along and happen upon an old castle that's not a tourist trap or anything special, just an old castle from a time when castles were normal, not photo-op amazing.

After hiking, we go to a restaurant and order pasta. A glass of the house red is actually less expensive than a Coke. Compared to London and Paris, we can live the good life here for cheap. The hostel we're staying at is also inexpensive. My plan has been to mix in so-so motels with roughing-it price-is-right hostels. Tate and I have not been budgeting carefully or really even paying attention to what we're spending, and while we've been mindful not to go out to pricey dinners and always opt for cheap drinks, a part of me knows that the reason I'm not paying careful attention to what we're spending is because I don't want to know.

After dinner, we get another glass of wine and enjoy the night air and the sound of the ocean crashing down on the rocks below us. When we finish our wine we each order a glass of grappa, which neither of us has ever had before, but I read that it is a traditional Italian drink and thus feel it is our duty to have some to experience Italian culture fully. The grappa comes in a variety of flavors, so I assume it's going to be like Schnapps. I order the hazelnut and Tate gets the strawberry. Turns out it's not anything like Schnapps. Oh no, it's about two hundred proof stomach-lining-burning serious alcohol. I enjoy it, but by the time I'm done drinking it, the world is spinning.

"I love it here," I say, hazy with alcohol.

"Yeah. I think Paris has been my favorite place so far, but this is pretty great, too."

"I wish I didn't have to go back to work." Just thinking about having to go back to work makes my relaxed mood vanish, replaced by a tight knot of stress and anxiety topped with low-grade melancholy. "I just cannot wait until the economy gets better and I can get a new job. Maybe working for a publisher or a magazine. I'd probably take a big pay cut . . . Or maybe I could finally get a job at a newspaper as a reporter. Anyway, I'd get a less stressful job so I have more time to write. I just . . . can't wait for my real life to begin."

"It's all real, Jadie."

I change the subject because I don't have a comeback for what she said, but later, when we're back in the room and I'm lying in bed in the dark, these four words echo through my mind. *It's all real, Jadie.* Of course she's right. I've been living my life in a dream state, just trying to get through the day, fantasizing about someday in the mythical future when I'll be disciplined enough to write every day. I know I have to start doing those things not someday but today. I have to stop living my life like it is on hold, as if one day, poof! all my dreams will magically come true.

In the morning, I wake up smiling. I haven't smiled first thing in the morning in a long time. Usually I wake up and think about going in to work and wonder, *How will my self-esteem be trampled today?* Then I groggily force myself through coffee and a shower, thinking bitterly of how I'll spend nine hours of my day, plus two hours in traffic, working my butt off to make a few rich white guys who own the company richer. Plus, since I stopped working at the Greenhouse and started working at an office job, I've put on weight. I don't run around at the office like I did at the restaurant, obviously. And I have a bad habit of eating when I'm bored, and no matter how busy I am at work, it's always a bored kind of busy, and so getting lunch or going for a snack is so much more interesting than whatever work it is I'm supposed to be doing. I feel like I give the office my mind—all my ideas and creativity for how to design our clients' Web sites and how to lay out and write the copy—do I have to give them my body, too?

For a while, things were really bad at work—I'd messed up on a project and my boss, Tina, was just giving me hell relentlessly, well after there was anything I could do about it. My moods were up and down, from day to day, hour to hour. I started keeping a journal of my moods to see if my depression was somehow related to my menstrual cycle, but it very quickly became clear: Sunday nights I started feeling anxious and blue, Friday afternoons a calm would descend, and I'd feel happy. It wasn't very hard to figure out what was bumming me out.

I went to a doctor explaining my symptoms. He set me up with anti-depressants, and they worked in that I wasn't so blue any more. But while they cut off the low lows they also cut off the high highs. Orgasms went from being like a waterfall to being like the drip drip of a leaky faucet. At the time I was still with Zach, and my sex drive just fizzled out. I got off the meds in part to see if I could salvage things with Zach, but also because when I thought about the fact that I needed to take drugs to make it through another day at the office, it infuriated me.

Tate and I go downstairs to the dining room for breakfast, which is included in the price of the room. Breakfast in Italy doesn't have much to it: just some rolls and coffee. An older woman and her daughter run the hostel. The daughter, Nicola, looks to be right around my age. We share the table with two women from Britain who are already at the table eating. We greet everyone with a "good morning" and I thank Nicola when she pours my coffee.

"This is a wonderful place you have here," I tell her. And it's true. The hostel is modest but charmingly decorated with an exposed beam ceiling and a large stone fireplace. The arched doors are painted a cheerful teal.

"Thank you. The house has been in the family for generations."

"You must love your job, always getting to meet new people from all over the place. Do you? Love it I mean?"

"Most of the time," she says with a smile that's hiding something, but I don't know what.

I tell her about my project to learn about men, romance, and dating. "Would you mind telling me your thoughts on Italian men?"

"Uh," she waves her hand in a dismissive gesture. "My advice: stay away, they will only break your heart."

"So you're not married?"

"I'm a modern woman. I own this business with my mother. I am too . . ." she struggles to find the word, "strong for many Italian men. They worry I leave them."

"I read somewhere that eighty percent of Italian men cheat on their wives," Anna, one of the English women, says. Anna has dyed her light brown hair red and is improbably tall, with endless limbs dangling from her narrow frame. She's pretty, but her long, thin nose and facial features give her face a horse-like quality.

"Eighty percent! But this is a Catholic country!" I say.

"It is true. Affairs are very common," Nicola says. "The men . . . they love their families, they are devoted to their families. The sex, it is something different. And, yes, it is a Catholic country . . . we still go to mass on the holidays . . . but the young people, we are not so religious as our grandparents."

"I don't get it. If cheating is so common in Italy, why is the divorce rate so low? I read that it's only twelve percent," I ask.

"Both wives and husbands, if they have an affair they are discreet," Nicola says. "But even if their spouse does find out about it, well, an affair . . . is nothing to ruin a marriage over."

I simply can't imagine casually accepting an affair and getting over it just like that. We discuss other differences between Italians, Brits, and Americans, talking about everything from food, to politics, to children. I learn that the birth rate in Italy is one of the lowest in the world. You need to have two kids, obviously, to replace mom and dad, and Nicola tells me that in some places in Italy the birth rate average is just barely more than one.

Our conversation turns to Europe in general, and Anna and her friend, Margie, tell me they've traveled all over Europe. On this trip, they went to Germany before coming to Italy.

"Germany, huh? Do you have any insights on German men for me?" I ask.

"German men . . . German men . . ." Anna looks at Margie, her face twisted in thought.

"In general, I'd say Germans keep much more to themselves than say, the Italians," Margie offers.

"It's cold there. Everyone is bundled up and in a hurry to get someplace warmer," Anna adds.

"It's cold? Even at this time of year?"

They both nod.

"Anything else about Germans?"

"I'm trying to think . . ." Anna says. "One thing I noticed is that when we went to the clubs and started shaking our butts, the guys looked at us like we were doing a striptease or something, like they'd never seen anyone grind their pelvis in public. We really had to tone it down. The Germans just kind of hop up and down when they dance. So if you want to snag a German male, don't dance provocatively. That's my advice."

"How about Europeans in general. Any insights on marriage or dating?"

"I have friends from all over Europe," Margie says, "and one thing that strikes me is that all of my friends have been in long-term relationships for years, but only one is married. I'm thirty-one and my friends are around my age, too. The one friend who did get married only got married after she got pregnant. Yeah, you know, now that I think about it, I remember Bela, she's Hungarian, she commented once about how Americans are marriage crazy."

"I wonder why?" Tate says.

"I wonder if it's because in Europe they have universal health insurance and that sort of thing so they don't need to get married," I say. "I mean after all, in the eyes of the law, marriage isn't about love but money and property and tax benefits."

Anna says I might have a point and tells me about how in France there's this policy that lets gay couples and unmarried people register and get tax, welfare, and inheritance rights just like married couples would.

We talk for several more minutes, until Anna and Margie say they need to get going so they can catch their train.

I smile, feeling happy. I'm learning new things—my brain is working in a way it hasn't since college—and relaxing. Going on this trip is the best decision I've made in a long time.

5

Florence, Italy

How's this for mortification: when I was a kid, my parents drove a Volkswagen bug they'd painted in pink paisleys. Needless to say, I walked a lot as a kid. Getting dropped off at school? No, I don't think so. Come blizzard, hail, or thunderstorm, I walked to school, you'd better believe it.

Not that my attempts to disassociate myself from my parents worked, but you couldn't fault me for trying.

My parents were both artistic, and so to some extent they were forgiven their eccentricities. But I noticed how the townspeople looked at them, and I did my best to be the opposite of my parents and fade into the background. My parents were like male birds that get all the bright, shiny, notice-me! feathers, and I was the female bird, plain and brown and hiding in the shrubbery, hoping the predators wouldn't notice me.

The thing is, if you're going to be weird, you have to either be oblivious to what society expects of you, like my parents, or you have to be confident in your uniqueness. I am, I'm afraid, neither of these things. My parents were—and still are—happy people. Happy I think precisely because they don't give a hoot what people think of them. But I didn't inherit this quality.

Take, for example, how, on the train to Florence, I'm

sitting here with my journal open, staring out the window, trying to find the words I'm looking for, and I don't notice that there is a young, pretty woman (Eastern European of some kind) who is hoping I'll notice her and move my backpack from the empty seat next to me. Finally she clears her throat and I notice her, and I jump up, apologizing madly and trying to get my stuff out of her way only to dump my open bag everywhere and then bumble around trying to gather everything up, mumbling apologies the entire time.

When I finally get my mess cleaned up so she can sit down, I spend a good twenty minutes feeling like such a dork my chest feels tight with anxiety.

We arrive in Florence in mid day and find a hostel to stay at. Tate says she wants to take a nap.

Nap! Nap! What heresy. Doesn't she know we have a limited time in Europe and there is no time for sleep!? Granted, I'm tired too. Last night the loud raucous voices of drunk hostel dwellers kept me up late and this morning the shriek of sirens woke me early. I tried to get back to sleep, but the rumble of garbage trucks was so loud it sounded like they were mowing the building down piece by piece with us in it, which made returning to sleep impossible. Even so, I know I'm too excited to sleep, but I say okay.

Tate falls asleep in moments. I lie down and will myself to sleep.

One, two, three, sleep! I command my body. One, two, three, sleep! But it's no good, my body is pulsing with the excitement I feel every time we come to a new town and everything is new and anything is possible . . .

But at some point, I must fall asleep, because I wake up

an hour or so later, feeling infinitely better and more relaxed and rested.

The first sight on our agenda is the Duomo, which takes about seven minutes of our time. We take pictures of the outside of it, with its green, pink, and white marble facade, and then take pictures of the copy of the door designed by some famous Italian guy on the Bapistry across from the Duomo. The doors have these panels that look three-dimensional even though they're basically one-dimensional. Then we go inside the Duomo, take a look around at the few tapestries that remain, and that's it, we're done. Neither of us have enough interest in seeing the religious artwork in the museum in the back to shell out the few bucks it costs to look at them, and we sure as hell aren't about to climb the four hundred and something stairs to hike up to the top of the Duomo, view or no view—I'll buy the postcard, thanks.

Next stop is the Uffizi gallery. We have to wait in a staggeringly long line, and then hike up approximately a jillion stairs to get to the museum. I have no idea how people in wheelchairs get anywhere in Europe. Everything there is to see is at the top of many flights of stairs. I have to use the bathroom, and I see a sign with an arrow pointing which way to go, so I grab Tate and we follow sign after sign until we've walked all the way through the museum and are at the exit. We haven't even started looking at art yet and my feet and legs have been done in by the stairs and the epic journey to find the WC. I work out regularly, but no amount of fitness prepares you for the arduous rigors of sightseeing.

We see about a thousand more Madonna with Child paintings and a jillion zillion pictures of St. Sebastian and other religious stories that neither Tate nor I know the history behind. My parents weren't religious, which means that my background didn't include the religious education most people I know got.

Not being religious in a small town was another thing that labeled me different. One Fourth of July there was a town potluck that was held at the church and though it was ostensibly secular, everyone there, except my folks and me, were members of the church. I was pretty young at the time and painfully shy. As the other families entered, the party-goers would immediately welcome them, embracing them into the fold. No one ever greeted us, though. We lingered to the side, waiting, until Mom basically herded Dad and me into the fray and foisted herself on a couple of startled women, forcing them into a conversation. I watched how the women reacted to her and realized for the first time that, compared to the other women, her skirt was too short and her laugh was too loud. She was too vibrant. She was like a red, pink, and green piñata in a room filled with gray.

By the time Tate and I are nearly done with the museum, I don't care if I ever see another religious Renaissance painting in my entire life. I don't care if Raphael painted it or if Joe Schmoe painted it, I'm sick of it all. I know that to make a living, artists got commissions from people with money, which just happened to be the popes running the churches, and so they had to paint what they were told to, but if they could have gotten funding from folks who told them they could let their imagination run wild, I think millions of us modern tourists would be very grateful indeed.

We finally get to the Botticellis—the *Birth of Venus* and *Allegory of Spring* and some other works I haven't seen before—and there we find an empty seat on the bench out in the hallway and collapse. I intend to stay on this bench for several hours. I never want to walk another step.

The ceiling, like many places we've seen in Europe, has paintings covering every inch, but I'm on art overload right now and it could be the Sistine Chapel and I wouldn't care, but Tate is studying the ceiling intently.

"That guy is looking into a mirror and jacking off," she says after a few minutes.

"What?"

She points up to a corner of the ceiling on a panel just overhead. "That guy reclining on that chaise lounge kind of chair is holding a hand mirror in one hand and his dick in the other."

"No way," I say, scanning the section of the ceiling she's talking about. Then I see the reclining guy, who does indeed have a hand mirror in one hand. I squint. His other hand couldn't possibly be . . . but it does really look like it. I study the ceiling with an I'm-going-to-need-Botox-soon squint.

"I think you're right! Holy shit!"

"And that guy over there is about to shoot an arrow directly up that guy's butt."

I look over to where she's pointing, and sure enough, there is a naked guy bent over and smiling mischievously, and another guy taking aim directly at his rear end. It's probably just a result of me being exhausted from sightseeing, but it strikes me as wildly funny, and I start laughing. My laughter is probably disproportionate to the actual level of humor of the situation, a product of fatigue and weariness, but Tate starts laughing too, and it all just seems funnier and funnier until we're sniggering raucously.

At some point I realize we're making a spectacle of ourselves, becoming an exhibition along with the da Vincis and the Rembrandts and Caravaggios. So I grab Tate and pull her outside with me, and that's when I notice I'm ravenous. She tells me she's hungry too, so, stupidly, we stop at one of the touristy restaurants not far from the Ponte Vecchio, the bridge where there are a ton of jewelry stores selling gold and silver jewelry and is absolutely teeming with tourists. Everything seems expensive, so we just get cheese and tomato sandwiches that are pre-made and warmed in the microwave and turn out to be edible but a far cry from tasty. We have to pay extra to sit at a table rather than take the sandwiches with us. It's less than a Euro to do so, but the principle of it grates on my nerves. We have nowhere to go and we're tired, so we just pay it.

After we've rested, we take off out of the heart of the tourist neighborhoods that are crowded with pricey designer clothing shops like Dolce & Gabbana, Gucci, and Bruno Magli. I like this area much more than the touristy section. We walk past bars crowded with Italians all standing at the counter eating their lunches. It seems so contradictory that the Italians—who are known for working to live rather than living to work like Americans, known for taking it slow and spending lots of time with their friends and family—should have this policy that it costs extra to sit down to eat your lunch or drink your coffee. Standing up is not at all relaxing to me. But, as with so many important global matters, no one consulted me when they were making up the rules. (And woe be to all of us because of it, I dare say.)

As we stroll around, Italian men whistle quietly or nod to Tate and me, calling out, *"Bella, bella."* Usually I find men catcalling annoying or creepy, but with the Italian men, it feels almost like they are putting us on pedestals, just tipping their hats at us, that kind of thing, so it doesn't bother me. And frankly, at the place where my self-esteem is now, I'll take whatever I can get.

Tate and I spend the entire afternoon walking around, then we find an out-of-the-way trattoria. It's small and dim, with high ceilings and stone walls.

The waiter hands us our menu and asks us what we want to drink.

"Water, no bubbles," I say. (They're always trying to pawn off that yucky carbonated stuff on you over here in Europe. I don't understand the obsession.) "And a half liter of red wine."

The waiter gives me a puzzled look, which baffles me, and I watch him curiously as he walks away.

"You confused the shit out of him," Tate says.

"What do you mean?"

"When he handed you the menu, you spoke to him in French. You said, 'merci.' "

"I did?"

"So then he switched to French, asking us what we wanted to drink, then you switched to English."

"I did?" I think back over the exchange. I didn't even realize he was speaking to me in French. I knew that he was asking us what we wanted to drink, so I just answered him.

"That poor guy," I say with a laugh. "No wonder he was so confused."

We enjoy the inexpensive wine and good bread and when our pasta comes—it has a creamy cheese sauce, peas, and asparagus—it is divine, and it more than makes up for the lackluster meal we had earlier in the day.

After dinner, we head to a crowded outdoor bar overlooking the Arno River and Oltrarno, Florence's left bank. House music fills the air and pitchers of Sangria fill the tables.

We've only been there a few minutes when two Italian men approach our table.

"My name ees Piero. This ees Giulo. You are American, yes?" the one says.

"Yes," I say.

"Ees very busy here. May we join you?"

I look at Tate. She shrugs.

"Sure."

Both men are handsome and well dressed. Piero, with his confident, sexy smile, is particularly yummy. They both have short, highly gelled hair and are both slim, just like every other young Italian male we've seen so far. I must confess to you at this point my weakness for chocolate brown eyes, of which Italian men as a group have the most intoxicating I've ever seen.

Piero looks into my eyes with his own heart-meltingly delicious ones and asks me where I'm from, how long I'll be in Florence, that sort of thing. I'm vaguely aware that Giulo and Tate have started their own conversation, but they could be discussing strategies for colonizing Mars for all I know.

I ask Piero several questions about Florence and Italian culture in general. He tells me some interesting stuff, like how in Florence, tourists outnumber the residents fourteen to one. Fourteen to one!

Piero gestures a lot as he talks and at one point he jabs a big blond backpacker who was just passing by, making the backpacker stumble a little, and his face is a comical contortion of surprise as he falls into someone at the next table over. The domino effect of their surprised expressions is hilarious. The backpacker recovers quickly and Piero apologizes. The backpacker nods and smiles back— no harm done—and continues on his way.

"Why do Italians use their hands so much? It's a health hazard," I say.

"*Scusi?*"

I use my hands and demonstrate, jabbing them around like an orchestra conductor. "Italians. They use their hands a lot. Why?"

"It ees our history," Piero says.

"It used to be that Italy had many city states, many dialects. To communicate, we need our hands," Giulo adds.

"You like Italy, uh?" Piero asks.

"I love it. It's beautiful. The people are friendly. We just had the most scrumptious dinner. If we can eat like that for every meal, I may never leave the country."

He tells us we need to try a restaurant down the block. "Their *prosciutto al forno*, it is *delizioso*," he says, smacking his fingers to his lips.

"Prosciutto, that's ham, right?"

"*Si*."

"Tate and I don't eat meat."

"Ees no problem. There is much fish in Italy. At Pierluigi, the octopus carpaccio . . ."

"We don't eat any seafood. No dead animals."

This throws him. "Why ees this?"

Every time I tell someone I'm a vegetarian I have to have this conversation, and I'm not in the mood to go into it all, so I just say, "We just don't like to eat dead stuff."

I think he notices my exasperation because right away his facial expression becomes more solicitous. He smiles. "It ees okay. I do not eat much meat myself. Mostly *pesce*, fish, uh?"

This is a very common statement from a guy before he sleeps with me. During the first few weeks I'm dating someone before we sleep together, he always orders vegetarian dishes. Then we sleep together, and bam! the next time we go to a restaurant, what does he order? Steak. Without fail. I am not the first to observe this and I won't be the last, but in my twenty-seven years on this planet I have learned this: a man before you've slept with him and a man after you've slept with him can be two very different people.

And so it is no surprise to me that Piero is back-peddling, first recommending a ham dish and then saying he hardly ever eats any animal flesh other than fish. I know it's a natural human reaction to change your viewpoint to match the person's you are talking to. When you're talking to someone with different views than you, unless you're looking for a fight, suddenly you tone down the rhetoric to avoid conflict. Still, I'm feeling like Piero is playing me, doing what he needs to do to get me in bed. Even though a romance with a sexy man with an accent was just what I was hoping for on this trip, Piero's just not doing it for me.

Piero and I talk for a while more, but soon he starts pressuring me to come back and see his apartment. I have to say I'm intrigued to see how the locals live, but I know what he wants, and it's not what I want. Well, it is what I want, but not tonight, not with him. When his sales pitch becomes infuriating rather than merely annoying, I grab Tate and we head to another bar.

For reasons that elude me, at this point Tate and I start drinking martinis. Turns out this is a very, very bad idea.

I start talking to a New Zealander who is half white, half Maori (I asked because his coloring and curly hair are so interesting and because, let's face it, I'm nosy). Even after he tells me his name twice, I still don't catch it—it's an unusual name and the bar is loud, but I'm too embarrassed to ask him to say it again. It's something with a "P"—Pomade? Pimento? Apoplexy?—Whatever it is, I think of him as Pomegranate, though naturally I don't say that to his face. Tate starts talking to a Russian jewelry maker with nine fingers. He's wearing a black beret and a thick gold necklace. At some point in my conversation with Pomegranate, I look over at Tate and see she's wearing the nine-fingered Russian's beret, and she looks so ridiculous, this tiny waif of a thing, her big brown eyes lost under this enormous and preposterous excuse for head wear, and it strikes me as so funny I nearly fall off my chair (or maybe it's just that, by this point, I'd had a few).

By some miracle, in the morning Tate and I wake up in our beds at the hostel fully dressed, without a sign of any naked nine-fingered Russians or New Zealanders named Pomegranate.

Phew!

We sleep in, trying to recover from our debauchery the night before. Even after I wake, I lie in bed for a while, waiting to feel human.

I finally will myself out of bed and get into the shower, and it makes me nostalgic for home. The showers here pale compared to showers back home. Here, water comes out of the shower head at a pace reminiscent of baby's drool. These are the kind of things that make me think fond thoughts of America. Then I think of the monuments we've seen in Europe that mark the dawn of civilization, the Renaissance era, and the most important pieces of art in history, and I think about the Colorado History Museum being all in a froth of excitement over about a whopping one hundred years of history, taking great pains to display pictures of men in their cowboy hats and showing images of mines and mining equipment and I roll my eyes and think, oh puh-lease, you call that history?

We head over to the Accademia, where the statue of David is. There are a few rooms of paintings, but basically the six bucks we shell out is to see David. The room we walk through to get there is lined with Michelangelo's statues of six prisoners. The books say the statues are unfinished, but I like them as they are, struggling to get out of their stone jails, their chests and torsos heaving and straining toward escape, their heads and limbs fading into the rock.

I've read that Michelangelo went to the quarries personally to pick out the marble blocks he would then sculpt. The sculptures were already there, he said, he just needed to chip away at the extra rock to reveal them.

As I marvel at David, instead of feeling awe-inspired, I feel a cloud of depression descend. Michelangelo sculpted and painted and was even an architect. His work defined an era, and not just any era, mind you, the *Renaissance* era.

I just want to write travel articles. Unlike Michelangelo, who took a blank canvas or a plain hunk of marble and turned it into something so spectacular that pilgrims from around the world line up for hours to see his work hundreds of years after he'd created it, I just want to write about stuff that already exists. I'm not creating something out of nothing; I'm just reporting on what is already there. That hardly seems like a very big accomplishment, yet I'm so pathetic I can't even succeed at that.

We finish with the museum in an hour and are then stumped for what to do with ourselves. I'm so sick of other tourists, I can't face another tourist attraction right now. In the guidebook, it says there is this amazing view of Florence from this square just outside the city where there is another copy of David in the center of the plaza. For some reason I have it in my head that this place is an off-the-beaten-track place unknown to tourists.

Um, no.

We take the half-hour bus tour to the plaza (watching the insane Vespa-riding Italians zip through microscopic clearances between the bus and other cars with absolute fearlessness) and tourists just mob the place. The tourist stands selling plastic copies of David are as ubiquitous here as back in the heart of Florence. The stands sell aprons of David minus the head (meaning it focuses on his very famous genitalia), and aprons of headless women in nipple rings and garters. In other words, just the sort of things you'd expect the city that launched the Renaissance to sell.

There *is* a nice view of Florence—the creamy yellow buildings with red barrel rooftops broken up with the large red dome of the Duomo—but after we take a few pictures and spend about two minutes scanning the horizon thoughtfully, we get the point already and retreat to a bench where the only view is of tourists' fat butts bending over the railing. After a few minutes, we decide to take the bus back into town. There is an accident or traffic jam of some sort and it takes forever to get back, and by then we are famished.

For dinner, Tate and I walk to a small restaurant with a red awning and green plastic tables on the outdoor patio. The waiter comes to take our order and hands us our menus and again I say *merci*, only this time I catch myself and then say, "Uh, I mean, *grazie*." I don't know why I keep speaking French to the Italians. It's like, what do I think, because I sort of know one foreign language, I can use it in any old foreign country and it should be understood?

Turns out the waiter's English skills are almost as minimal as my Italian.

"You drink?" he says.

"Huh? Oh, we'd like a bottle of red wine and a bottle of still water with some lemon," I say.

"Lemon water?"

Lemon water sounds very frightening somehow. "No, no, just plain water with a lemon." I pantomime squeezing a lemon.

His expression is completely blank, but he nods. The nod in no way reassures me that we've communicated, however. He turns and walks back into the kitchen.

"Why do I get the feeling he's just pronouncing the

words phonetically and he's going to go back there and just repeat the sounds we made without having any idea what the words mean?" Tate says.

"Because I'm pretty sure that's exactly what's happening."

As we peruse the menu, consulting our phrase book constantly to translate, the maitre de sits a cute guy who is by himself at the table beside us.

Over my menu I take peeks at the guy, who, because he is wearing a baseball cap, baggy shorts, and Tiva sandals, I'm quite certain is American. He has sexy green-brown eyes that are the color of a thirsty plant and brown hair that curls a little at his neck. He's in good shape, with the thick veins of an athlete studding his forearms just like Michelangelo's David.

Tate and I discuss what we want for dinner, deciding to begin with bruschetta, and then we decide to split a pasta for our first course and the eggplant parmesan for our second.

I glance over at the guy who is sort of staring off into space. I wonder if he's bored or lonely and if we should invite him to join us. I should try to strike up a conversation with him—just to help a lone traveler keep from feeling lonely, naturally.

Before I can think of an opening line, our pasta is delivered in this enormous bowl; it's enough food to serve a banquet hall of people.

"Did we accidentally order the family size?" Tate asks.

I shrug. "I have no idea, but this is a ridiculous amount of food."

"What about leftovers?" It's the guy sitting next to us. He's smiling, obviously amused at our reaction. My heart does a little jig of excitement: he's talking to us!

"I'm all about saving money on the road, but I can

barely bring myself to carry an extra T-shirt in my back-pack, let alone six pounds of pasta that will be a congealed lump in about two hours," I say. "Do you want some of this? Seriously, you'd be helping us out."

"Thanks, but I already ordered. I've got my own vat of pasta coming."

I'm disappointed and momentarily frantic that this is the end of my conversation with him. "Ah, uh," I stumble, anxious not to let the conversation end but not sure what to say next. "So are you traveling alone?" I spoon some of the pasta onto my plate and take a bite, savoring the thick noodles with wilted spinach with gorgonzola in a white wine sauce.

He nods. "I'm spending a few months traveling before I take over my father's business."

"Wow. That's cool."

He shrugs. "I don't know . . . the business is a restaurant in Ithaca. I never really saw myself as following in his footsteps. I'm thinking maybe I'll try to make it a chain. It's a dipping grill—you get skewers of food and several sauces to dip them in. I'm thinking maybe I'll try to turn it into the Starbucks of dipping grills or something."

"I've heard Ithaca is a great town. Is that where you live now?"

He shakes his head. "I live in Iowa, which is where I grew up. My mom still lives there. She and my dad got divorced a long time ago. You know, I feel like I'm pouring out my whole life story to you and I don't even know your name yet. I'm Justin."

"I'm Jadie. This is Tate. I'm sorry if I'm prying. I'm a journalist, so I'm trained to be nosy."

Justin's food arrives, and while it's a hearty amount of food, it's not in the trough Tate and I somehow managed to get. Our food is delicious and the house red wine is cheap and unbelievably tasty, and when you add the view of this yummy boy with the green-brown eyes and sexy smile, I decide that I'm very happy indeed.

"So what do you do in Iowa?" Tate asks Justin.

"Right now I'm bartending. I've had sort of an odd career path, to say the least."

"How so?" she asks.

It flashes through my head that she might be interested in Justin, too, and I suddenly feel very territorial about Justin and annoyed at Tate.

"Well, after I graduated from college, I got a job working as a programmer for an Internet company."

"Ugh. I survived working at an Internet company. Barely," I say.

"Yeah? I didn't last there long. A couple years after I started there the company got bought out and I was laid off. They gave me a pile of severance money, so I just kicked back and lived the good life for a while. I played my guitar and wrote some songs, wrote a lot of terrible poetry." (Editorial side note: I love that he writes poetry, terrible or otherwise.) "I hung out with friends and traveled around the U.S., visiting buddies of mine, that kind of thing. Finally I decided I was ready to look for a real job again. I looked really hard for several months, but the economy was in the toilet and I couldn't find anything in my field. So I took a job as a bartender. It was pretty fun, but then last year my father died."

"I'm so sorry," Tate and I say together.

"No, it's okay. We were never really that close. Anyway, he left his restaurant to me. His manager has been running the place. I've spent a lot of time this last year thinking about whether I want to take it over. I really don't want to leave Mom behind, but she won't move from the house she's lived in for the last thirty years. She says she's lived in Iowa her whole life and it's where she intends to die, that kind of thing."

"You don't have any siblings?"

"It's just me."

"Is that why you decided to go ahead and take over the restaurant?"

"I just finally decided it was time for me to grow up and get a real job. I don't know, running a business might be cool. Maybe I'll get my MBA at some point, I don't know."

"That sounds great. How long are you traveling for?"

"My plan is to travel until Christmas and then start my new grown-up life in the new year. These are my last few months of being able to do whatever I want, having no responsibilities, seeing the world. How about you?"

"We just have a little less than three weeks, and then it's back to our real lives."

"When you go back to your real lives, what is it you'll be doing?"

"Tate waitresses and I write travel articles and work at a company managing the creative end of things, the design and the copy for Web sites."

"Cool."

"Well, I don't know about 'cool,' but after working at the craziness of the Internet company, anything seems normal and functional by comparison."

"Crazy how?"

"When I started with the company—I was the sixth employee—the offices were located in an airplane hangar because the rent was cheap, but our offices perpetually reeked of gas and when the planes were being fueled we'd all get woozy from the fumes. If we ran the coffeemaker and the microwave at the same time, there would be a power surge that could destroy a day's worth of work and keep us in the dark for hours. Squirrels regularly chewed through our power cords, and every time it rained our offices flooded—we'd get to work in the morning to find large chunks of the ceiling floating in a puddle on our desks."

"That's nuts!" he says.

"Tell him about Crotch Boy," Tate says with a smile. She gives me an encouraging look that I know means, "Go for it!" and I feel awful for my bitchy territorial thoughts earlier.

"Crotch Boy?" Justin asks.

"When the venture capital started coming in—there were no profits to speak of, of course—it suddenly became critically important that the staff bond in a series of team-building activities. The first thing we did was a mandatory company meeting at an adult 'fun' center. We were all supposed to play ice hockey, and since none of us had any hockey gear, we were told to play just in our gym shoes, without any safety equipment. Can you imagine? I pretended that I was getting over a knee injury to get out of it. From the sidelines, I watched one coworker after the other take a series of nasty spills. This one guy, he worked in sales, he was so intent on winning that he took this dive over the president of the company and his jeans ripped open at the crotch—I'm not talking a small hole, it was a gaping opening—and he just kept right on playing totally unfazed. Let me say right now that if my pants tore open at the crotch and my tighty whiteys were aglow for all of my coworkers to see, I would not be *unfazed*, I would be *fazed*. For the rest of the day, through the dinner and the after-dinner-drinks schmooze fest, he just wore a napkin over his crotch like a loin cloth and went about his day like nothing was wrong."

Justin and Tate, who has heard this story a million times, laugh. Tate is such a good friend to still laugh at my little anecdotes after being subjected to them a million times.

"After the ice hockey game, it looked like a hospital scene out of a WWII movie—everybody was hurt, just everybody, and the injured people lined the hallway of the rec center, moaning and nursing their wounds. The two marketing managers limped along; the HR director held a cloth to her cheek to staunch the flow of blood from a gaping wound; the quality assurance manager was wheezing, straining for breath as he attempted to refill his lungs with oxygen after an ungainly nose dive on the ice. It was bad. And the thing of it was that we'd have to do these kind of team-building events all the time. And they were always making us go to these happy hours and plying us with alcohol before we hit the highway to commute home. I think they'd read about how Internet companies in Silicon Valley were big into the work hard/play hard sort of thing, and they were trying to be like them. Then things started going downhill and the team-building activities and mandatory happy hours abruptly stopped. The company had several rounds of layoffs, but I managed to get the job I have now before getting axed."

"I thought that my experience was nuts, but I think yours wins for most crazy."

"How was yours nuts?" Tate asks.

Before he can answer, our eggplant arrives. I'd forgotten that we'd even ordered it, and I've barely touched the food I already had because I was too busy trying to make Justin think I was witty. I take a bite of the eggplant, which is covered in gooey melted cheese and tomato sauce and is decadent and heavenly.

"Mostly it was that the CEO was a lunatic," Justin continues.

"Lunatic how?" Tate asks.

"Well, one time a bomb threat was called into the HR

department. There were two HR ladies who worked there, and so they went to the owner and told him about the call. The two HR women, the owner, and the vice president evacuated the building but didn't tell any of us about the bomb threat because they didn't want to risk the loss of productivity."

"You're kidding!"

"It gets better. One of the HR ladies was seven months pregnant, and the CEO tried to get her to go back into the building and find the bomb."

"He sounds like a great guy. A real gentleman," Tate says.

"I can't believe he wouldn't tell his employees there was a bomb threat. That's one sleazy manager you had there."

"The more I learn about corporate America the more I'm grateful I don't work at an office," Tate says, shaking her head.

"I know what she means. I used to work at the same restaurant where she works," I explain to Justin, "and sometimes a colorful character would come in, but corporate America is like an outpatient clinic for the mentally insane only they fool people by wearing suits instead of straight jackets."

Justin and I keep talking about the good and the bad in office life. I, naturally, have no shortage of negative things to gripe about. "And working at an office makes me fat," I say, continuing my litany of complaints. "I don't have as much time to work out as I used to."

"Do you have a gym at your office?" Justin asks.

"No. I go to a gym nearby."

"That's probably for the best. There's something about having to be seen naked by your coworkers that's really disturbing. When I worked at the Internet company I worked out at the company gym and it was so distressing—I'd be tying my shoe and look up and there is the HR director toweling off his Johnson about a centimeter away from my face. I just do not need to see that. Personally, I think they should create pods that contain both a shower and a little changing area slash locker, so you could go into your individual pod and never have to see your coworkers private bits."

We joke around some more about work and then he says, "Well, think of it this way, you'll be able to leave corporate America soon and just be a writer."

"That's the plan."

"I like travel magazines. Maybe I've read something of yours. What have you written recently?"

Recently—the word slams me like a meat cleaver, whump! I suddenly realize that the last time I had something published was well over a year ago, and that was an article I'd sold nearly a year before that. I've been writing here and there over the last couple of years, but all of my clips came in the years just after college when I didn't work nearly such long hours and I wasn't yet beaten down by how tough the business of being a writer is. Basically, since taking the job at Pinnacle, I've claimed I was a writer based on the few measly clips I got a long time ago.

"Actually, not that much recently. I'm hoping this trip will get me back into it."

"That's cool. Did you want to be a travel writer as a way to pay for your travel or did you want to travel so you had something to write about?"

"Both. I've always liked writing and I've always loved travel and learning new things, especially other cultures' traditions. In my family, it was just the three of us. Well, Mom had family in California, but they'd had some falling out and she stopped speaking to them long before I was born and hasn't seen them in years. Anyway, we didn't really have many traditions in my little family. We didn't go to church, things like that. In school there was one Jewish kid—one—and for some presentation she told us all about all these Jewish traditions—like at weddings how they break the glass, the chair dance—and these traditions were performed by generation after generation. They had this link that connected them to all these people in the past, all these people in the future, people who hadn't even been born yet, and I thought that was so cool. I guess I just like learning about other cultures and seeing what I like and adapting those things to my own life."

The three of us keep laughing, talking, eating, and drinking for at least another hour or two, never getting stuck in an awkward silence or mentally groping around for something to say. When I tell a story, Justin and Tate laugh in just the right places. I feel witty and fun and nothing at all like the quiet girl I am at the office.

When at last we've requested and received the bill, Justin asks where we're staying.

"It's the . . . I don't know how to pronounce it." I fumble through my dog-eared guidebook and point to the hostel we're staying at. "How about you?"

"I haven't actually found a place to stay yet, but I figure if worst comes to worst I can sleep on a bench outside or something, do the true backpacker roughing it thing. Do you want to pick up a bottle of wine and hang out in the courtyard at the hostel or something?"

The last few hours have been wonderful, but when he says this, I feel even happier, and I can't hide my smile.

Then I remember Tate. "I don't know, Tate, what do you think?"

"Yeah, sure, that sounds good." I try to read her expression, her body language, trying to discern whether she really doesn't care or if secretly she's irritated that I'm paying so much attention to this stranger, but as far as I can tell, she's okay with whatever we decide to do next.

"We don't have to hang out at the hostel. We can . . ." I begin. Despite the fact we're in another country and there are a zillion new things to do and see and experience, I can't think of a single other way to spend the rest of our evening.

"It's okay. Let's get some wine," Tate says.

We stand and when Justin turns to leave the restaurant, I mouth to Tate "Thank you."

We get a bottle of wine and head back to the hostel courtyard, where we claim a picnic bench. There is a group of rowdy backpackers at another table, and we just smile and wave and say hi, and they do the same. Hostels may not be the most luxurious of places to stay, but I love how friendly everybody is. The energy of the people makes the dirty floors and warped mattresses immaterial.

I start to tell Justin about some of the things we've done and seen so far. He says that he's never been to London or Paris, but that he plans to hit those cities at some point on his trip.

"Paris has been my favorite. Every street is beautiful, but there's one street in particular I liked. It's called *rue . . . rue . . .* Tate, what was the name of that street with all the produce stands and bakeries?"

"*Rue* something, I can't remember."

"Me neither. God, I hate when I just draw a complete blank like that. We were just there a few days ago. I can't believe I can't think of it." I sit there in silence for a moment, feeling like an idiot.

"Don't worry about it. It happens to everybody," Justin says. "It can be the dumbest things. One time I forgot how to spell 'who.' I was like, I don't *think* it's H-O-O. Another time, I made the mistake of actually *thinking* about how to tie my shoes while actually trying to tie them. It turns out I don't actually know *how* to ties my shoes, I'm just some idiot savant who can *do* it. I just sat there for maybe ten minutes trying to figure out how to tie my shoes. I tried to fake myself out, to just do it without thinking, but by then it was too late. It was pitiful, a grown man just staring at his shoes without a clue. Finally I just fashioned some pathetic knot so I could leave my house."

Both Tate and I laugh. I like that he can admit he does stupid shit, that he's not one of those guys who need to brag about himself to look good.

God he's got sexy eyes.

"So how many days do you plan on spending in Florence?" I ask.

"I don't really have a plan. I'll just move on when I feel like it."

"That's basically our plan," Tate says.

We talk about other cities we've seen on other trips, and the conversation comes back around to New York.

"Are you excited about leaving Iowa or are you going to miss it?" I ask.

"I like Iowa, there's a lot I'll miss, but in some ways I'm really looking forward to getting out of there. But I worry about leaving my mom alone. Right now I live about an hour from her. She contrives little projects around the house for me to help with, something to get me to drive out for a Saturday, but I think mostly it's just that she's a little lonely."

He tells a hilarious story of trying to help her install a new sink and everything that went wrong, making a project he thought would take a half hour last all day. It involved pipes exploding with water all over him and everywhere and other irritating mishaps.

"That's when I learned that I'll paint, I'll do carpentry, but I won't do plumbing," he says. "I just don't plumb."

Then he tells another story about trying to help her paint her bedroom and all the little things that went wrong and the dozens of trips to Home Depot he had to make. As he talks, I think about how sweet and kind he is, looking out for his mom like that.

I could move to Ithaca—I can be a travel writer stationed from anywhere. It's not like I've got some great job waiting for me in Boulder. But I'd miss Tate. Maybe Tate wouldn't mind moving to New York . . .

We keep talking for hours, until somewhere along the way Tate begins nodding off, and even though I feel happier and more alive than I have since I can remember, I notice that I'm exhausted, too. I can't suppress a yawn.

"God, sorry," I cover my yawning mouth with my hand. "I guess I should probably get some sleep."

"Yeah, that's a good idea."

"Oh! You never found a place to stay!" I say.

"That's okay. I'll find something."

"Well, maybe you could sleep with me. I mean you know, sleep sleep. Tate, would that be okay with you?"

"Whatever. I'm going to be gone to the world the moment my head hits the pillow."

"Really? That would be great. Thank you," Justin says.

We walk to our room. Once inside, I feel I'm suddenly in this awkward role of hostess. I excuse myself, saying I'm just going to clean up a bit, and duck into the bathroom and brush my teeth as best I can in four seconds flat, then I quickly wash my face, neck, and armpits. I pause only long enough for a quick glance in the mirror, and I wish I hadn't. When I was talking and joking around with Justin and Tate, I felt sexy, pretty, confident, and witty. Looking in this mirror, I feel grubby and plain and road weary.

Mirror, mirror on the wall.

Shut.

The Fuck.

Up.

Fortunately, I don't have time to worry about what I look like and I return to the room where Justin is waiting, sitting on the edge of my bed, which is small and narrow and covered with a nubbly blanket that has seen better days.

"Is it okay if I strip down to my boxers?" he asks.

Tate appears to already be asleep, but even if she's not, I know her well enough to know she wouldn't care if he ran around the room totally naked. I nod. "Yeah, sure."

He smiles. "I didn't want you to think I'm some exhibitionist or something."

He turns to take off his clothes and I turn and take off my bra through my sleeves without taking my shirt off. If I could bottle the feeling of taking off an underwire bra at the end of a long and sweaty day, I'd be a zillionaire. Freedom!

I get under the covers and lay on my side, facing the wall, feeling excited and nervous and shy. Justin gets into bed beside me. We lie there for a few minutes, my heart thumping in painful awareness of just how close Justin is.

"Would it be okay if I put my arms around you?" he whispers. "Just hold you, I mean," he hastens to add.

I nod and breathe the word "yeah" in a barely audible whisper.

He gently traces his fingers along my arm, then he wraps his arms around me, holding me tight. I put my hand on his forearm, doing my best to embrace him back despite not facing him and not really having access to my arms. I love the feeling of his forearm, the muscles, the spattering of hairs that are somehow both soft and wiry.

I ache to feel his erection against me, but that part of his body is too far away. I imagine turning around, kissing him like the sex-starved maniac that I am, and tearing his clothes off. Instead I just enjoy how good it feels to be held by another human being, the warmth of his body against mine.

True to his word, he is a gentleman, and he doesn't try for anything more than a good night embrace. Eventually, we both fall asleep, and when we wake, I am still wrapped in his arms.

I turn to face him. He is already awake, and our eyes are about a micron apart. We smile at each other and study each others' faces, squinting at each other in the bright early morning sunlight. Have I mentioned how cute this boy is?

Although I have to say, I can't believe I went halfway around the world only to fall for a boy from Iowa.

"Good morning," he says.

"Morning."

"Would you and Tate be up for touring around the city today?"

"I'd love to. Let me see if Tate is up for it."

I look over at the other bed at Tate, who is awake and lying on her bed doing nothing. Her ability to do nothing is something I don't understand about her. When I have down time I write or read. That's relaxing to me. Doing nothing would drive me mad.

Tate shrugs her consent when I ask her if she minds hanging out with Justin, and after a shower and a quick breakfast of rolls and coffee, we head out to see the town.

Justin suggests we rent Vespas to get around.

"Do you really want to drive around a foreign city with some of the craziest drivers on the face of the Earth?" I say. Ever since I was four years old and I climbed on a recently parked motorcycle and burned my thigh on the exhaust pipe, I've been wary of anything mechanized on two wheels. Even bicycles are sort of intimidating. I know how pathetic that sounds: Jadie Peregrine, adventurer, world traveler, and fearer of bicycles. What can I say, I'm a complicated woman.

"I think it's a great idea!" Tate says.

Ordinarily, I like Tate's adventurousness. But now that I feel compelled to do something that terrifies me so that I won't look like a wimp in front of Justin, I find this quality of hers highly irritating.

"Uh, okay then," I say.

When we get to the rental place, Justin asks the vendor for two scooters. I correct him. "Three, you mean."

"I thought you could ride with me."

I feel like I shouldn't like him making this assumption, this decision without asking me first, but a part of me is flattered—it's like a declaration that he sees us as a couple.

I climb on behind Justin and hold on to him for dear life, well aware of my breasts pressed against his back.

We zip along the cobblestone roads, past fountains and marble statues, my hair snarling around my face. Tate's excited screams and squeals fill the air. I look over at Tate and smile at her, a smile that is filled with more joy than I can remember in recent history. Tate reminds me of Audrey Hepburn in *Roman Holiday*, with her delicate frame, big eyes, and graceful features. She would be a dead ringer for Audrey if Audrey had a tattoo and a nose ring and was only five feet one.

After a few hours of racing around the city, we spend the afternoon walking around the Pitti Palace, where the powerful Medici family once lived. The Medicis were these rich people who basically shelled out the bucks to let the Renaissance artists create their art.

We get eyefuls of walls so covered in paintings in such thick gold frames I can't imagine how the walls can support them all. Then we head out back to where the Boboli

Gardens are. The park is filled with statues, fountains, and trees. Stray cats are everywhere and there is an endless array of stairs to climb. After hiking up approximately eight million stairs we're treated to a spectacular view of the city and the palace, but our feet are aching.

We return the Vespas and walk the few blocks home, sharing a bottle of water, passing it back and forth. Back at the hostel, we collapse on the bench of the outdoor picnic table.

"Would you guys be terribly offended if I took my shoes off? My feet are killing me," I say.

"Take your shoes off. Give me your feet," Justin says. "I'll rub them."

"Don't be ridiculous, my feet smell so bad the odor could kill a small child. Anyway, my feet are filthy and we're going to eat soon."

"I can wash my hands. Hand 'em over, I mean it."

I'm embarrassed, but I take off my sandals, swing my legs up onto the bench, and place my hot sweaty feet in his lap.

He rubs my foot and it feels amazing, but my first reaction is not pleasure. I know it sounds ridiculous, but I realize as he massages my feet that it's been more than a year since someone has given me a massage. It was just over a year ago that I broke up with my ex, and ever since it has been nothing but lackluster first dates and awkward tangles with lesbians. How could I have possibly gone this long without the touch of another human being? I've been living my life like a zombie. The touch of Justin's hand is like the prince's kiss, bringing me back to life at last.

After resting, we clean up and head out for dinner, a little early by local standards, then head out to a club to hear live music. We get there too early, so there are hardly any people there yet and nobody is dancing, but before we've even had a drink, Tate takes a liking to one of the songs and asks us if we want to dance.

"Uh, not yet," I say. I don't need to be buzzed to dance, but I do need at least a small crowd to get lost in. "I'll join you in a little while."

"Well, I'll be back then." Tate smiles and slides off her stool and goes down to the small dance floor. She's a great dancer. It's not that she has fancy moves, but she's graceful and beautiful and simply captivating to watch. I love that she's one of those free spirit types who can feel completely comfortable dancing all by herself.

For a moment, I'm at a loss for conversation. "I love music," is the best I can come up with.

"Me, too."

"Well, of course, you play guitar."

He nods.

"Did you ever want to be in a band?"

"Not really. I mean every now and then when I'm at a concert where a band is making a stadium of 20,000 people go nuts, I think *that'd be cool*. But in reality, no. I mean I play around with some friends every now and then. We'll play songs together at parties. But even getting a few songs together for a Christmas party or something takes so much work and practice. And musicians are notoriously flaky."

"Hey, what's wrong with being flaky?"

"Nothing, unless you're trying to make a business out of it."

Justin and I spend the next hour talking about our past, our future, about nothing at all. We talk about high school memories, college antics, our parents, our families, and with all the talking we've done over the last twenty-four hours, I feel like I know him well—better than some people I've known for years. As we talk, I watch a cute

Italian guy approach Tate and say something. She smiles and they start dancing together.

Eventually, Justin and my conversation hits a momentary stall. In that moment, I look into Justin's eyes, and he returns my gaze with a smile.

Kiss me, kiss me, I mentally urge, but he doesn't kiss me. Instead, he asks me to dance.

The dance floor has filled up by now, so I say sure and follow him out to it. We sidle up next to Tate. "Hey girl," I say.

"Hey. Jadie, this is Lucio. Lucio, this is Jadie and Justin."

"*Ciao,*" he says.

"*Ciao.*"

Even though I'm not at a museum or a palace right now, there are still many sights to take in. The sight, for example, of Justin's ass. It's concealed in baggy shorts, unlike the Italian males' asses, which are universally clad in tight jeans. (I haven't seen any Europeans wearing shorts; it seems to be a purely American thing, at least at this time in the season, when the shocking heat of the summer is fading and the weather requires a light sweater at night.)

Still, the loose shorts can't completely conceal the roundness of his butt, and they provide an excellent vantage point from which to admire his muscular legs.

He's a good dancer, able to find the beat and move smoothly, unlike the jerky twitch so many white American men pass off for dance. He doesn't take himself seriously, making jokey expressions that make me smile.

I turn, and Justin's body grazes mine. I jump a little; my pulse races.

Part of me is praying for a slow song; something to give us an excuse to get closer. As it is, our bodies are sort of orbiting each other. I'm painfully aware of the heat of him, the proximity of our bodies, how much I want to reach out and touch him.

After several songs, even the electric sexual tension isn't enough to stave off exhaustion—my body's way of reminding me about my late night the previous evening—and I can hardly do anything more than sway to the music.

"Are you getting tired?" I ask Justin.

"I'm having fun, but I could definitely catch up on some sleep."

Then I turn to Tate and say into her ear, "Tate, I'm beat. Do you mind going home? Are you into this guy?"

"He's cool, but . . ." she shrugs, her expression indifferent. She turns to him. "Lucio, it's been fun. I've got to go."

"*Bella*, I will walk you home," he says.

"No, that's okay, Justin here will protect me. Good night." She kisses him on his cheek. He continues to protest, making exaggerated facial expressions like he's devastated, but he doesn't follow us as we leave.

Justin and I walk home hand in hand. Tate walks beside us humming and singing.

Justin holds me back a little so Tate gets a little ahead of us, and then he whispers in my ear, "When you were in the shower this morning, I went to the front desk to see if they had a single room. They did. I took it."

The meaning of this is not lost on me, nor is the breathy way he imparts this information. Again I feel the tumultuous mix of excitement and nervousness and expectation that has been raging through my veins at regular intervals since I met him just over twenty-four hours ago.

"I'd really like to spend another night holding you in my arms," he adds.

My face is flush with heat, and I feel incapable of speech. Fortunately, we're practically back to our room.

Justin walks Tate and me to our door. Tate goes in. I linger a moment and give Justin the one-minute signal with my index finger. I open the door to the room and say to Tate, "Justin went and got his own room this morning, and I was thinking I'd sleep with him tonight. Just sleep," I add, though I'm not totally sure about that last part necessarily.

"'Kay." It's only one syllable, but I detect something in it. Disappointment? Disapproval?

But I don't know what to ask her to figure out what she really thinks, so I just say, "I'll see you in the morning. Sleep tight."

I close the door, take Justin's hand, and we walk the few steps across the dirt yard to his room. I feel giddy to the point of trembling. I love this part, when everything is thrilling and new.

Inside, I watch as Justin strips down to his boxers, admiring his flat stomach and broad chest. I take off my bra and shorts and climb under the covers at the edge of the bed, facing away from him because, stupidly, I feel too nervous to look him in the eye.

I'm in a guy's bed, wearing only a T-shirt and underwear, and feeling completely naked. I'm very aware of my breasts now that they've been liberated from the polite constraints of my bra, my nipples against my shirt, my breasts moving freely.

Justin gets in to bed next to me, my back against his front, just like last night. He pulls my hair away from my neck and kisses my neck lightly. It feels good, but I think it's more the excitement and the anticipation of what's going to happen next that makes me moan, a sound he takes—rightly—to mean I want him to go on.

The intensity of his kisses increase and he gently sucks the back of my neck, and that—that makes me writhe.

At last his hand ventures beneath my top at my waist, then up to my rib cage. Finally he slides his fingers a few inches higher, cupping my breast. My nipple hardens in his palm and I twist my head enough that we can kiss, then turn completely around so we're facing each other. We spend a great deal of time discovering each other's bodies with our hands, until I'm out of my head with desire and I ask him if he has a condom. He does; he retrieves it from the depths of his backpack, tossing clothes and underwear all over the place in his effort to find it. I am both grateful they are there and a little disconcerted. I'm on the pill to make my periods less horrendously painful—I've been on the pill for five years now—but I always make guys wear a condom. I have a pathological fear of AIDS, so I'm happy he has protection with him, but the thought flashes through my mind that if he hadn't found me, he'd just be using his condoms with somebody else.

The thought disappears as soon as it comes. He enters me slowly, teasing me, driving me insane.

It feels so good to have him inside me, but it's an interesting challenge to make love on a bed this tiny—when we change positions we have a few near tumbles off the bed that are marked with giggly *oopses!* that in no way detract from our passion.

He comes within moments of when I announce my orgasm with a guttural moan, a sound I only realize must have come from me after the fact.

It takes several minutes for our breathing to return to normal.

We fall asleep for minutes, sometimes hours, here and there over the course of the night, but the bed is so tiny that if one of us moves, we bonk each other in the head. If one of us breathes a little loudly, it's like a siren in the other's ear. But I'm so happy right now, I don't care about sleep.

In the morning, our eyes sting from lack of sleep. We make love yet again, slowly, with lots of gazing into each other's eyes and smiling at each other.

After Justin does the awkward full-condom, flapping-dick waddle to the bathroom he returns to bed and we embrace, spending a ludicrous amount of time smiling stupidly at each other, staring into each other's eyes and studying each other's features in extreme close up.

After breakfast, Tate, Justin, and I walk along the banks of the Arno river. Now that we're hanging out with Justin, the Italian men lay off with their declarations that we are *bella bella*. Justin is our man barrier.

We can't figure out what to do with ourselves, so we decide to take a day trip to the Leaning Tower of Pisa. It's an hour-long train ride away and then a quick walk into town to see the tower. The first thing I feel is a little betrayed when I see the many enormous cables that keep the tower from falling down. I feel like I can see the puppeteer's strings when I want to believe the puppet is moving on its own accord, dancing on air.

Apparently the tower was intended to be the campanile, bell tower, of the nearby duomo. It wasn't quite finished being built when the soil just abruptly dropped out because the area was unstable from having once been under water. The tower keeps slipping a few more inches each year, but the tourists don't stop coming, no matter how many cables it takes to keep it from crumbling down entirely.

We also visit the duomo, which is filled with religious art, surprise surprise.

Just walking around the city itself is fun, too. The art, architecture, doorways, and balconies all have the effect of making me smiley and content. The buildings are old and not always in the best state of repair. I'm not sure what it is exactly that appeals to me so much about the place: That it's charming? Quaint? So different from everything I know in the States?

When we've had our fill of Pisa, we take the train back to Florence and find a restaurant recommended in our guidebook.

Tate and I order salads of spongy buffalo-mozzarella cheese, fresh Roma tomatoes, and basil leaves covered with olive oil and a pinch of salt and pepper. We eat our salads with crusty bread and house red wine. I wish Americans knew about real bread like this instead of the sorry excuse of Wonderbread-type crap. If touring Europe were mandatory for Americans, Wonderbread would be out of business and U.S. restaurants wouldn't dare serve that mushroom-like Astroturf excuse for bread on the table with meals.

After dinner we decide to hit the clubs. Tate and I retreat to our room to get cleaned up the best we can, but it's really a pointless exercise. We have no sexy or pretty clothes to change into. We have no make-up. We only brought sturdy T-shirts and sweaters and our most practical underwear. I long for my closet back home—I can think of a dozen things there that I could put on, a myriad of footwear choices to select from. I'm sick to death of these same few T-shirts, the same pair of jeans, the same sweater I've worn nearly every day of our trip.

"I'm officially sick to death of every item of clothing in this stupid backpack," I announce. "I don't have anything to wear to a club."

"Here," Tate says. She tells me to put on my red T-shirt

and to tuck it into my jeans. She takes her black silk scarf that she sometimes uses to cover her head with and wraps it around my waist like a thick belt, tying it in a big knot on one side. It's not much, but it does make me feel a little prettier. Of course Tate can put on any kind of ripped ragged clothing she wants and she always looks cool enough for the clubs. She puts her hair up in her decorative chopsticks, puts on a black tank top; baggy, knee-length, olive-colored shorts with cavernous pockets; and black shoes that look like ballet slippers.

As we get ready, I casually say, "So, what do you think of Justin?"

She smiles. "I think he's nice."

That's it? Where's the squealing and jumping up and down? I'm finally getting nookie after an appallingly long dry spell, I think some squealing is in order. But that's not Tate's style. Nor is it her style to ask personal questions. But I'm about to burst here, so I just spill the details.

"We slept together," I say.

"Yeah?"

"Yeah. And it was great. He's a great kisser. It was so much fun. We didn't get any sleep at all. It was not easy making love on that tiny bed. More than once one of us would have to rescue the other person from falling off the bed. But we could just laugh about it, you know?"

"Good. Good for you."

"What about you, are you going to try to find some romance on this trip?"

"Oh, you know, guys on the road—you can't trust them. I mean Justin seems great and everything, but . . ."

I'm abruptly irritated with Tate for bringing a storm cloud to my parade. What does she mean you can't trust guys on the road? Sure you can. Some of them anyway.

I look in the mirror and give my hair one last fluff, then I tell her we should get going.

For once, we get to the club late enough that the place is hopping and we hit the dance floor first thing, and I feel so happy with life that my irritation with Tate fades promptly away.

Tate hooks up with an Italian guy who is a few years younger than us and tells us he just finished his mandatory military service. He is really cute and seems sincere. He doesn't posture or preen like Piero did, trying to get attention. He works at his father's restaurant, a business he will take over one day.

Justin and I are dancing hard, both sweating like crazy. I look over and see Tate is kissing Gino. I smile. Life is good.

Tate seems to have so much fun with Gino that I'm as surprised as he is when she tells him not only that she doesn't want him to walk her home, but that she doesn't want to take him up on his offer to have dinner at his family's restaurant tomorrow night. Having dinner with locals sounds great to me, but nope, she's not interested.

As we walk home, Tate covers her hand with her mouth. "I can't believe I made out with a stranger in a bar. That is so very MTV Spring Break of me."

"Oh whatever," I say. "You're in Italy. A little saliva swapping with a handsome Italian man is a requirement. It's like going to Rome and not seeing the Sistine Chapel."

"Unless of course you've got a dashing Iowan to smooch," Justin says.

I smile at him and squeeze his hand.

* * *

At the hostel, though I want desperately to spend the night with Justin, I can't bear the guilt of abandoning Tate for a second night in a row.

"I'm afraid I'm going to have to say goodnight, Justin. I'm going to go back to the room with Tate."

He looks disappointed. This pleases me.

"You can spend the night with him, it's no big deal," Tate says.

"No. Don't worry about it. I could use some real sleep." Which is true.

I give Justin a goodnight kiss.

Even though I'm exhausted, the moment I'm under the covers, I find myself too giddy to sleep. I want to talk to Tate about every second I've spent with Justin, but if I just spend the night talking about him, it's no better than if I'd just gone to his room and left her alone yet again. I'll hold off on reporting every touch, glance, kiss, and emotion until I can write in my journal in the morning.

"I'm having the greatest time on this trip. Are you?" I say.

"Yeah. I'm glad you asked me to come. I think I needed to get away for a while and I didn't even realize it."

"Yeah? Why?"

"I don't know. I think maybe you were right, we needed some adventure. I needed a change. I was in such a routine."

"Me too. I really feel inspired to write. I think this trip has kick-started my muse."

"Good. That's good to hear. I'm happy for you."

Moments after our conversation pauses, I hear Tate's heavy breathing, letting me know that she's asleep. I try to do the same, but I keep thinking about Justin. What if he wants to go on to Paris or something when Tate and I have barely seen anything in Italy yet? I try to get my mind off Justin, but then I immediately start thinking about my other obsession, which is fantasizing about how great life will be when I make it as a writer, when I'll be able to wake up whenever I want, work out, drink coffee in idle leisure, and then spend several hours writing. Then I'll make dinner for my future husband and myself. I never cook now, but in my new life, I'll learn how because I'll have time to. Then Husband and I will talk and laugh and make love, and spend the rest of the evening reading or watching a DVD. It will be bliss.

After a fruitless hour of not sleeping, I quietly get out of bed, close the door behind me, and run across the lawn of the hostel to Justin's room. I knock lightly on the door, worried that I may be waking him, but he opens the door wearing nothing more than a smile.

"I was hoping you'd change your mind," he says, and takes me in his arms.

No matter how much sex Justin and I have, I want more, more, more.

In the morning I wake before he does. I slip out of bed and go to the bathroom where I splash water on my face to try to wake up. When I stand up and dry my face, I see Justin in the mirror walking up behind me. He's also naked; his penis is semi-erect. I smile at him in the mirror. He offers a devious half-grin in return. He kisses the back of my neck and positions my arms on either side of the sink, his hands over mine. He caresses my bottom with his penis and in moments he's totally hard. He slips on a condom and enters me from behind.

It is, without question, the perfect way to start my day.

6

Venice, Italy

I'm thrilled—and relieved—when I mention to Justin the possibility of going to Venice next and ask if he'd like to come with us and he says yes. Then I realize I haven't checked with Tate to see if it's okay with her if Justin tags along with us.

I scurry back to Tate's and my room and watch Tate sleep for what seems like days. When she finally wakes, I smile a smile that is too big and too enthusiastic and Tate picks up on it right away, giving me a questioning look.

"What's up?" she asks in a voice that is both groggy and a little wary.

"Oh, nothing. I . . . I was just thinking maybe we could go to Venice next."

"Yeah. Sure. Great."

"Yeah? Okay. Um, yeah, so I was also thinking maybe—"

"He can come, Jadie. I don't mind."

"Really?"

"Really."

I'm so happy I actually squeal. (I'm not proud.) I run over to Tate and hug her tight.

"Jadie . . . I can't breathe."

"Oh sorry." I loosen my grip and leave her to shower and pack while I do the same.

For the entire train ride to Venice, I can't stop thinking about having sex with Justin. Images keep flashing through my mind—Justin's facial expressions that look like pain but I know are pleasure, the groan/murmur sound he makes when he comes, watching him as he grinds his pelvis into mine.

The entire three hours of the trip I think these thoughts. I can't focus on the view, write in my journal, or interview female train riders for their insights on international romance. Good sex does a whammy on your ability to concentrate. Not that I'm complaining.

In Venice we find a hotel that's not too far from the train station. We ask for two rooms, a single and a double, and then comes an awkward moment when the clerk asks us whether we want two single beds or a double in the double room. The three of us look at each other, perplexed.

"Why don't you two take the double room?" Tate offers. Oh how I want to hug her.

"Are you sure?" I ask. Tate has seemed happy enough to share me with Justin so far, and she's not the kind of person who harbors secret resentment but doesn't tell you about it until she's so damn pissed she could spit on you. Still, I hope that she's not furtively feeling like a third wheel and putting a smile on her face to cover up feeling left out. I pull her aside a few feet and whisper. "You really don't have to do this. I came on this trip to be with you, you know."

"It's cool, Jadie."

"Are you sure you're okay with this? With all of this? With us hanging out with Justin all the time? Am I neglecting you? You can tell me the truth."

"I don't mind." We look at each other, me trying to figure out if she's telling the truth. Then she says, "This might be your great love, and even if it's just a great romance, Jesus, we're in Venice, you should be with your guy."

Have I mentioned that I really and truly love this girl? And "great love" and "great romance"—these words will zip through my mind for the rest of the day.

"Thank you," I say, giving her a hug.

We dump our backpacks in our rooms and then head out to explore the city. There are no street signs here, since there aren't really streets, just signs indicating which way you go to get to a landmark like St. Mark's Square or the Rialto bridge.

Everything but everything looks run down in Venice. Every building needs a coat or ten of paint and at least some minor repair work. The shutters on the buildings look like they were put on in Medieval times and then never painted or touched again.

Still, it's a beautiful city. Justin describes it as "picturesque decrepitude," which sums it up nicely.

There are endless narrow stone alleys, and the buildings are painted in cheery pinks, rust-oranges, and clay yellows. Even so, the main thing I think as we walk is *everything is so run down*. The day is somewhat overcast, so that may have something to do with my reaction.

There are millions of bridges everywhere, all with steps to get up and down them. We watch tourist after tourist struggling to negotiate the stairs with their luggage, and I feel savvy for having only brought a backpack.

We follow the signs to St. Mark's Square. To get there we are herded past half a million stores all selling Mardi Gras masks or things made from glass—vases, decorations, jewelry, etc., and the closer we get to St. Mark's, the more mobbed with tourists the area becomes.

St. Mark's Square is an open plaza the size of two football fields covered on three sides by buildings that were once white but are now half black from dirt or pollution,

I'm not sure which. On the fourth side are the domes and mosaics of St. Mark's Basilica. We order preposterously overpriced cappuccinos and listen to the pigeons serenade the lovers, artists, and tourists that fill the square. We watch little kids feed the pigeons and chase them around. One little three-year-old sprinkles his bird seed with a little too much vigor and is attacked by a Hitchcock-*Birds*-type swarm of them that land on his head, shoulders, and arms while squawking like mad. The kid screams and runs away, squealing with laughter.

Eventually our rumbling stomachs pull us away from the people watching and we walk a ways (there aren't really "blocks" here) and find a pizza place where we order pizza and beer and have a lively discussion about whether it would be feasible to start our own town called Beer, Colorado. We figure we'd need a post office because naturally it will be popular for people to come to town and have their letters postmarked from Beer. Our income, we figure, will mostly come from the bar that will be the focal point of our town and from the endorsements we're sure to get from Budweiser or another company that we're convinced will want to buy the rights to be able to say "Brewed in Beer, Colorado," on their bottles and all their advertisements. Justin says that by the time we've got all the paperwork to launch our town, he'll have had experience running a restaurant, so he can be the manager of the bar. Tate, of course, will be the cocktail waitress, and I'll edit the weekly newspaper, which will be ninety-eight percent beer ads, and two percent propaganda posing as news about fun things to do in Beer and the health properties of beer and other alcoholic beverages.

Even though our conversation is stupid—we're not exactly figuring out a way to achieve world peace or something—I feel really happy. I love that Justin is volunteering to come to Colorado to run our mythical bar in our mythical town. It may all be made up, but the possibility of Justin coming to Colorado still thrills me.

After dinner we find, oddly enough, an English pub that is amazingly not filled with tourists but Italians who are glued to the television screen watching soccer. The volume is set to ear-puncturing levels, I think so the two bartenders can keep up with the game while continuing with the arduous task of doing their jobs.

Here in Europe, you can order your beer in a normal size pint or a little micro-size, and inexplicably, all the Europeans order the mini-training-wheels size beer.

"I don't get it," I say. "If you're going to order beers that small you'd be going up to the bar every two seconds. I think we should let them know they've got the option of ordering a normal size beer."

"Also, I think somebody should let the Venetian boys know that the eighties are over. What's up with these hairdos?" Tate asks.

I follow her gaze to the two guys who are ordering beers at the bar. One has his hair trimmed short on the sides with a bouffant of curls shellacked with gel on the top of his head in a style that reminds me uncannily of Jon Cryer's hairdo in *Pretty in Pink*. The other guy has a crazed mop of long curls popping out all over his head; the only explanation is that he belongs to a little-known religious cult that strictly forbids its followers to look into mirrors or own combs or hairbrushes of any sort.

A collective groan from the bar patrons is so loud and unexpected I nearly fall off my bar stool. "What happened?" I ask Justin and Tate, who are facing the television, like every other patron in the bar except me.

"Nothing. Nothing ever happens in soccer. Somebody *almost* did something exciting, but the exciting thing didn't actually happen," Justin says. "I don't get the fascination with soccer over here. It's the most boring game ever created. They run around for a couple hours and at best they get one or two goals that whole time. The goal is huge. You'd think it would be easy to get the ball in there, but no. No goals. Not ever."

We have another beer and joke around about soccer and bad hair, and eventually we endeavor to find our way home, which turns out to be no easy task. Finding the Rialto Bridge and St. Mark's Square was no real problem because there were a million signs pointing to them. Our hotel, however, is not by any landmark we know of, so there is nothing to guide us back. Thank goodness there are three of us because just when an alley looks to me like any other alley, Tate or Justin will say, "I remember that restaurant!" or "I remember that sign!" then when the two of them look like they have no idea which way to turn next, I'll remember that we'd had to go over a wooden bridge and pass such and such a hotel to get to St. Mark's Square earlier in the day so we have to go back over or by it to get home. Only twice do we wander down Medieval alleys that end in a dead end and then have to backtrack.

The next morning we walk around the residential part of Venice, which is much prettier and less run down than the tourist parts. Italian parents push their babies in strollers or sit at sidewalk cafés with red and white checkered tablecloths and green bottles of spring water taking the place of centerpieces. Laundry flaps in the breeze everywhere on lines hung outside apartment windows. I can't imagine how they can get their clothes dry while simultaneously keeping them pigeon-shit free, but apparently they do because every apartment building is adorned with laundry.

After lunch we decide to return to the tourist hell of St. Mark's Plaza. We visit St. Mark's Basilica, squinting to see the details of the gold mosaics decorating the dome-vaulted ceiling. Then we head next door to the Doge's Palace. The first floor is where the Doge (the guy who used to rule Venice) and his family lived. Today the living quarters, like the rest of Venice, look tired and worn out. The silk wallpaper is ripped and faded, and the signs (with merciful translations in English) explain that most of the art on these floors is not original. There are lots of marble fireplaces—practically one in each room we visit— that are carved and decorated intricately, and those hint at the splendor that once was. There are several halls where the law-making aristocratic types either made laws or hung out waiting to make laws. And the Chamber of the Great Council is enormous—one of the largest rooms in Europe, so the signs say. It houses the largest canvas painting in the world—*Parardiso* by Tintereto.

Eventually, I get sated on the art and the gilt and I want to get to the dungeons. Basically, the Doge lived, worked, and condemned people to life in prison all from the comfort of his own palace.

At this point in the day, we've been on our feet for hours, and I just want to get through the place to somewhere where we can rest. We're practically jogging through the rooms when we go through one and I see a painting and say, "That looks like a Hieronymus Bosch. Hold up you guys." I consult the sign. "It is a Bosch! Oh my gosh! I love him!"

I point to one of the paintings, noting how Bosch is warning against the deadly sins, with humans writhing, being tortured and carted away to hell. Bosch worked in the 1500s, but his evil-looking creatures look like the stuff of modern cartoons or comic books. While his work was religious like the other artists of his time (though some might argue he was poking fun at the church in a way subtle enough to get away with it), his work is so different and innovative it's a welcome change from the endless parade of Madonna with Child-type paintings we've seen on this trip, and even Tate gets into pointing out interesting details in the piece.

Eventually we move on and get to the Bridge of Sighs, which crosses over a canal to the prison. We take some pictures of the eerie stone cells and then we all agree it's time to get home for some rest.

As we exit the palace, I look at my watch so I'll be able to time how long it takes us to get home. It's 3:02 in the afternoon.

We walk and walk and walk, taking turns that seem logical enough. It's maddening trying to get through the narrow alleyways packed with tourists. A group of four will walk four astride, taking up the entire width of the alley, and then one of them will stop abruptly to window shop. Dozens of times we have to stop dead in our tracks—and we're only going at an old-person's shuffle sort of pace to begin with—to avoid ramming straight into someone who has stopped suddenly in front of us. Often their arms will be draped with bags and they'll turn so quickly their bags go whirling around, building up maximum velocity with which to whump us in the head. Parents use strollers to steamroll people in front of them, clear-cutting a path for themselves, knowing that since their weapon of destruction has an innocent and adorable baby at the helm, there will be no retribution . . . or justice.

Then we're suddenly spit back out onto the Molo, the pier. We turn around, and what do we see? That we're about one hundred yards from where we started walking exactly forty-five minutes ago. Which just happens to be on the complete opposite side of the city from where our hotel is.

The three of us trundle to a bench where we collapse, dejected and defeated, bemoaning our fate.

"I do not want to have to go back through that mob of tourists," Justin says. "We'll find some other way home." He opens the map and studies it, then he looks around to find where we are on it. "Okay, we're here. To get home, we need to take a right, then a right, then a left, then a right, then another right, and a quick left and a . . ." he sighs dramatically, expelling hours worth of exhaustion. "It's hopeless. These maps can tell you where you are but not how to get to where you want to be. We'd have to take about fifty-eight rights and lefts to get home."

"Let's just go back to St. Mark's Plaza and follow the same route we did last night. We got home last night. We can get home again," I say, trying to seem cheerier than I actually am.

And that's what we do. We get home at 4:39, an hour and forty minutes from the time our feet had already been waving white flags and begging for mercy. Justin and I collapse on our bed and stare at the ceiling without speaking for a good forty minutes before we can even muster the energy to speak. It's like we've just survived a harrowing event and are still reeling from the effects.

"Venice is a city that whoops your ass," Justin says at long last, his eyes still wide from the trauma we've undergone.

"It's brutal," I agree.

Out of the corner of my eye, I see Justin extend an arm to retrieve a book from the nightstand beside him. I do the same, using as few muscles as possible to fetch my book.

It is two more hours before we can bring ourselves to move from our supine positions, where the only part of our bodies that we move are our fingers to turn the pages of our paperbacks, and even then our leg muscles are so sore and tight we immediately agree that we should go to the restaurant that's about thirty feet away from our hotel for dinner, and we don't care if it's touristy and over-priced; we ain't walking any more today.

Tate readily agrees to this plan when we knock on her door down the hall, and the three of us stagger the few feet to the restaurant and eat thin slices of pizza and drink exorbitant quantities of house wine.

Everything is expensive here except the wine, but the meal and the wine are tasty enough. Everything is going well until I say I'd like to take a gondola ride after dinner. Justin rolls his eyes and declares this hopelessly touristy and overpriced.

"I know, but I want to do it anyway. It's not like there's a lot of stuff to do here at night. It's my treat."

"I can wait for you guys somewhere. A bar or back at the room," Tate says.

"No, I want all three of us to go."

"Come on, gondola rides are supposed to be romantic. I'll be in the way."

"Tate, I'm not kidding, I want you to come. Come on. Please, please, please. It's my treat."

I finally wear them down.

The cost is exorbitant as Justin had warned, but the gondolier is a ham, and he keeps us laughing for most of the ride. He expertly zips around, making hairpin turns I simply couldn't imagine doing in a boat.

"Why is everything so expensive in Venice?" I ask him.

"Venice ees the most expensive city in Italy to leeve in and to visit. It is an island, zo everything must be brought in by boat. It costs extra, no?"

"That makes sense."

The gondolier doesn't sing, which I'm secretly happy about, but he does answer my questions when I have them and occasionally offers tidbits about the city with-out prompting. The ride gives us great views of the canals.

Afterward, we return to our hotel. I don't know what Tate does with the rest of her night, but as for Justin and me, we just read until I start thinking about the folly that was our day—that moment when we arrived on the Molo and turned around to see that we were just yards from where we'd begun, seeing the Doge's Palace and the granite columns topped by St. Theodore, the first patron saint of Venice, and the lion of St. Mark—and I start laughing. I just keep laughing harder and harder until Justin asks what's so funny.

"We walked and we walked and we walked and then we hit the canal, turned around, and that moment, that horrible moment we realized we were a hundred yards from where we started! Ah ha ha!" I'm laughing so hard I'm crying, and Justin joins me.

"It's only funny now that we're home and off our feet, relaxing comfortably in bed," he says, still laughing, and this is so true I laugh even harder. We laugh for a good long time, and even after we stop, little giggles burble their way to the surface from time to time until I finally escape into sleep.

The next morning, as Tate, Justin, and I wander along the pier a vendor approaches and asks us if we want to see a glass blowing museum on Murano, a nearby island. He says the vapretto (basically a bus in boat form) ride will be free, which makes me immediately suspicious, but we have time to kill and life is all about accumulating experiences, right?

Well, was I right to be wary. The "museum" turns out to be a showroom full of kitschy glasswork—pink flamingoes and green kittens and the like. A salesman immediately latches onto us like a wet T-shirt and relentlessly hounds us, telling us he'll give us the best prices on the island.

At first we try to be nice, explaining about how we're

backpacking and anything we bought would be crushed in moments.

Salesman: "I ship it to you."

Me: "We're not interested, thank you."

Salesman (holding a ridiculous piece of glass of a woman in a red dress that is unbelievably expensive): "This one, ah? It is beautiful, no?"

No. Not even close.

Me: "We don't have enough money."

"I will bill your credit card in three easy installments!"

Like he's doing me a favor.

On and on he goes. I don't even want to look at the glass because every time I glance at something he becomes convinced I cannot know happiness until I buy this particular piece. He's hounding Tate with equally aggressive techniques and suddenly she explodes, "We're not fucking interested! Leave us the fuck alone!"

Tate storms out of the shop and Justin and I follow—me looking back at the gape-mouthed salesmen, smiling, doing my best to look contrite.

Tate is walking back to the ferry stop as fast as her little legs can take her. She's walking so fast that Justin and I fall far behind her.

"Your friend is quite the little tough ass," Justin says. "Is it because she's so short, it's like some kind of a girl version of a Napoleon complex?"

"I think Tate's tough act is about her having needed to be tough all her life. Her mother died when she was a little girl and her father died when she was, I can't remember, twelve or thirteen, something like that. She got sent to live with her uncle in Boston, but she didn't like it there, so she ran away. She came back to Denver, where she was originally from, and she just kind of lived on friends' couches and in their basements through high school."

"You're kidding."

"I'm not kidding."

"What was so bad at her uncle's that camping out in friends' basements was better that living with him?"

This is something I've often wondered about. Was he abusive? Too controlling for a free spirit like Tate? Tate won't say. "I don't know. Tate doesn't talk about her past. I've tried to pry, believe me. She changes the subject every time."

When we get back to Venice, Justin says he's tired and would like a nap before we get lunch, but when he and I get back to our room, he pulls me into a hug, gives me a deep kiss, and tells me to take off my clothes.

I feign surprise. "Why Mr. Devlin, I thought you wanted a nap. Surely you haven't gotten me alone in your room under false pretenses?"

"I have been wanting to get you out of your clothes all morning. You have no idea how much self-control it's taken me not to grope your breasts all day," he says, cupping them. He releases me and goes to his backpack to get a condom. I pull off my clothes and lie on the bed, waiting.

"Fuck!" he exclaims.

"What's wrong?"

He groans. "I meant to buy more condoms. We're out."

I consider telling him that I'm on the pill. I need more background on what I'm getting into here, so I ask, "How many sex partners have you had where you didn't use condoms?"

"Two. Both long-term girlfriends. Why?"

"Did you cheat on them or did they cheat on you?"

"I definitely didn't cheat on them and to my knowledge, they didn't cheat on me."

He's from Iowa. What are the odds he could have something? Surely Iowans are a wholesome people?

"Do you think you could pull out?"

"Definitely. No problem."

I notice that he doesn't inquire about my sexual history. Is he telling the truth about having unprotected sex with just two people? I decide to risk it. "Okay, you can come inside . . . I mean don't *come* inside, but you can enter."

I lie naked on the bed and watch him take off his clothes. He climbs onto the bed, stroking my leg with his hand as he crawls up to where I am. His fingers are teasing my inner thighs; he takes my nipple in his mouth. At last he plunges his fingers inside me until I'm more than ready for him.

He enters slowly. "Jesus that feels good."

It sure as hell does, though he comes before I can. When he does—all over my stomach—it's with a particularly primal cry of pleasure.

It's not until we get dressed and leave the room to meet Tate that I notice a tell-tale coil of Justin's hair springing out from the middle of his head that says clearly, "we've just had sex." For a second, I feel embarrassed, but then I just smile at him, my co-conspirator in pleasure.

The three of us decide to return to St. Mark's Square to visit the bell tower. We're almost there when the telltale cramps hit: diarrhea.

"Guys, I need a bathroom, right away," I announce.

But of course as would follow Murphy's law of travel, when I need a bathroom desperately, there are none to be found. We walk and walk and finally I see a sign pointing in the direction of a bathroom. We have to walk the equivalent of several blocks before we actually reach it, a distance that would be merely irritating in other circumstances but is downright dangerous at this particular moment. I leave Tate and Justin and dash into the bathroom only to discover it's a pay toilet. I send a silent prayer up to heaven that I have a few small coins. I ferret around in the darkest corners of my money belt, first pulling up some coins from London with the queen looking stern and royal, then finding a couple quarters, until at last I find a fifty-cent Euro piece and am allowed entrance to the bathroom.

When I exit the stall, I tell myself that the crisis is now over, and join up with Tate and Justin.

The three of us wait in preposterous lines to take the elevator up the campanile, the bell tower, not because we particularly care, but because we don't have anything else to do but see the city and so, lemming-like, we do what everyone else is doing. From time to time my stomach spasms threateningly again. In between the stomach contractions, I feel fine, and do my best to convince myself that my illness has passed.

But as time passes, between my burbling stomach and the mad crush of tourists battling to get to the view, I decide that I hate everyone in the world, with the exception of Tate and Justin. I hate all of humanity, all the people who are crushing me and fighting their way up to the top of the tower. Then *I* get to the top, and the view is so breathtaking I stop hating all the other tourists, and even forget, for the moment, about my ornery stomach. Red rooftops extend all the way out to the horizon. I can see the Dolomites a hundred miles away. To the south is the open sea and the Grande Canale. To the east is the courtyard of the Doge's Palace. Next door are the eastern domes of St. Mark's Basilica. I take lots of pictures, though I know no photo can accurately capture the beauty or what it feels like to be here right now.

When we've been sufficiently dazzled by the view, we start heading back to the hotel. We're not far from the hotel when we collectively decide to sit down for a drink, but just as we sit down at the bar, my stomach feels like a rag being rung out by two angry hands and I feel like my intestines might explode right here in the restaurant.

"I'm so sorry, you guys. I'm not feeling well. Something's going on with my stomach. I'm going to go back to the room to moan and writhe for a while. You guys stay and have fun."

"Don't be silly, Jadie. We'll come back with you," Justin says.

"No, stay, have fun. You can check on me in a few hours, before you get dinner. There is no reason for you guys to be locked up in the hotel room just because I'm not feeling very well." I'm doing my best to not let out an explosive fart that would no doubt detonate the room with an unconscionable odor. This is so freakin' irritating. It's not like we're in some third-world country and I went around drinking filthy water from random locations. There is no reason for me to have gotten sick. Of course in the middle of a wonderful romance on the road I get a crippling case of diarrhea for no apparent reason from no apparent source. It is clearly a metaphor for my life. You think life is going well: Bam! Take that! Here's a pile of shit. *Deal with it.*

"I wouldn't mind going back to the room and getting some rest," Tate says.

"Seriously, I wouldn't mind either," Justin agrees.

"Yeah? Okay. Thanks."

The walk back to the hotel only takes ten minutes, but it seems like ten hours. I'm trying my damnedest to walk normally, but it ain't easy.

As soon as we get up to our room I make a beeline for the bathroom. There is only the tiniest thin door between Justin and me, and the room is so small that for all the auditory shield the door can provide, Justin might as well be in the bathroom with me.

I run the water on full blast, though I doubt that it can do much to mask the torrential spluttering sound, but it's all I've got.

God this sucks. I've known the guy for just a few days. We're having the perfect romance, and now I'm in the midst of the most unromantic ailment I could possibly get.

Finally I go out to the room where Justin is. I lie beside him on the bed. He embraces me. "I'm sorry you're not feeling well. Is there anything I can do?"

I shake my head.

"Do you want me to get you some medicine?"

I shake my head again, more vigorously this time. I so, so do not want to send my new lover out into a foreign city to buy medicine for this particular disease. Anyway, if I took medicine, I would be acknowledging that I'm really sick and that this isn't just going to go away in a few minutes, which I'm quite certain it will.

But a few minutes later when I'm racked by another painful cramp, I can't bear it anymore and say, "If that offer about you getting me some medicine is still good . . . would you mind?"

"Of course not. I'll be right back." He kisses me on the forehead and gives me a parting hug.

Fifteen minutes later or so he returns, carrying a small box of pills in a small paper bag. I gratefully take a pill and wash it down.

"Was it hard finding the pharmacy?"

"No. I just asked downstairs where one was."

"Oh. Smart. Well, thanks."

"No problem, babe." He gives me a sweet smile; I smile weakly back. I can't shake the fear that Justin will decide hanging out with me is more trouble than it's worth and ditch me. But I can't think of that right now. I can't think of anything but how awful I feel. Vaguely I take note of Justin, who is lying beside me, picking up a book. I just lie there, clutching my stomach, staring at the ceiling.

At some point, I fall asleep, and when I wake, my stomach still feels off, but it's a million times better than the blinding pain I was in before. I feel almost human.

"I'm feeling a little better," I tell him.

"Good!" He puts his book down and rolls over on his side, propping his head up on his elbow so he can look at me. "Do you have any idea what made you sick?"

"No. I didn't really eat anything different than you and Tate, did I?"

"I don't think so. Speaking of eating, I'm getting kind of hungry. I don't suppose you're up for getting a bite?"

I appraise the stomach situation. It's been several hours since we've eaten, but my stomach is still too messed up for me to tell if I'm hungry. "Maybe I could get a snack. Plain pasta or something. I'm up for going with you guys, anyway."

"Great, let's go get Tate."

We go to dinner at a place not far from our hotel and share our table with three backpackers. (In Italy, small tables are often pushed together and you're frequently seated right next to complete strangers.) They haven't ordered yet, and they ask us if we want to join them for dinner, and we say sure. They explain how they all met— they've formed impromptu friendships over the last few weeks on the road that are difficult for me to keep track of. Pete from Australia and Ben from England became friends in Rome, or maybe it was Brendan from Ireland who Pete met in Rome and Ben he met in Siena, I can't remember. My stomach ailment hasn't completely gone away, but at the first return rumble, I pop another pill, which keeps things in my intestines from exploding.

The waiter comes and takes our orders and brings a liter of the house red wine. After Pete and Brendan have poured us each a glass and we've all sipped it and proclaimed it delicious, Pete asks us where we're from.

"We're from Boulder, Colorado," Tate says, "And he's from Iowa. We met Justin in Florence a few days ago."

"Abandon your friend for a guy, did you?" Ben says to me.

"No, no!" I protest, a bit too emphatically. "The three of us do everything together. Well, not *everything*." This elicits laughs from everyone.

"Brendan, Ben, tell me, how is it possible that a beautiful girl like Tate hasn't been swept away yet?" Pete says.

"It's inexplicable," says Ben.

"Totally incomprehensible," says Brendan.

"Many guys have tried," I say, "but Tate, she's a tough one, I tell you."

As we talk, I watch Pete watch Tate, and watch Tate smile, fluttery-eyed at the attention. We learn Pete is twenty-six and that it took him eight years to get through college because he worked full time as a waiter to put himself through school, and he had to take a year off here and there to save money.

"I wait tables, too," Tate says.

"Oh, so you have the silverware dreams then," Pete says.

"Silverware dreams?" asks Brendan.

"Folding silverware into napkins," Tate explains. "You have to roll a million before you leave for the night, so they're ready for the next day, and then when you go to sleep, you have visions of silverware and napkins dancing in your head."

Pete and Tate are off, talking about their respective jobs, in their own world, and the rest of us become mere spectators for a few minutes until our first courses arrive.

We discuss what each of us has ordered—I got the gnocchi, Tate got the mushroom ravioli, Justin ordered the cracked red pepper pasta, both Pete and Ben got the spaghetti alla Bolognese, and Brendan ordered the rigatoni alla something or other that has bacon and pecorino on it.

As we dig in to our meal there is another pause in the conversation. It's just a blip, a moment, but it makes me uncomfortable, so without thinking I say, "So, what do you all do for a living?" Ahh! Ahh! Did I just say that? That's so damn American of me!

"Right now I'm Pete Roberts, world traveler, esquire. I graduated from college about three months ago and took off right after graduation. It's expensive to leave Australia, so when an Australian travels abroad, we mean it." Pete is very cute, with black eyes and curly black hair that reaches his shoulders. I'd guess he's about 5'10", and he's got a powerful build, with thick muscular arms and legs. He's just scruffy enough to fit right in in Boulder.

We learn that Ben does something corporate and financial and Brendan is an aspiring police officer who currently delivers bottled juice to grocery stores and restaurants and things.

"So, you are from Colorado. Italy must be really hot compared to what you're used to," Pete says.

"Why would you say that?" Tate says. "It gets wicked hot in Boulder in the summer."

"Isn't Colorado really cold?" Pete asks.

"In the winter in the mountains, yeah, but it's actually a lot milder than most places in the States," Tate says.

"I thought Colorado was gray and freezing all the time," Brendan says.

"Other people we've met on this trip have said that," I say, "but actually, Colorado has an average of three hundred sunny days a year. It gets cold for about three months in the winter but almost never gray."

"That sounds like a place I just might like," Pete says.

"It's a good city. It's kind of . . . odd there," I say. "If you're not outdoorsy, you probably shouldn't visit. Everybody there is always like, 'Woo-hoo! Let's go run a marathon!' or 'Woo-hoo! Let's go hike a fourteener!' ".

"Fourteener?" Pete asks.

"A mountain that's around fourteen thousand feet tall."

"Feet? What's that in meters?"

Meters? Meters? I'm from America, what does he think, America is some modern, first-world country that uses fancy schmancy, easily-divisible-by-ten standard measuring systems that are used by about every other country on the globe?

"I have no idea. They're tall, I know that much," I say feebly.

The conversation morphs over the course of the night as conversations do. I realize that my knowledge of international affairs is pitiful. I know nothing about what is going on in their countries, but they know everything about us. We get on the topic of television, and they all applaud *The Simpsons*. Pete is also a fan of *Malcolm in the Middle* and *The Bachelor*, a show I'm mortified to learn has been exported. I'd really prefer that that be America's private shame. This is about the time I realize that America is the modern-day equivalent of the Roman invaders who spread their culture, politics, and traditions around the globe due to their powerful armies and economic strength, only instead of bringing architecture, aqueducts, and superior building materials to the world, we're conquering cultures with *Baywatch* and *Terminator 3*.

I can't believe how much fun I'm having. We're talking with people from as far away as Australia and Ireland, and when I'm in a diverse group of people, I fit right in. Around my coworkers, I never have anything to contribute to the conversation. They talk about how they spent their weekend remodeling their kitchens or golfing, and I'll say, "I read a great book over the weekend. It's called ____. Have you read it?" And they'll say, as if it makes them important and not dullards who are willing to allow their brains to atrophy from lack of use, "I don't have time to read. I'm too busy." Then they go back to talking about Titleist golf clubs and I go back to staring at the wall, feeling like I'm back in junior high, a socially handicapped outsider.

We go through two more liters of wine over the course of our meal. I look over at Tate and Pete, who haven't stopped talking all night. Pete is asking her about what happens to her nose ring when she gets a cold.

"Does the nose ring come out all covered in boogers? Come on, you can tell me."

"Ooh! You're being gross! Stop it!" she says, laughing and lightly slapping him on the arm.

Tate and I have certainly done our share of flirting on this trip. It's fun, that charge you get when you find someone attractive and, more important, feel like they find you attractive. I realize that none of the guys Tate has met so far on this trip has had the effect on her that Pete is having. She's usually not a fluttery-eyed type, but she can't stop smiling, and the way she looks at him goes well beyond friendly.

"I'm just kidding with you," Pete says. "I thought about getting my ear pierced once, but then I realized I don't like pain. That's why I don't have any tattoos, but I see you can take pain with the best of them." He points to the wave on her arm. "Do you have any others?"

She shows him the rose on her ankle.

"Lovely. Any others?" His tone is provocative.

Tate bites her lip. "One more. But very few people have seen it."

"What do I have to do to get a peek?"

"You either have to get very, very lucky or you have to get me very, very drunk."

"Waiter! Waiter! Another round of drinks over here!" he pretends to call out, his arm waving maniacally in the air, but the waiter is nowhere to be found.

Tate laughs. "So you don't believe in luck?"

"Hey, I figure I should cover all my bases."

It's nearly eleven by the time we've finished our meal and paid the check. I'm lethargic from so much pasta and wine and I tell the group I've had fun tonight, but that we should get going so I can get some sleep.

"But Tate, you don't have to rush home until you're ready," I say.

"I'm ready to go." She stands. "It was fun talking to you guys. Have fun on the rest of your trip."

Now I'm really confused. That's it? Doesn't she even want to see if she can arrange to see Pete again?

When Tate, Justin, and I get outside, I say, "Tate, what about Pete?"

"What about him?"

"You guys were getting along so well."

"Yeah, I just . . ." she shrugs.

"Justin, could I talk to Tate alone?"

"What? Oh sure, I'll just head back to the hotel. I'll catch up with you there."

When he's out of earshot I say, "Tate, don't you want a little romance? Several guys have been interested in you on this trip and you always go home alone. I mean you're allowed to, it's just kinda . . . weird."

"I don't know . . . we're on the road, it's not like anything could go anywhere."

"But you specialize in relationships that aren't going anywhere."

"What's that supposed to mean?"

"I mean it's been seven years since you've had anything like a boyfriend. You're young, you should be falling in love and having fun."

"It's not a big deal."

"Tate, I don't understand why you're too scared to open yourself to a relationship . . . or at least a little romance."

"I'm not scared!" she snaps.

"Yeah, Tate, you are. You always have been."

"Fuck that! Fuck you!" With that, Tate marches back inside.

Okay, that didn't go as well as I'd hoped. I've always known Tate had this fiery side to her. I know that she acts like a bad ass as a defensive mechanism. She pretends like nothing can hurt her as if faking it can make it so, but right now I want to throttle her.

I see her talking with Pete and watch them come outside together.

"Don't wait up for me. I'm staying with Pete tonight," Tate says.

"Tate . . . can we talk about this? I didn't mean for you . . ."

"Good night. I'll see you in the morning."

Shit. I do not want her to go off and sleep with some guy just to prove to me she's not afraid to. Shit. Shit. Shit. Shit.

I struggle to think of a way to stop her, but I can't think of anything I can say or do that would do anything but make her more determined to do whatever it is she thinks I don't want her to.

Defeated, I return to the hotel room where Justin is waiting.

"What happened? What was that all about?" he asks.

"I'm not even sure," I say. I sit on the edge of the bed, my mind whirling. "Tate . . . normally she's really easy-going but sometimes, out of nowhere, something will happen or someone will say something and it just triggers this really defensive reaction in her."

Justin looks perplexed, as if he can't understand this crazy world of female friendships. Then he shakes his head as if shaking the tension of what happened between Tate and me off and gets ready for bed.

I'm waiting for him under the covers, my mouth tasting like I ate a garlic clove raw but I can't bring myself to care enough to muster the energy to brush my teeth. He climbs in beside me and begins groping my breasts, kissing my neck, and murmuring excitedly. I take my underwear off and pull him on top of me. I try to moan convincingly. It doesn't take him long to come, and for that I am grateful.

It takes me a long time to fall asleep.

In the morning light, my little tiff with Tate the evening before seems far less dire than it did at the time, and I'm in a surprisingly good mood.

Justin and I gaze into each other's eyes, smiling contentedly. "You've got the most beautiful eyes," he says. I love that he says this first thing in the morning, when I've got breath that could curdle metal, messy hair, and a face with pillow-imprint lines like zebra stripes. He's not trying to get me into bed or get something out of me, he just tells me this out of nowhere and the compliment buoys me. There is a part of me that aches for him to tell me that he loves me. I want him to tell me that I'm the most amazing woman he's ever known, and he doesn't know how he'll be able to be away from me when the trip is over and would I consider moving to New York to be with him? But he doesn't say anything more. Instead he begins communicating with his hands, mouth, and body.

We make athletic love and when we finish and are trying to arrange ourselves on the microscopic bed Justin falls off, stumbles, and rights himself, using his arms for balance.

"Perfect dismount!" I pronounce.

He struts around, posturing, with an I-meant-to-do-that expression.

"Bravo, bravo! Perfect ten!" I say.

He leaps back on the bed and smothers me with kisses and tickles and I giggle like I did when I was a little girl, when I could laugh and enjoy life without worrying about what other people thought of me or whether I was living up to my potential and accomplishing what I should with my life. I laugh like I have no worries in the world, and right now, I don't.

I get dressed, putting my skirt on for a change of pace, hoping it'll make me feel sexier than my usual uniform of shorts and a T-shirt. I make myself as presentable as possible with no make-up or beauty aids to assist me in my quest.

Justin and I are dressed and ready to head out to find something for breakfast when there is a knock at the door. It's Tate.

"Hey," I say.

"Hey. Can I talk to you?"

"Of course."

I tell Justin I'll be right back. As soon as I close the hotel door behind me, Tate smiles.

"I'm sorry about last night."

"I'm sorry, too. I didn't mean—"

"No, you were right. I'm glad I went back and got him. I'm glad I spent the night with him."

"Yeah?"

"Yeah. It was fun."

"Did you get some?"

She smiles. "We didn't do *it*, but we did *stuff.*"

I know that's as much detail as I'm going to be able to pry out of her, so I don't try for more. "Well, good for you. So you like him?"

"Yeah of course I like him, but it's not like this is going to go anywhere. I'm not taking this seriously. We'll hang out for a little bit, have some fun, that's all."

I don't say anything to that. I don't want to think about how in a couple weeks we'll be flying home while Justin's plan is to stay until Christmas and then move to New York.

"Pete was wondering if it would be cool for him to hang out with us today," Tate says.

"Of course. Let me get Justin and we'll be right over."

A couple minutes later, Justin and I are at Tate's door. She opens it, and we see Pete on the bed, flipping through our Europe guidebook. "We were thinking we could go to the Santa Maria Gloriosa Dei Frari," Tate says. "It's a church."

"The book recommends it," Pete adds.

Tate takes the guidebook from Pete and reads aloud, "The Frari is large with high ceilings. There are paintings and marble sculptures along the sides. The altar is surrounded by old stained glass. . ."

Ugh. Another church. I can't bear it. Italy is chock-full of big ornate churches with marble statues and paintings and stained glass. I have had my fill.

"I'm not really in the mood to see another church," Justin says, echoing my thoughts. "What do you think about letting me have Jadie to myself today?"

Tate and Pete exchange looks. "What will I do with you when I have you all to myself?" Pete says in a lascivious tone. "Suddenly going to a church seems unnecessary."

I swear to God, I think I catch Tate actually blushing. Oh the rejuvenating powers of lust.

So we go our separate ways for the day and Justin and I spend several hours just wandering. In the late afternoon, the sun-washed tourists thin out, especially in this off-the-main-drag area, and it feels like we've got the city to ourselves.

Justin and I meander through the endless alleys and cross dozens of bridges. We're just talking about heading back to the hotel when we come upon an abandoned palaggio (a large house), a not uncommon occurrence in Venice, a city sinking into the sea more and more each year. From what I've read, my guess is that the endless flooding from the Adriatic has caused foundation problems that are apparently too expensive for the family who own this palaggio to maintain, so this once-splendid house simply sits vacant, its once-gleeful rococo ornamentation now showing more wood than gilt.

"Let's see if we can get in," I say. Justin scans the canal for boaters, but there is nobody in sight. He puts his shoulder to the door and gives it a shove. It doesn't move.

"Try the window," I say.

He grunts, struggles, but it's no good. "Oh well," I say. It would have been an adventure, checking out an abandoned home, but it's no big deal.

Justin and I link hands and continue walking, turning down an alley next to the abandoned house. We only make it a few steps before Justin exclaims, "Hey!" I follow his gaze to the broken window. The gap is easily big enough to fit through.

"Let's check it out," Justin says. I follow, excited.

Slipping through the window, we enter a wide, moss-covered hall. Many Venetian merchants once lived above their warehouses and received goods directly off the canal and stored them for reshipment. This house might have once been such a place. I imagine crates of spices and gems being transported down the hall. What might have once been a series of stalls that would have held the merchants' goods was now occupied by moss, giving the rooms the feel of some strange oceanic apothecary.

A quick look around reveals a marble staircase leading to the upper floors. I start up the stairs, and I can feel Justin's eyes on me as I climb. He follows behind me on the stairs and wraps his hands around my waist.

The second floor is barren, but it's clear this was once a wealthy home. Wallpaper peels from the wall and here and there are remnants of gilt. Some past renovation had injected a room with a Wedgwood blue ceiling, though we can only see the colors in the faint light leaking in through the windows facing the canal.

There is an old, though clearly not original, rod iron balcony. Slipping away from Justin, I push through a creaky glass door and take a test step out onto it. It seems solid enough, so I move to the edge and lean out, resting my arms on the rail.

Justin slips his hands up my shirt around my breasts. He nuzzles my back and presses himself against me again. I am already ready for him.

He removes his hand from under my shirt and reaches his hand up my skirt; his fingers find their way between my thighs. He pulls my underwear aside, slipping his fingers inside me, and I lose myself in how good it feels. I hear Justin unzip, then the rustling sound of him pulling his pants down, just a little. He puts his hands on my hips and I feel his penis touch my skin. He slips around for a couple of seconds, searching for the spot, and then enters, starting slow, then quickening his pace.

We find our groove, with Justin gripping my waist, pulling my body toward him as he plunges himself inside me. Within minutes my arms and stomach are quaking, and I groan loudly as I come. Justin suddenly buries his cock as deep as he can, then pulls out just as abruptly and comes with a bellowing groan. His breathing is ragged, and he mumbles something into my back, where he's rested his head.

Snuggling back, I lean into him until he pulls away. My skirt drops back down between us and as I half turn my head to kiss him. He gives my breasts a last squeeze. We walk hand in hand downstairs and back out the window into Venice, which, from my perspective, lives up to its reputation of being one of the most romantic cities in the world.

Before Pete, Tate, Justin, and I get some dinner, I tell Pete I need some time alone with Tate.

"So you can talk about me?" he says.

"Not just you. How self-centered. Also so we can talk about me." I give him a smile and a teasing wink.

Tate and I walk to a grocery store not far from the hotel so we can stock up on bottled water. The tap water in Venice is supposed to be safe to drink, but I won't even drink tap water in America. The connotation of tap water being poisonous is just too strong for me. Anyway, after my little bout with my stomach ailment, I'm not taking any unnecessary chances.

"So," I say as we walk, "have you gotten some yet?"

"Jay-*dee*," she says in a whine, as if she can't believe how intrusive I am. (To which I say, how long has this girl known me? Being intrusive is what I do.)

"Okay. Just a sign then. Like they do in baseball. If you've done it with Pete, tug your ear twice."

I wait.

"If something happens with Pete, I'll tug my ear."

I smile and nod my head, satisfied.

Pete, Tate, Justin, and I get some dinner, then we meet Ben and Brendan at this pub that is very narrow and has a garden in the back. We're in the garden, drinking beer, and somehow it comes out during the course of the conversation that I'm a travel writer.

"I'm talking to women about how men, dating, romance, and marriage are different in different parts of the world. Obviously, I'll be working on this project for the next several years before I have an exhaustive body of data. I'm just starting."

"What's the most interesting thing you've learned so far?" Ben asks me.

"Well, one thing I've found really interesting is that the countries that have the lowest divorce rate—Italy, France, and Spain—also have a much more tolerant view of extramarital affairs."

"Are you saying everyone should start tolerating affairs?" Brendan asks, smiling. "I think it's a great plan."

"No. Definitely not. I could never look the other way. It would be too devastating. I just think it's interesting, that's all."

"Have you interviewed any men during your research?" Pete asks.

"Um, no," I say, abashed.

"Leaving out fifty percent of the population! What kind of researcher are you?" Ben says.

"Um, a bad one I guess."

"We're here to help," Brendan offers. "What do you want to know?"

"Ah, well, why don't you tell me about your worst dates ever."

"Oh, I have one. That's easy," Brendan says. "I was going out with a girl for the first time. We'd met at a bar, and she seemed really cool. So I went to pick her up for our first date, a proper date, with dinner and everything, and when I picked her up, she seemed really out of it, but I thought, well, you know, I don't know her well, maybe this is just how she is. But it turned out she was drunk. One drink at the restaurant and she could barely sit upright. She was totally fluthered."

"Maybe she was just nervous," I say.

"I was too. Nervous she was going to pass out and wet herself in public, for the love of God! I had to practically carry her back to the car past a whole street full of people. 'Twas mortifyin'."

"How about you, Ben? What was your worst date?" I ask, chuckling.

He thinks a moment. "Well, I don't know that there was any one single date that really stands out, but there was a girl I dated for a few weeks that was certainly memorable. She's the only girl I've ever dated who, if I saw her in public, I'd hide behind a plant to avoid her."

"Why?"

"She was just a little freaky."

"Freaky how?"

"Well, for example, I had these toys on my window sill and she asked about them and I joked that they were my pagan shrine, and she said, 'You're a pagan! I'm a pagan, too!' I told her that I'd been kidding, I'm not really a pagan, but she was off, telling me about her pagan shrine and how she was a practicing Wiccan. That's witch to you and me. That's about the time I broke it off."

"Paganism isn't that scary," I say.

"What is it?" Justin asks.

"It's when you believe that God is in everything. Every tree, every blade of grass, every desk and chair," I say.

"Aren't your parents pagans?" Tate asks.

"No. They don't believe in anything."

"You weren't raised in any religion?" Justin asks.

"No. Were you?"

"Lutheran."

"Do you still go to church?"

"No. But I believe in God. Do you?" he says.

"I don't really know what I believe. No, that's not true, I believe that people should just try to be the best people they know how to be, and if there is a god, he or she will understand that we did our best."

Pete says he's not sure what he believes, either, but if he's going to follow a church, he wants one that believes that its holy people follow a vow of poverty. "Money is the root of all evil, after all. So, to help everyone out, I was thinking I'd start a religion where the deal is that everyone will give all their money to me so I can personally save them from the bonds of materialism."

"That's very noble of you," says Ben.

"It's a big responsibility, I know," Pete says, nodding at the significance of it all. "But I think I'm up for it."

"And naturally you'd insist that all of your female parishioners sleep with you," Justin says.

"Well yes, of course, but only for ritualistic ceremonial purposes."

We all laugh and joke and tease each other over a couple more beers. I really like Pete—his humor and his intelligence. I think maybe this time Tate went and found herself a decent guy.

* * *

Justin and I sleep in the next morning. I wake first and hop in the shower. I'm dressed by the time he gets out of the shower and I'm just putting my birth control pill to my mouth when Justin emerges from the bathroom with a towel around his waist and his wet hair combed back.

"You're on the pill?" Justin says.

"Yeah. Just for my cramps, though."

"Why won't you let me come inside you?"

"I just thought if you pulled out it would be an extra caution, you know?"

He shrugs, irritated. "Do you know how hard it is to pull out at that moment? You're not exactly thinking straight at that particular point."

I feel abruptly guilty. I probably am being overly cautious. If he had something, he probably already gave it to me.

"I . . . I . . . you know, we should go get Tate and Pete and head to the kitchen before it closes for breakfast."

We go to their room and when Tate opens the door, I look at her expectantly. She smiles and tugs her ear twice. I raise my eyebrows up and down and smile my approval.

At the kitchen table, as we butter our rolls or slather them with jelly, I say, "I was sort of thinking we might head for Rome next."

"Pete's already been to Rome," Tate says, a stricken expression spreading across her face. She is *so* falling for this guy.

"Ah yeah, never want to see that place again," he jokes. "I wouldn't mind, really. I threw my coin in the Trevi Fountain just like everybody else to assure my return to the city. I didn't think it would be this soon, but I'm game, if you'd have me."

Tate exhales. "But what about Brendan and Ben?" she asks.

"They're all right, but I've found myself a beautiful woman. On the road, I go where the wind blows."

I look at Justin. I know I shouldn't be thinking about a future with him beyond the next day or so, but I can't help it. I can so easily picture moving to Ithaca with him. I'll get a job waitressing and get serious about my writing while he goes to school . . .

It sounds odd, but quitting my corporate job to go back to waitressing has a strange appeal to me. Getting a physical job that doesn't deplete my creative intellectual energy . . . it sounds like heaven.

"Justin, what do you think?" I ask.

"I definitely want to go to Rome. Absolutely."

So we're agreed, Rome it is. We'll leave in the morning.

We spend our last day in Venice visiting the Peggy Guggenheim museum. The museum is in the house she called home for the last thirty years of her life and has works by Picasso, Kandinsky, Chagall, Mirò, Ernst, Dalì, Rothko, and Klee. I'm a modern art fan, particularly the surrealists, so I'm in heaven.

"I don't get it," Tate pronounces at Albert Gleizes' *Woman with Animals*. The picture is a cubist painting of a woman sitting with her dog and two cats. I really like it; the thing about cubism is that it puts into practice something I very much believe: sometimes you have to look at things from multiple perspectives.

"Look at the repetition of motion—the dog's tail wagging—the painting has an energy," Pete says. He goes on to explain all this stuff about what's going on in the picture, pointing out stuff I certainly would have never seen on my own.

"Are you some kind of art history guru?" I ask.

"Nah. I just like art. I took a few classes, that's all."

"What did you study in college?"

"Graphic design."

"So you *are* an artist."

"Well, a commercial artist. I do work with stained glass for fun on my own. I've sold some pieces, too, but I'd have to really work to get that side business to a point where I had a steady enough stream of clients that I could live off of that."

"I didn't know that, about the stained glass. You'll have to show me how you do that someday," Tate says.

We move on and take in *Windows Open Simultaneously*, an abstract painting by Robert Delaney. The only way I can describe it is to say that it's made up of fragments of color, like boxes of various colors thrown together but highlighted with light like you'd get from the sun pouring in through the window.

"I'm sorry, it seems like a three-year-old could do that," Tate says. "I don't get it."

"You, Tate Moran, are a plebian," I say jokingly. She seems a little hurt by this, her eyebrows furrowing. "I'm just kidding, Tate, you don't have to like it. I like it. I don't even know why I like it. The pretty colors, I guess. I could be an art critic. *Look at the pretty colors,*" I say in the tone of someone who is painfully slow, trying to make fun of myself to get myself out of telling a joke that didn't go over.

"It's kind of like the stained glass I work with," Pete says. He goes on to point things out in the painting, the use of color and form, what he thought the artist was trying to accomplish. Tate listens patiently, not getting annoyed like when I tried to point things out to her at the Musée d'Orsay in Paris. I wonder if it's because she's falling for Pete.

Pete says, "It's like light pouring in from a window, see?"

She says, "Yeah, I can see that," nodding her head thoughtfully. Either I should be annoyed that she's listening to a guy in a way she wouldn't listen to me or I should be happy that she is letting her guard down a little and opening herself up to learning new things. I decide to be happy.

That evening after dinner, when Justin and I are back in our hotel room, I take off my blouse and bra just as Justin is walking by to turn off the light. He stops, strokes my breast, and bam, insta-hard-on. I lead him over to the bed, pulling him on top of me. He enters with . . . how to put this . . . with no introductory warm-up-type moves.

Several minutes later, he says, "Do you want me to pull out?" I know what he wants me to say. It probably doesn't matter if he comes inside me.

"You can come inside me."

With a few more thrusts, he does just that in a grateful explosion of pleasure.

"God, that was fucking phenomenal. You're phenomenal. You're amazing."

I smile and hold him close.

It turns out that the train to Rome goes right back to Florence first. We sit with two American backpackers, who tell us their names are Dori and Susan and that they were in Rome before coming to Venice, taking our trip in reverse.

"We're heading to Rome next," I say.

"Uh," Dori says, making a pained facial expression.

"What does that mean?"

"Well, Rome is an amazing city obviously, but it's exhausting. There are beggars and thieves everywhere . . ."

"The beggars are really aggressive," Susan says. "Rome is mecca for Catholic tourists, so they know tourists are in a charitable mood."

"The Romans themselves are pretty friendly though."

"Did you get to date any Roman men while you were there? The reason I'm asking is because . . ." and I explain my project.

"We didn't," Dori says. "We were actually visiting my girlfriend, who moved here a year ago when her husband was transferred here for work. Her husband is from California and she was obviously married when she came here, so she hasn't dated any Italians. I'm trying to think if I have any stories that might help." She pauses, her face scrunched in thought. "The only thing I can think of is about Italian workmen. My girlfriend wanted some work done on her house. She figured it would take two weeks. It ended up taking four months. She e-mailed me updates through the whole ordeal. Whole weeks would go by when the workers wouldn't show up. When they worked they worked hard, but like if it rained or something, they'd say, oh sorry, we can't work today. There were delays in getting the supplies from the suppliers, and then August came around, and of course all of Italy shuts down in August as the Italians take the month off for vacation. Italians just aren't into money like Americans are. They don't worry about shutting their business for a half hour here and there so they can take a coffee and cigarette break. They don't think about sales they might be losing from closing their store for a while. Is that at all helpful?"

"Yeah, any insight into different cultures is interesting to me. I'm not sure how it's all going to fit together, but I can't know too much. Really, anything you can tell me about any culture would help."

"I have a story about the Dutch," Susan says.

"Yeah? I'd love to hear it."

"Well, so the deal is that when I was in college I spent a semester abroad living with a Dutch family. Let me tell you, it was quite an experience. I had a very conservative suburban Midwestern upbringing. I was a nineteen-year-old virgin at the time, and boy oh boy was it an eye opener. The Dutch are a very . . . *open* people. The family I stayed with had two little kids and only one room in the house. Host families are required to give the visiting students their own room, so they moved a bed into the living room for themselves and gave me their bedroom. One morning I got up to use the computer, which was on the desk in the living room, and their four-year-old son was watching television and they're going at it just a few feet away from him. I was mortified."

"Right in front of the kid?" Tate says.

She nods. "And they have very graphic art, graphic television. It was so funny when I went back to the States and listened to all the American politicians railing against what alleged libertines our country is filled with, because it's just not true. We're puritans, not libertines."

I pump her for more details about the Dutch. Then the conversation turns to specific talk about where we've been on our trip and where we're going. We share with them our tips on places to see and avoid in Florence and they share their advice on Rome.

In Florence, we wave them off. It's just another hour and a half until we're in the heart of Rome.

7

Rome, Italy

When we get to Rome, we stop at several hotels before finding one that has two rooms available. It's pricier than we'd like to pay, but by this point we're all sweaty from walking around in the heat. My back is hurting from the weight of my backpack and my back is so slick with sweat my T-shirt is soaked, so we say we'll take it.

The four of us agree to meet in forty-five minutes. Tate and Pete go to their room and Justin and I go to ours. We shower and change and I brush my teeth and tell Justin I'm going to go downstairs to the front desk to ask them where a good place to go to dinner near here is. It's only a little after five, yet I'm already hungry. I'll have to wait until 7:30 when restaurants open up for dinner. Still, there is no harm in being prepared.

Our hotel is pretty fancy, with mirrored hallways, marble floors, and high ceilings, and I admire the art, architecture, and decoration as I make my way to the concierge's desk. There is a large group of swankily dressed Italians talking to the concierge in a life-or-death fever pitch of emotion that comes to an abrupt halt when I show up. The group of five men and women and the concierge all turn to look at me like I'm the Antichrist, and for a moment, I feel like I'm stuck in one of those dreams where you show up to school naked and everybody knows it but you.

"I'm sorry to bother you," I say. "I was just wondering if you knew a good place around here to get something for dinner."

Well, do they ever. Voices from all six of them begin shouting out recommendations and deeming others' choices ghastly in varying degrees of passable English, but after several minutes and many arguments they come to a conclusion that they can all agree on. Then they ask me about how I like Italy. I chat them up, imagining myself to be worldly and wise.

I go upstairs and glance at myself in the mirrored hallway. Of course I hadn't bothered to look in the mirror on my way down, only now after holding a conversation with several hip Italians for twenty minutes do I look, and what do I discover? That when I brushed my teeth I'd dripped a foaming heaping mound of toothpaste on my left breast. It looks like I have just finished nursing a rabid dog.

How do I manage to do these ridiculously mortifying things more or less every day?

I go to Tate's room and tell her what happened, and she collapses on the bed with laughter, and I start laughing too, but I'm secretly relieved I'll never have to see these people again in this lifetime.

I decide not to tell Justin. I just go back to our room and covertly change into one of my last clean shirts.

Our hotel is not far from the Trevi Fountain, so the four of us stop there on our way to the Spanish Steps and take pictures of each other throwing coins into the fountain along with several hundred other tourists.

To get from the Trevi Fountain to the Spanish Steps, you don't need any sort of map, simply follow along with the crush of tourists slurping gelato.

The Spanish Steps are steep and clogged with people. We hike up them and walk a short ways to the Borghese Gardens, where we wander around for an hour or so. As opposed to the Boboli Gardens, these gardens have the distinct advantage of not having millions of steep stairs to climb and they are also free, and for once so far in our trip through Italy, here the locals outnumber the tourists.

There are lovers on practically every bench draped lavishly across one another—she strewn across his lap or he across hers in poses reminiscent of Michelangelo's *Pietà*. Other couples are rolling around in the grass, and my eyes bug out when I see a girl with her shirt pulled up over her breasts as she makes out fervently with her boyfriend. To keep Justin and Pete from getting a free show, I say, "Hey, look at the hot air balloon over there!" and it's true, there is one on the ground that's most certainly decorative rather than functional. I feel very certain that the guys are just as happy to take in this view as any of the other ones afforded in this particular area.

When we've killed enough time that it's finally late enough for the restaurants to open, we head back down the Spanish Steps to get dinner. Several times in our short journey, a young Italian couple stops abruptly in front of us on the sidewalk to kiss each other with an enthusiasm that requires their entire bodies, not just their lips. Their public displays of affection are lavish and unapologetic. I love it.

I feel like I've been mainlining on bread and pasta these last few days, so I order a salad and linguine with vegetables. My dinner is tasty, though the vegetables in the linguine are hopelessly overcooked. The Italians know about fresh ingredients, hearty bread, and flavorful wine, but they could learn a thing or two from the Greenhouse about how to cook a vegetable.

The restaurant we have dinner at is playing bad '70s American music, and I comment on how odd it is how many stores and restaurants we've been to play American music.

"American music from the '70s until today," I say in my best approximation of a radio announcer's voice.

"What's weirder is when there's American music on commercials on TV," Pete says. "You do this double take, like, wait, where am I? What country am I in?"

"American music on Italian TV?" Tate says. "You would never have Italian music playing on American TV. Never."

"And we've had almost no trouble getting around without speaking any Italian. I know exactly three words in Italian: *Ciao, grazie,* and *rigatoni.* I mean we've only been in big cities, so I'm sure that's part of it, but everyone here speaks a little English," I say.

After dinner we return to the steps after first buying beer from a street vendor selling beer, water, and snacks.

We sit in the middle of the stairs to get an optimal vantage point to people watch. Near us is an enormous group of German students in their late teens, and two of the guys are actually singing bad American songs *from a songbook.*

"I can see suddenly getting the urge to sing," Pete says, "but to actually prepare ahead of time and bring a songbook?"

"Do you think maybe they're hoping that some cute girls will join them in singing? Like maybe it's a ploy to pick up girls?" Justin asks.

All four of us turn to watch the German kids sing Roberta Flack's "Killing Me Softly."

"Well, if that is their strategy, it's a very, very bad one," Tate says.

Early on, the young Italian guys seem to contradict stereotype—they seem positively terrified of women. They sit with their sunglasses perched on top of their short, highly gelled and styled hair, and they hold a cell phone to their ear with one hand while a cigarette dangles from the fingers of their other hand. Over the course of the night, they seem to build their courage—or maybe it's just that they've had time to plot their moves and make their game plans—and we watch the guys make their plays on young foreign girls. I would love to hear precisely how they make their moves, but the ambient noise is too much for me to hear specific conversations.

For a good hour or two we watch East Indian salesmen selling—successfully—all manner of crap. We watch tourists from all over the world, German teenagers singing and getting drunk, Italian boys hitting on blond-haired girls from faraway places, and then we head for home and a good night of sleep.

In the morning, we attempt to take a bus to Vatican City, but all of the buses that go by are so packed with people—and inescapable armpit odor—that *I* can't even fit on the bus, let alone all four of us. Finally, Tate and Justin figure out another bus route that also goes to the Vatican, and when that one comes around, there is plenty enough space for the four of us.

St. Peter's Basilica blows me away. Unlike the other palaces and churches that we've seen on our trip that were used to impress people a couple hundred years ago, here's a building that's actively wowing people today. It's clean, nothing is faded, there is Michelangelo's *Pietà* in the corner, his dome over there, works by Raphael sprinkled here and there, and statues, marble, and paintings all over the place.

I am less impressed by the Vatican museum. It may well be that it's not the museum's fault, it's just that by this point in our trip I've been so inundated with art and culture it feels like I'm cramming for a final exam I didn't know about until just a few days before I had to take it. Touring the museum is mostly about managing our tempers in hot, crowded rooms where tourists use their elbows to get by us even though there is no place in front of us to go or else we'd be there already. There is nothing to do but shuffle slowly along. Clusters of tour groups routinely stop in the middle of these rooms, further blocking traffic, and doors from one room to the next are often so narrow that only one person can get through at a time.

I begin to feel like getting through the museum is some kind of trial we need to overcome to get to the reward— the Sistine Chapel. And when we finally get to it, it is such a thrill my irritation diminishes as awe takes its place.

It is so, so nice to be able to put together the pictures I've seen in books into a 3-D space where I can feel the depth and size and how all the panels work together to form a cohesive work.

We stare at the ceiling until the pain in our cricked necks becomes too much to bear, then we get through the rest of the museum at a sprint and catch the bus back to our hotel, where we get tasty, cheap sandwiches far away from the tourists mobbing Vatican City.

I say I'm desperate for some clean clothes. Tate says she, too, is out of clean clothes.

"I could wash some, I guess," Justin says.

"You don't have to. Tate and I could have a girls' night, just the two of us, and you guys could head out on the town. I'm just beat from all the traveling. I think I'll be asleep by nine."

Justin looks over at Pete. "What do you think?"

"Well, I don't know if I can bear an entire evening away from Tate, but I'd be up for tooling around the city with you."

So it's decided: for tonight, Tate will hang out in Justin's and my room and we'll do laundry, watch TV, and get to sleep early.

We see the boys off and start washing our clothes in the tiny hotel sink. I use an empty film container to stop up the sink since there is no plug, and we use the small plastic bottle of Tide I've carried in my backpack all the way from America to clean the clothes.

As we wash our clothes, I say to Tate, "Do you think we have to worry about the guys meeting other women tonight?"

She shrugs. "If they meet other women they'd rather be with, I guess it would mean they were never that into us in the first place."

"So what are you saying, it would actually be a good thing?"

"Wouldn't you rather know how they really felt?"

"No!" It's so obvious! Of course I don't want to know. How can Tate have such a cavalier attitude?

We continue to wash clothes and the image of Justin chatting up another, prettier, more fashionable girl becomes more and more clear in my mind. What madness let me let the guys go off by themselves so Tate and I could spend the night alone? I should have said they could have a boys' night—but they couldn't leave their hotel room to do it.

We wash every single item of clothing we have, until the two of us are wearing nothing more than our underwear. Wet clothes drip from every conceivable place—

the shower rod, the closet rod, the chair, the ceiling fan. Once we've completed our domestic chore, we sprawl across our beds and turn the TV on. I try to remember to watch a little television when I'm on the road. The great monuments, works of architecture, paintings, and statues can tell you about a nation's history and its past, but television can tell you about its current culture.

It's clear Italians spend no money on television. For one thing, a lot of the shows are from the U.S. and dubbed in Italian. All the women who do the voice-overs have super-sultry voices and the men have booming, commanding voices. The shows that do seem to have actual Italian origins have the hammiest acting I've ever seen.

I am absolutely, completely enthralled. I find bad Italian acting just as captivating as the Sistine Chapel, the Vatican, and the Coliseum. When it comes to dramatic spectacle, the Italians have it going on.

As Tate and I watch bad Italian television clad only in our underwear, we suddenly hear the lock to our hotel room door being unlocked. I grab a pillow to cover my chest and do my best to shimmy beneath the sheets, shrieking the entire time.

The door opens and a husky blond man and a husky blond woman start to enter. They are startled when they see us and begin shouting in some mystery language.

"This is our room!" I shout. "What are you doing in here?"

"They gave us keys!" the man says in heavily accented English. "They said this was our room."

"It's our room! They must have a duplicate set and given you the wrong keys." I feel preposterous wearing a pillow and bedding as my attire and I have this horrible fear that the hotel staff are going to say that the mistake regarding the room lies with Tate and me, and we're going to have to shamefully switch rooms dressed in sopping wet clothes, our arms draped with sodden articles of clothing.

The man and woman are clearly as mortified by the situation as we are, murmuring excitedly to each other. I think they also are trying to say something to Tate and me, but even though they can speak English, in their dismay they've forgotten to do the translation.

I know only a short period of time has passed during this awkward exchange—it can't have been more than a matter of seconds—but it feels like it takes approximately forever. Finally the man and woman begin backing out of the room mumbling apologies in English. In the man's nervous excitement, he reflexively switches the lights out, making Tate and me scream again. He instantly realizes what he's done and switches the light back on, but this time he accidentally turns the ceiling fan off as he does. He realizes he's made yet another mistake and turns the fan back on, but the on/off motion dislodges a pair of my wet underwear, and it goes flying off—directly into his face, where it clings like Saran Wrap. The three of us women are shrieking and he's muttering incomprehensible exclamations. I can't do anything because I'm naked except for the pillow I'm covering myself with. He peels my underwear off his face, flings the offending garment on our floor, and apologizes, closing the door behind him.

I have to catch my breath after that ordeal, and when I do I ask Tate, "How many extra sets of keys do you think they have?"

She shrugs.

I pull the top sheet off the bed and tie it around my shoulder and wrap it around my body, toga-like. "Just in case there are more keys out there," I say by way of explanation. Then I sprint across the room and lock the door and stare at the lock as if I can will it to keep out any additional unexpected visitors.

"Good idea." Tate pulls her sheet off her bed and does the same.

Then I return to bed and sit there feeling ridiculous.

"Well, you know, 'when in Rome,'" I say.

This strikes Tate as hysterical, and she cracks up. In between laughs she says, "Oh my God, the expression on that guy's face was hilarious when he walked in . . ."

"The one night we're just sitting here naked on our beds! Of course that's the night the hotel gives somebody else our room key."

"When the underwear hit that guy in the head . . ." She reenacts him grappling with the sodden underwear, stumbling around like a drunk, trying to pull it off his head like it was some kind of face-hugging eight-legged monster, and we laugh some more.

All night, every time Tate needs to get up to get a glass of water or change the TV station, she reenacts the blond man's battle with my underwear, and we roar with laughter all over again.

Eventually we go to sleep, wearing our toga nightwear and hoping like hell we don't get any more unexpected visitors.

Over breakfast, I recount our little adventure from the evening before with the boys, and then we spend our morning visiting the Coliseum and the Forum. I'm impressed by how extensive the ruins are, but I have no idea what we're seeing—it basically looks like a few standing columns, parts of buildings, and rocks that are in an organized pattern on the ground. Eventually we find a guide to give us a tour, and she helps bring the ruins to life.

When we're done touring the ruins, we begin an epic journey to find someplace to pee. The only bathroom we can find by the Coliseum is out of order, so we walk and walk until we finally find a public bathroom. On this last point, I will say this: Rome's bathrooms are squalid and a good many of them don't have toilet seats. What I want to know is this: why do they think this is optional?

I suggest we spend our afternoon visiting the Appian Way, the oldest road in Rome, which leads to the cata-combs. The four of us huddle around our map, which only has certain roads listed and thus is of minimal use. It's more like an abstract painting that gives you the *feel-ing* of where you are rather than actually telling you. But it does list where the bus stops, and Pete says we can catch the subway to the pyramid of this guy who built it as a monument to himself when Egyptian things were all the rave in Rome, and then we can walk the rest of the way. Our impressionistic map doesn't include the Appian Way because it's actually south of the city. Going to the pyramid will get us at least to the southern part of town, so we agree to this plan.

We stand on the hot and crowded subway for what seems like a very long time. Then we finally get to the pyramid, snap a picture or two, and find a public map to figure out which way to go next. We take every possible wrong turn we can make until we finally figure out which way is the right way to go.

And then we walk. And walk. Along a very busy, unat-tractive street, with the sun absolutely bearing down on us. I'm sweating my ass off, and on most nights when I've needed a sweater, Justin has been sweating, so I know he's got to be in his own private blistering hell right now.

My feet and legs are tired from walking all morning. We rested for lunch, but once your feet hit that "I'm tired and achy" wall, rest can get you a little farther, but the damage has been done. It takes a good eight hours of sleep to recover fully, and a half hour of resting while eating our paninis didn't do it for us.

"My foot is hurting," Justin whines. "The top of it. I think I may have pulled something."

"I'm sorry. Did you twist it or something?" I say.

"I'm not sure. It's like the top of my foot is just, I don't know, it feels sprained, or something."

"Well, should we turn around?"

He doesn't answer.

We keep walking and walking and walking. We must have taken a wrong turn. It's after five and I, for one, am getting hungry.

Tate says the words aloud, that she, too, is getting hungry. But she says it as an FYI. Justin quickly devolves into full-out whine, and we decide to abandon our plan. I'm mad at myself for not getting a better map and figuring out a better way to get to the catacombs. But we just march back home in silence. We won't see the Appian Way on this trip.

Justin keeps complaining about how hot he is, how hungry he is, and how much his foot hurts.

Both Tate and I, when around someone unhappy, immediately get more cheerful, even if we're just as miserable as the loudly unhappy person.

"I'm pretty sure we're really close to town. About ten more minutes and we'll be able to put our feet up and stuff ourselves silly," I gush in the manner of someone who spent four years as a waitress and can give somebody a smile even when I'd prefer to spit on them.

We finally get to the subway and ride back close to our hotel. By now, the restaurants have opened and thus salvation is near. We stop at the first restaurant we come to, and Tate and I stop to look at the menu. Tate shakes her head.

"Let's look at another place," she says.

"It's Italian. How can it not have something vegetarian?" Justin says, his irritation crackling through the air.

"It's got a couple things, but they're cream-based. I'd like something light."

"Well, I'm just going to order a great big steak."

"That's fine, order whatever you want," she says.

"Why do you have to make such a big deal out of not eating meat anyway? Humans have been eating animals since cave-man days. We wouldn't have survived if we hadn't been able to hunt."

"Well lucky for us we live in modern times and can make choices based on ethics and not mere survival," she says.

Some background on Tate: she's a very live-and-let-live kind of person. She doesn't care what you believe or what you do as long as you don't try to convert her to your way of thinking. She's never evangelical about what she believes, never gives speeches about what she wishes people would eat or do, but when someone tells her she's wrong or the way she's living her life is stupid, the gauntlet is thrown, her hackles are raised.

One time when I still worked at the Greenhouse and we were just slammed—people were waiting halfway down the block for a table—two poorly dressed young men who were fundamentalists of some kind came in and started asking us if we'd found Jesus. I remember thinking, *I have to find my breakfast burrito for table five, what are you talking about, finding Jesus?* I was too busy running around to hear the entirety of the exchange, but I did hear Tate when she finally exploded in a voice that boomed through the restaurant, "Look, buddy, I'm trying to get these people fed and make a living. We're incredibly busy right now if you haven't noticed, and you're totally in my way, yammering on about my immortal soul. Why don't you just go to Hell and I'll plan on meeting you there someday. Now get out of here!"

Applause erupted through the restaurant, and the hush-puppied crusaders were shocked into leaving us alone, exiting the place with indignant, Well-I-never! type expressions.

I think about that line a lot. *Why don't you just go to Hell and I'll plan on meeting you there.* For one thing, I think it's a pretty funny line, but for another thing, it represents a spunkiness in Tate I admire and wish I had more of myself.

The four of us walk a little ways until we come upon another restaurant. Its menu is only in Italian, but I read that if we want to eat well, we should only go to restaurants with menus in Italian, not translated into five languages. It takes us a while to translate the menu with the help of the small Italian dictionary I've brought. I can sense Justin getting more and more irritated. Finally all four of us agree and go inside.

I peer at Justin over the top of my menu. He still looks grumpy. Maybe a little food and rest will improve his mood.

Justin orders the liver and onions. I don't know if I'm imagining it, but it seems like I detect a so-there tone in his voice. It occurs to me that this is the first time he's ordered red meat since I met him. The rest of the time he's ordered fish or eaten something vegetarian.

Tate and I struggle to communicate with the waiter, who speaks very little English.

"*Sono vegetariana,*" I say. *I am a vegetarian.* "She is too." I point to Tate.

On the menu, the waiter points to a dish called "*Involtini di pesce sprada alla messinese.*" I don't know what the rest of it means, but I know "*pesce*" is fish.

"No *pesce*, no *pesce*," I say.

"Ah? Si." He points to "*tortini di vari tipe di verdue.*"

"What is it?" Tate asks.

"Pie with many vegetables. No fish," he says.

"Okay, I'll have that," I say, relieved that all the effort of finding a restaurant and something I can eat has at last been taken care of.

"Me too," choruses Tate.

The waiter smiles, nods, and leaves now that the ordeal is over.

"Why are you vegetarians anyway?" Justin says in an accusatory tone.

"It's how I was raised," I say.

Justin's testiness goes from a roiling boil to a slow simmer over the course of the meal and a few glasses of wine, and all I can say is thank god for Pete, who could be in the eye of a hurricane and still keep the conversation going without ever slowing down his rapid-fire jokes and quips.

At some point, Pete asks where we should head next. Justin says he's always wanted to go to Greece.

"Greece sounds great!" I realize as the words come out of my mouth that I was a little too enthusiastic with my delivery. All three of them give me looks like, *whaddya think, you're auditioning for a "Go to Greece!" commercial? Calm down.*

"We can catch a ferry," Justin continues.

"Greece sounds good to me," Pete says. He looks at Tate.

"Hey, I'm just here for the ride. I'm game for anything."

After dinner when we're heading back to our hotel, Justin invites Pete and Tate to our room. While the guys look at maps and through the guidebook to map our

strategy of how we should get to Greece, I ask T
"What do you think it meant, how Justin acted tonight?"

"What do you mean?"

"He was really snappish."

"He was tired and hungry."

"Do you think he's changing his mind about how he feels about me?"

"Do you even know what he thinks about you?"

Hmm. She has a point. "Well, however he feels, right now he likes me enough to hang out with me and I don't want him to start thinking hanging out with me is more trouble than it's worth."

I want to dissect Justin's mood tonight, but Tate's not the kind to go over and over an event or conversation to attempt to deduce what it may or may not have meant. She's more like a guy that way, just shrugging things off rather than doing what most women do with emotional wounds: add salt and pick at it—pick, pick, pick, pick, pick, pick— until a small abrasion becomes a gaping, bloodied gash.

That night, Tate goes back to the room Justin and Pete shared last night and Justin spends the night with me. We push the two narrow single beds together and have me-chanical, so-so sex. I know we've been having sex twice a day and sometimes more, but it seems unfair that sex can get routine in merely a week, and I fall asleep feeling grumpy and confused.

In the morning, we have good sex, much better than last night, at least I think it is. I wonder if Justin thought last night was good. There are times when you know that you are both totally in sync, your bodies instinctively knowing how to meet the other's to maximize the plea-sure for both of you, but with bad sex, it feels like an experience you're having all on your own. And he comes even if the sex has been like a dance where you just keep stepping on each other's toes, never finding the right beat.

But today, we're both obviously out of our heads with pleasure, and when he collapses on the bed, he says, "God, I'm so glad I found you."

I'm so happy—whatever happened last night was a blip, an aberration, a product of being tired, hot, and hungry. Everything is okay between us again.

"I'm glad I found you, too." We do our stupid insane-with-happiness smiles at each other for several minutes.

Our next stop is Brindisi, where we'll catch a ferry to Greece, but we take a detour down to the Calabria region of Southern Italy because Justin heard about a place where we can go white-water rafting. I see his point about wanting to do untouristy things, but our time in Europe is dwindling, and I want to see as much of it as I can, so I'm a little irritated by all the preparations and time it takes to get this day trip set up. All these phone calls, and paperwork, and haggling about money and figuring out a time to go . . . *ugh.*

But once we get everything done (it's nearly two and the sun is searingly hot), and we're finally on the raft, it's such a beautiful day that my irritation fades and I'm back in a contented frame of mind.

Our guide is a gorgeous young Italian, which also doesn't hurt my mood. He's slender but his muscles are powerful; he's extremely fit. His attempts at English are valiant but largely mystifying. At least we can understand the most important words, like his commands for whether to paddle forward or back.

I'd gone white-water rafting in Colorado once before when I was in high school. At the time, there had been a drought, so the river was placid and calm, and we tooled tranquilly down the river enjoying the scenery and the beautiful day. That's what I was expecting here, but there are a number of rapids and going through them is both terrifying and fun.

We're heading through a class-four rapid when we come up against a sort of standing wave that Danilo, our guide, tells us we need to blast through. (This is an English word he's mastered: Blast! Blast through!) We blast through it all right and then promptly crash into a rock. I'm trying to focus on following Danilo's commands about paddling but in the middle of the frantic chaos of getting through the rapid, I realize that Justin has fallen out of the boat. My heart becomes instantly epileptic. I can't see him. I can't see his body. Where is he?

Moments later he bobs up, thank God, but I'm still frantic. I want that boy in the boat. It takes at least several minutes for Danilo to get a grip beneath Justin's armpits, around his chest, and hoist him in. Justin slides in like a dying fish, shivering and wet.

"Thank God, thank God, you scared the shit out of me. Are you okay? Did you hit your head?" I hover over him, gripping his arm as if to ensure he's really there.

"I don't think so. I think I'm okay," he says, but he looks stunned.

"Next time, be sure lean into boat. That way if fall, fall into boat," Danilo says. He had told us this before we even set off down the river, but now the message has officially hit home. Suddenly, the rapids aren't fun, they are frightening potential harbingers of death.

"Oh, I'm all about leaning now," Justin says, righting himself on the side of the boat and readying his oar for more. Eventually, my breathing returns to normal and my heart stops doing the rumba, and I enjoy the rest of the trip, though when we go through the next couple of rapids, I lean into the boat so far I practically give myself a hernia. I don't care. I don't want to go diving into the drink. Before Justin's tumble, I'd been having fantasies of becoming some extreme sports wild girl jock. Turns out I have not an extreme-sports-adrenaline-junkie molecule in my body, I now realize, as I tremble from my head down to my river-soaked Tivas.

We take a bus to the youth hostel we're staying at in town, where we shower the river off of us. I volunteer to go get picnic supplies for dinner while Justin, Pete, and Tate nap. I'm tired, too, but too wired to sleep, story of my life.

I buy wine, cheese, and bread, a meal that I could happily live off of exclusively for years. You'd think Tate and I would have become enormous subsisting on a diet made up largely of wine and cheese, but we walk so much that I actually feel like I've lost a few pounds. This trip is making me feel lighter in every way.

I return to the room where I watch Justin sleeping, a goofball smile plastered on my face. Finally he blinks into consciousness. He returns my smile and pulls me in for a kiss.

"All that adventuring wore you out, huh?" I say.

"And made me hungry. I'm starving."

I don't want to knock on Tate and Pete's door in case they're still sleeping, so I just slip a note under their door that says they should meet us in the dining room when they're ready.

Justin and I go to the dining room where there is a long, communal table. We sit near three female backpackers from Canada who are in their early twenties and who are pretty in a skinny, natural way I find particularly annoying when applied to women who are not me.

They describe their day hiking and we tell them about rafting. Justin tells them about how after we crashed into a rock he went flying out of the boat.

"The river was pouring straight into my chest and was pressing me up against a rock . . . underwater. I was not floating. I was not moving beyond the rock. I was just plain stuck. I felt around above me and realized that I had spent a moment or two under the raft . . . I sort of pushed against it, or it was carried by the flow of the water, I don't know . . . at any rate, it moved a little. I was still underwater and decided to abandon the notion of floating and try to stand up. I tried to stand but I couldn't feel the bottom of the river at all. I then started sort of pushing back against the rock to try to get to the surface, and somehow our guide managed to catch hold of me by the shoulders of my life vest. He pulled my head up a little so that I could get a few breaths of air, then I got turned around and we collectively hauled my soggy ass into the raft. Somehow I managed to keep my paddle the whole time, which I think was probably due to the G.I. Joe kung-fu death grip I put on it as I realized I was going into the water. And before this all happened, I was sitting there sharing the boat with Jadie and Tate having manly thoughts of someone (not me) winding up in the water, thinking I'd be the heroic one pulling the person back into the raft. Well, it turns out that someone did go in the water (me) and the women who were still safely seated in the raft more or less watched the guide save my ass. Typical."

Everyone laughs and again I'm struck by the thought of how much I like that Justin can just be himself and admit he does stupid things. Have you ever had a boyfriend who misses a shot in tennis and blames the racket? I feel lucky to have found a non-blame-the-racket guy who can admit that sometimes in life we miss easy shots, and it's not the racket's fault but our own.

The three Canadian girls are joined by two guys, one of whom is evidently the boyfriend of the blond girl, Jodie (this insight was garnered when he repeatedly thrust his tongue down her throat).

Jodie tells the guys, Chris and Todd, about how we went rafting and Justin nearly died or at the very least had some scary moments along the way. Justin repeats his story more or less verbatim, but leaves off the line about how he'd been thinking manly thoughts of rescuing us only to need to be rescued himself. I thought that was the funniest, most entertaining part, so I chime in. "Yeah, it was funny, Justin was saying earlier how he'd been having manly thoughts of rescuing me or Tate, and then he was like, and who goes into the drink? *Me*."

Justin flashes me an irritated glance as the rest of the group laughs and for a minute I don't know what I've done wrong. He was the one who said it first, it was his joke, I was just repeating it. Then it hits me: before he was talking to a room of all women, being charming and showing his vulnerable side. Now there are men in the group and the rules have changed. Great. I've just emasculated my . . . what is he—boyfriend? Lover? Lover sounds grown up and worldly, but really, I'd prefer boyfriend.

I realize this: I no longer feel as comfortable around Justin as I did before.

Part of the reason I was attracted to him in the first place was that from the moment he first smiled at me, I felt like I could say anything to him. We talked and laughed so easily. And of course there was instant, powerful attraction that in and of itself turned my brain to mush. Now I'm afraid I'll say or do the wrong thing.

The conversation continues, evolving and circling back around to earlier themes, and eventually Justin seems to be laughing and happy again, but I still sense that he's feeling annoyed with me. I do my best to not worry about it, and just enjoy the fun conversation and the caressing winds.

8

Athens, Greece

We take a train to Brindisi and then catch a ferry to Patras, Greece, overnight. We are lucky that we get a tiny cabin on the boat, but the accommodations are far from comfortable, and by the next morning on this seemingly endless journey, both Justin and I are crabby and we take it out on each other by squabbling over stupid things.

"My neck hurts from that awful pillow," he gripes. This is his eightieth gripe this morning, and I've had enough.

"You say that like it's my fault or something," I snap back.

He gives me this irritated glance that could melt titanium, and I worry again I'm being too much trouble and he won't want to be with me anymore.

"I'm sorry. I didn't mean that," I say. "Let me rub it."

The back rub leads to me going down on him and this leads to sex. We clean up in awkward silence, get dressed, sling our backpacks over our shoulders, and go outside to the deck to wait for the boat to dock. I discover that I didn't clean up enough after our little romp this morning and now my underwear is soaked and I don't have any clean underwear to change into.

I've always thought there was something of a semen barometer that could tell you how things were going in a relationship. If his semen sliding out of me turns me on, things are going well. If it irritates me, things aren't going well.

Things aren't going well.

From Patras we catch a bus that takes us to Athens. We get rooms at a hotel and as Pete and Justin are asking the concierge some questions about where the subway station is, Tate and I take the keys to our rooms and head upstairs. We hit the button for the elevator and step into its tiny, narrow confines. We press the button for the fourth floor. The elevator goes up and Tate and I wait patiently for the doors to open, which they don't. Instead we're taken right back down to the first floor. We exchange perplexed glances at each other, and I for one feel retarded. A man gets on, hits the button for the third floor, and when it stops, he pulls the door open himself. Ah ha! The secret! Tate hits the button to the fourth floor and this time we manage to get off the elevator like old pros.

The four of us take naps to recuperate from the epic journey it took to get here, then we head out to see the town. There are tons of stray dogs and cats running around everywhere here, but otherwise Athens is all shiny and clean. Even their subway is gorgeous, if you can believe it. When they were digging to build the subway, they came across a bunch of important ancient artifacts, and so they built a museum in the subway displaying their findings. Can you imagine the grubby American subways sparkling clean with historic artifacts adorning them? The glass would be broken and full of graffiti in seconds.

Also, there is marble everywhere here. I ask a shop keeper how they can afford to use marble all over the place, and she tells me marble is cheaper than wood here. I mean even the gas stations' floors are marble. Imagine! And everyone here parks as if they'd had sixteen shots of ouzo before leaving their car at some ludicrous angle on the sidewalk or wherever they feel like.

All day Tate, Justin, Pete, and I walk around the city saying things like, "Ah yes, to get to the bakery we want to turn left at the Parthenon," casually using some of the most important monuments in history to guide us to the coffee shop or wherever. It's impossible not to trip over history here.

At one point in the day we actually visit the Parthenon instead of just using it as a landmark to find food and coffee. Our footsteps crunch on the dusty land between the temple called the Erechtheion, which has six maidens for columns, and the Parthenon itself.

I bring my guidebook and read out loud to Tate about how Greek builders used the optical tricks to construct it, making the long sides of the building slightly concave so that the columns appear to be in a straight line when viewed from a distance. Apparently, straight lines appear to bend from a distance so when you use unstraight lines everything balances out. "Neat, huh?"

Tate gives me a withering stare. She wants to just enjoy the beauty of the place without learning about all the behind-the-scenes historical stuff. Tate is the only person I know who doesn't want to know how the magician does it or how special effects work; she just wants to enjoy it, reveling in a total sense of suspended disbelief.

We decide to sign up for a bus tour that will leave in the morning to see some of the important ancient sites of Greece that are in small towns a few hours from Athens and then we're off for a night on the town. We go to a coffee shop that also sells alcohol. Ouzo is the cheapest thing on the menu. I've never had it before but I've heard it tastes like black licorice. Because it's cheap I decide to give it a try and decide the cloudy white drink, while not my favorite beverage in the world, isn't bad.

There is a table of three women nearby, and I ask Justin, Pete, and Tate if they mind if I go to talk to them. They don't, so I approach the women and tell them about what I'm researching.

"You're learning about love, like how to do it?" says one. The other two laugh. All three women are smoking, all have long hair, and two of them have tinted their hair a plum color that seems to be very popular among Greek women.

"No, more like how men and love and dating and relationships are different in different parts of the world."

"Why?"

"Like I said, I'm a writer. It's a new take on travel writing—sort of travel writing meets romance."

"Romance is a good thing," the woman says. "Sit down."

"Thank you, thank you so much. My name is Jadie Peregrine." I flip my notebook open. "What are your names?"

"I'm Voula," says one woman. "This is Adreana and Alexa," she gestures to her friends.

"So, I guess to start, tell me a little about Greek men."

Voula laughs. "Greeks . . . I would say we're more traditional than Americans. More family oriented." Her English is fantastic. There's barely a trace of an accent. She's curvy and solid and beautiful, and I covet her outfit—jeans with a thick belt that rests on her hips and a sleeveless black turtleneck sweater. "Women run the house, men run . . . everything else." She laughs again. "But women work and have careers. We are not *passive*. We are *traditional*."

We talk about Greek weddings, Greek customs, and even Greek food, and the conversation, while interesting, is veering off the topic so I steer it back by asking them what their worst date was like.

"My worst date was with an American," Voula says, taking a long drag on her cigarette.

"Uh-oh." Somehow I feel personally responsible when Americans behave badly abroad.

"He was a lawyer, working in Greece for an American company. He was not really my type, but I figured I would get a free meal so, what could it hurt? We went to a movie, but this man, I have forgotten his name, he did not speak Greek, so he did not understand any of it and he talked the whole time. Halfway into it, he grabbed me and kissed me with this wet messy kiss—"

We all groan in sympathy. We've all been there.

"I tried to push him off me, but he kissed me three more times. I was like this," she flails around in her chair and we all laugh. "It was awful. I left him right after the movie, so I did not even get my free dinner."

"Surely it's not just American men that are oafs. Adreana? Alexa?" I ask.

"My worst date, it was a favor to my father," Alexa says. Her accent is slightly thicker, her "r's" roll out. "He was the son of one of my father's colleagues. He had greasy hair and was just . . . not handsome. But that is not what made the date bad. What made it bad was that on our way to dinner, he stopped off at his apartment . . . to get drugs! Cocaine! He said he got nervous on dates, and he asked me if I wanted any. As though I would take drugs from a strange man! I was so scared we would crash in the car. When we got to the restaurant, I called my mother and asked her to come get me. But while I waited for her, I went back to the table, and the man, he was talking very, very fast, and . . . like this, with his hands," she demonstrates him gesturing wildly. "He knocked over the bottle of wine all over the back of a woman's fur coat! My father did not ask me to go on any more dates with sons of his colleagues again." She concludes with a definitive wag of her index finger.

We talk and talk. Voula tells me that, because space is at such a premium in Athens, everyone owns small apartments, not houses, and these apartments are extravagantly expensive—parents pass apartments down to their children. Apartments! Not houses! Suddenly the housing prices in Boulder don't seem that bad. But despite the housing shortage, Athens doesn't have any skyscrapers because of the earthquakes. The highest buildings have four stories. Eventually, I tell them I don't want to monopolize their entire evening and I thank them for their time and I return to the table where Pete, Tate, and Justin are laughing. Justin seems to be in a much better mood now that he's gotten a nap and some food in him, and for that I am relieved.

The next day, Tate, Justin, Pete, and I get up at an appalling hour—my sleep schedule is completely messed up from the many, many ouzos we consumed last night—to catch the bus.

We hoist our backpacks on, totter around under their weight for a few minutes until we catch our balance, then we head downstairs, grab some ghastly excuse for coffee, and go outside where the bus is waiting for us and climb aboard.

There are about fifteen other people on the tour. One Australian family, a bunch of older folks from America, and us. One of the Americans is a woman from Texas who dresses so hideously ostentatiously that I can't stop staring at her with car-wreck curiosity. I'd guess she's in her mid-sixties. She wears her hair, which is dyed purplish brown, in three levels: in the front are bangs, on the sides her hair is cut so it ends just above her ears, then in the back it goes down to her shoulders. She has crepey from-the-bottle orange-tanned skin and wears a cheap leopard-print coat. She wears enormous rings on every finger and bracelets with huge tear-drop-shaped stones dangling everywhere. She has dark-tan knee-high stockings on and glittery gold moccasins. Her large purse has different colors of alligator-skin type patterns—bright pink, green, purple, black, gold—you get the idea. She is such a whirl-wind of poor fashion choices it boggles my mind.

The bus first stops in Corinth. There is nothing like experiencing places firsthand. You can look at pictures until you're cross-eyed, but until you climb and climb and climb, you can't really understand the enormity of the place, the depth and height and how it all fits in with everything else.

You have to be very imaginative when you explore the ancient ruins of Greece. You have to imagine the colorful frescos that once decorated the now-slate-gray rock. You have to imagine the castles and monuments in their en-tirety. Otherwise, they mostly look like a bunch of care-fully arranged rocks.

In Corinth, our guide tells us that the Greek city was destroyed and rebuilt by the Romans. So though we can't see the Greek city, the Roman city is pretty damn cool. We get to see the marketplace and walk on the same streets where Alexander the Great once walked. We learn about the baths and the irrigation systems the Greeks invented and get to see a toilet (a stone hole) Alexander the Great may well have used. For some reason, this delights Tate and me to no end, and I snap several pictures.

Next the bus takes us to Mycenae, where we visit the palace of this guy named Agamemnon, high king of the Mycenae. The entryway to the fortress is known as Lion's Gate because of the two lions facing each other carved into this triangular-shaped rock. We stroll around the fortress, checking out the panoramic view of mountains and green valleys and olive trees. I can easily imagine myself living in 1600 B.C. in this place, wearing a toga and sandals and resting on the veranda as some Greek male with rippling muscles fed me grapes. Yes, I think I'd fit right in in ancient Greece.

wonder what she'd think of what Mycenaen women really wore?

Next we go to the town of Epidaurus, where we visit an amazingly well-preserved 2,300-year-old open-air theater. The guide tells us to spread out across the theater. She stands in the middle and talks in a normal voice, and no matter where we are, we can hear her perfectly. The acoustics are amazing. How did the ancient Greeks know how to do this? I'm impressed.

We spend the night in Naupalia. There are no bars or anything close to our hotel, so we decide to spend a quiet evening relaxing in our rooms.

Justin and I lie in bed beside each other, he with a paperback and me with my journal. I keep waiting for a loving look from him, keep hoping that he'll start kissing me, touching me. I want him to want me. I want that reassurance, but it doesn't come.

What's going on with him? Have I done something?

Should I talk to him, ask him what's wrong? But what if there's not really any problem—maybe he'll think I'm being annoying and then there *will* be a problem. Maybe it's just better to act as if everything is okay?

In my journal I write down my jumble of thoughts, hoping that trapping my thoughts onto the page will help me make sense of what I'm feeling, but even after wrestling my vague concerns and ideas into concrete words, I'm no closer to understanding how I feel.

The next morning we head to Olympia, home of the Olympics. The roads here are frighteningly narrow, yet our bus driver takes these insane turns as if we're in a

Volkswagen Bug and not an enormous bus. Also, here, stop signs are taken as suggestions—not to slow down or stop, but to honk your horn crazily to alert other drivers that you're there.

I read aloud to Tate from the guidebook. "It says here that Greeks have one of the highest mortality rates due to car accidents in Europe."

"Thanks, thanks for sharing that little tidbit of information."

"No problem."

Olympia is much larger than the other fragments of ruined cities we've visited so far. We see the gyms (now just rocks arranged in a rectangular shape in the grass) where the athletes trained and the field where they competed. We see the spot where the torch is still lit for the Olympics today. After it's lit, runners take it to Athens, and then it's shipped over to whatever country is hosting the games.

I imagine the statue of Nike on the pedestal outside the temple of Zeus and the statue of Zeus (one of the Seven Wonders of the World, now destroyed) sitting on the throne inside the temple. I envision the athletes running through the stone arches to the field, like modern athletes coming through the locker rooms onto the court. This cheers me and temporarily gets my mind off Justin. Tate and Pete and Justin go sprinting along the old track while I take pictures of them, allegedly to capture the moment on film, but really to avoid getting sweaty and stinky and having to exert myself by running with them.

Our guide, Nia, tells us that if any of the athletes were ever caught cheating or in other ways deemed dishonorable, they'd have to pay to create a statue of Zeus (it wasn't cheap), and their names were carved into the pedestal of the statue so there would be a testimony of their bad behavior recorded for all of history. There are eighteen of these statues in all, though only the bases are left now. When you consider that the Greeks held the Olympics for centuries and centuries, up until some king deemed them pagan and did away with them, that's a damn good rate. Evidently the threat of disgrace was enough to keep most athletes in line. If only that worked today.

We take the ferry across the Gulf of Corinth, and spend the afternoon visiting the ancient sanctuary of the god Apollo on the slopes of Mount Parnassus in Delphi, a cliff-dwelling town beside fishing villages.

By the time dinner comes, I'm famished, but by this point, Tate and I are officially sick of Greek food already. Enough with the eggplant, Greek salad, spinach pie, and potatoes. In the small Greek towns, there are simply no other options. It's not like home, where on every corner you can opt for Chinese or Mexican or Thai or Indian or Italian. Here it's Greek, Greek, or Greek. I mean I want to absorb the culture, but if I have to eat one more damn Greek salad, I'll kill myself. At least we're not sick of the ouzo yet, which is a good thing, because they have exactly two choices of beer here: Amstel or Mythos. Oh how I miss Colorado, the micro-brew capital of the United States! Two beers? What kind of choice is that? And they're both light! After another dinner of Greek salad, red wine, and good bread, I suggest doing some window shopping.

Pete and Tate walk hand in hand ahead of us. I take Justin's hand in mine and we stroll along the cobblestone streets, peering into windows. We stop in one shop and I'm looking at postcards when a voice comes out of nowhere.

"Where you from?" a Greek man asks in accented English. I hadn't seen the man behind the counter before, but he must have been there all along.

"Colorado. The United States," Tate says.

"Americans! I love Americans!" he says.

This baffles me utterly. I thought all Europeans hated Americans, so I ask, "Why?"

"Because you always have money!"

Ah.

"I going to America soon," he continues. "California. I work there in the winter and come back here for summer. Come, come. I have restaurant next door. You taste my homemade wine!"

I'm wary. He's probably brought the rape drug back from the States with him. Why is he being nice to us? Surely it's because he wants to rape and kill us.

"No, no," I protest, "we really weren't . . ."

"Is free, I give you glass for free. Taste it! White wine? You like?"

So that's it. He'll give us a free taste and then try to get us to buy a bottle.

"I don't think . . ."

"Come on," Pete says. "Let's go." I glance at Justin, who nods.

I guess we're not really under any obligation to buy a bottle, and Tate and I do have two guys with us to protect us, so I relent and we follow the man next door.

The restaurant is dingy and small, with white-and-red plastic tablecloths and folded metal chairs. The floor is scuffed and the tile is worn—it might have been a cream color once, but now it's a defeated yellow from years of use.

"My name is Nick," the man says. That's a big surprise. Half the men we've met in Greece are named Nick.

Nick pours us each a glass of wine in plastic cups. "My son, he go to America for school. More opportunities there, in America. Me, I run this restaurant and the shop next door in the summer. I live upstairs. Come, I show you."

Everything I've ever learned in school tells me not to follow him, but somehow, he seems okay, so we do.

He has a miniscule apartment upstairs, which we don't actually enter. We stop at the patio, which overlooks the Gulf of Corinth. The sun is setting, and the view is gorgeous.

Nick's shop is worn, his restaurant dingy, his apartment tiny, but this view, Jesus, this view.

Nick shows us his mini vineyard of grapes that he uses to make his wine.

"Well, I leave you alone to enjoy your wine," Nick says.

Wait a minute. That's it? "Wait, wait, are you sure we can't pay you something? For the wine? For the hospitality?" I say.

"Enjoy the view. Go downstairs when you're ready."

"Come on, let us do something."

"Come back to see me! That is all!" And with that, Nick leaves us alone. No hard sales pitch, just a friendly invitation to enjoy the wine and the view.

And that's what we do. We inhale the salty sea air and watch the red and orange sky turn gray, then black. We stare at the stars in a dreamy silence.

When is the last time I stopped to watch the sunset or stare up at the stars?

We stay there well after our glasses of wine are gone, then return to our rooms, feeling relaxed and happy.

In the morning, I finish my breakfast early and leave the rest of the tour group inside the restaurant to use a phone booth, trying to arrange tickets on the Eurail. We'll have to haul ass to Hungary when we're done with the tour, and we'll only be able to spend one night since we're sacrificing an entire day traveling, and then to Germany, where we can spend just a night or two before taking yet another long train ride to Amsterdam, where we'll have just a day and a half before catching a ferry to England and flying home. The next few days are going to be almost exclusively spent on trains traveling, and I'm mad at myself for not having planned better, but there is nothing I can do about it now.

On the last day of our tour before we return to Athens we drive to Meteora, where there are twenty-some rock-top monasteries, but I don't even get my foot in the door of even one of them because as I go to pay the entrance fee, I discover that I don't have my money belt—and thus my passport or any money—with me. How could I not have noticed not putting it on this morning? But I *did* put it on this morning, I'm sure of it . . .

The phone booth. I took it off when I was calling the train station to reserve seats on the train to Hungary. I couldn't find my pen, so I took the belt off so I could inspect it with my eyes instead of essentially groping blindly at my navel. I found the pen wedged in the envelope where my plane tickets are, and then set the money belt on top of the phone as I scribbled down what time the train left.

I am in a foreign country with no money and no identification and no way to get home.

Panic: sets in . . . *now*.

"What's wrong?" Tate asks.

As soon as I say, "I left my money belt at the phone booth in Delphi! It has my passport!" I start crying.

Justin looks annoyed with me, and I'm instantly mad at him for it. I already feel like an asshole. I need to be given reassurance, not a hard time. "Look, Justin, you don't need to worry about any of this. I'll take care of all of this on my own. Justin, Tate, Pete, you go on inside and enjoy the monastery. I'll . . . I don't know what I'll do."

"Jadie, don't be ridiculous. I'll stay with you," Tate says.

Justin lingers for several seconds, looking unsure about what to do.

"Why don't you and Pete stay here?" I say. "There is no reason for all four of us to have to spend an extra several hours on the bus."

Justin nods. "I'm okay with that. Pete?"

Pete frowns. "All right. Tate, I'll miss you." He gives her a big hug and kiss good-bye. From Justin I get a hurried peck on the cheek. Justin and Pete go inside and I sit on the curb, crying, feeling stupid and powerless and scared.

Nia, our tour guide, notices that I am a crying heap of patheticness and comes over to ask me what's wrong. I tell her, which renews the torrent of tears that had, just a few seconds earlier, been reduced to a steady trickle.

Nia talks rapidly in Greek to Constantine, our maniac bus driver, then she tells me that she has to go inside to lead the tour, but that Constantine will make some phone calls and see what he can do.

Constantine clicks on his cell phone, though who he could be talking to I have no idea. All I can think about is some Greek bandit having his way with my passport and credit card, stealing my identity, causing me to go bankrupt, and spending all the Euros I had in cash.

"Do you know what a nightmare it's going to be for me to get a temporary passport to get my ass back home?" I say.

"It'll be okay," Tate says.

"Yeah, eventually, but having to get a new passport will mean hours of waiting in line, then probably several days before I can get it, which means I won't be able to see Hungary or Germany because there won't be time. We'll probably have to fly to England, which will cost hundreds of dollars, and of course I'll pay for yours because it's not your fault I'm an idiot."

Constantine, who doesn't speak any English, comes up to me and tells me something I can't understand, but he looks cheery, which I choose to take as a good sign. He then puts his hand out as if to say, "wait here," as if I had anyplace else I could go.

I watch him as he approaches several people outside the church. After talking briefly with a number of people, he and a man come walking back over to us. Constantine says something in Greek, and the man says in accented English, "You wallet is find at restaurant."

"What?"

"Person bring in wallet to restaurant. They have. All okay now," he pronounces with a nod and a smile, as if he were personally responsible for this good news.

"My passport, it's there?"

"Passport. Money. All there. All okay."

I hug Tate. Then I hug the man and Constantine, who genuinely seem as happy as I am about this, and I decide then and there that I love all Greek people everywhere, even if their small towns serve only Greek food. I'll eat Greek salad until the end of time. Imagine someone turning in my wallet and not stealing anything out of it! Imagine the restaurant keeping it without stealing anything out of it!

"Sir, could you ask Constantine how I might get to Delphi to get my wallet?"

He and Constantine confer. Then the man says, "He can no go. Group." He points to the church where the tour group is. "I take you."

"No! It's a five-hour drive! Can't we find a bus or a train or something?"

He considers this. "Maybe. I take you into Kalambaka. We see."

We follow the man over to the group he'd been standing with earlier and who are now standing there waiting for him to finish his business with us before either entering the monasteries or moving on to another one, I'm not sure which. He talks to them, pointing at me and Tate a lot, and the older men and women all nod, and the man, who introduces himself as Nick, surprise surprise, comes back and says he's ready to take us.

Tate and I follow the man down to the parking lot. He talks excitedly the entire time about how lucky it was that he was here (which I assure him is true, but I can't help smiling at the way he shamelessly laps up the appreciation and praise). He keeps talking all the way to Kalambaka, the town at the bottom of the base of the rocks of Meteora. There he finds a bus station and helps us get tickets to Delphi.

We say goodbye to Nick and thank him profusely, and then Tate and I sit on a bench designed for maximum discomfort to wait for the bus, which doesn't leave for two more hours. "So if the bus doesn't leave till two," I say, "we won't get to Delphi until seven at night, which means we'll have to spend another night there, and then catch a bus to Athens tomorrow, which is going to take hours, then we'll just turn around and have to take a twenty-one-hour train ride to Budapest. Ugh. I'm so sorry I messed up the last two days of our time in Greece."

"Don't worry about it. It's no big deal."

And I can tell from her voice that she's not just saying that, she really means it, and it is such a relief that she's not mad at me.

Because I'm plenty mad at myself. Now that the crisis of having my identity and thus entire future being annihilated by a villainous evildoer has passed, I'm really irritated by the prospect of another ten hours on a bus and another night in a small town where there is nothing to do.

We are silent on the bus ride there, and for once I'm grateful that Tate is not the kind of woman who is into dissecting emotions and feelings. My other girlfriends would be probing, asking what I thought it meant that Justin didn't come with us, how I felt about where things were at between Justin and me. I don't want to think about it, and frankly, right now I genuinely don't know how I feel other than a generalized state of unhappiness.

I look over at Tate, who is staring serenely out the window. I take her hand and squeeze it, my silent way of thanking her. She looks at me and we exchange a smile, then she turns again, looking out the window. I know I said I could have gone back to Delphi by myself, and I could have, but I'm really glad she is with me. She left Pete behind without a second glance, worried less about alienating a new boyfriend than being there when her girlfriend needed her.

In Delphi, I retrieve my money belt without hazard or fanfare. We get dinner immediately since we skipped lunch, then we go to the hotel we stayed at the previous night and get a room. I herd Tate down to the bar so I can get started drinking myself into oblivion.

We go to bed early, but I don't sleep well.

After another long bus ride, Tate and I get to the hotel in Athens. I'm already weary with travel and again I rue my stupidity of trying to see the entire damn continent in one month. Granted, I have no idea when I'll save up enough money to come back and see the many, many parts I missed and it makes sense to make the most of a trip, but it was so very goal-oriented-American of me to kill myself to take it all in in just a few weeks.

Pete and Justin aren't in their rooms. I leave Justin a note:

> *Tate and I survived our adventure to Delphi. Hope you somehow managed to have a good time without us. We're going to grab some dinner and then we're going to head down to the hotel bar. Meet us there, okay?*
>
> *—Jadie*

Tate and I find a place that serves a falafel-type pita sandwich. It's not like the falafel I've had at Middle Eastern restaurants, but it's tasty and cheap and with the inexpensive beer we order to wash it down with, it makes a good meal.

On our way back to the hotel we pass a McDonald's that advertises a McPita sandwich, which I just love. Tate and I snap a couple pictures of the poster and then I see a group of Greek Orthodox priests in their long, black belted-dress kind of outfits and black hats and I whisper to Tate to stand near them so I can pretend to take a picture of her when really I'm taking a picture of them.

It makes me feel mildly better to do these stupid, jokey things with Tate, but when we get back to the hotel and see Pete and Justin waiting for us in the hotel bar, I feel inexplicably nervous. Justin and I kiss, and I give him a tentative hug. I climb on the barstool next to him.

"So," I say, infusing my voice with a cheeriness I don't feel. "What did you guys do without us last night?"

"We didn't do much. We got some dinner. Got a couple beers. Went to bed early. That was about it," Justin says.

"Sounds like our night. How were the monasteries?"

"They were okay."

"Just okay?"

"Yeah. There was a lot of religious art. Exactly what you'd expect."

We nod at each other like two strangers.

I turn to face Tate and Pete, "So, what should we do on our last night in Athens? Tomorrow we're off to Budapest." I look back over to see Justin blanche. "What's wrong?" I ask.

"I . . . Jadie, I was thinking maybe I wouldn't go with you to Hungary after all."

"What?" He may as well have hurled a bowling ball into the pit of my stomach.

"I've been thinking . . . I mean, you are going to go home in a few days anyway, and I'm going to stay in Europe traveling, and getting all the way to Amsterdam by train in just a few days . . . it'll be exhausting. I was sort of thinking maybe I'd spend a few more days in Athens and then head over to Turkey."

I'm too busy reeling to say anything.

"Ah, how about Tate and I . . . we'll take a little walk around the city," Pete says. "Give you some time to talk."

Tate looks at me, waiting for me to tell her what I want to do.

"That'd be great," I finally manage in the hoarse voice of someone who is doing everything she can not to give in to her tears. "Why don't you meet us back here in, I don't know, twenty minutes."

"Yeah. Sure. We'll see you soon."

Tate slides off her stool and I watch as she and Pete exit. It's only once they are out of sight that I turn to look at Justin.

"So, I mean . . ." I begin stupidly. "I guess I can understand you not wanting to cruise up to Amsterdam in such a rush."

"Yeah, all those train rides and everything."

"Yeah." We look at each other. Well, I look at him. His gaze is evasive. "What about after your trip—do you think we'll be able to see each other after you get back?"

His eyes briefly bug out and his head rears back as if this question is shockingly out of the blue, which apparently to him it is. "You mean do the whole long-distance thing?"

"Well, I don't know. Maybe for a while. We can keep our options open. I'd be . . . I mean, a writer can work from anywhere, you know."

"What are you saying, that you'd move to New York?" his voice is getting shrill. I'm not taking that as a good sign.

"I'm saying we can keep our options open. I'm saying I'd like to see you again after if you want to see me."

He shakes his head. "I mean, yeah, we can keep our options open, sure. It's just . . . I'm going to be really busy, with the restaurant and everything."

"I'm not asking for a commitment, I'm asking if you'd ever like to see me again."

He stares intently at the table, then intently at something off to his right as he speaks. "Well, I mean, yeah, like if you were in New York or something, sure, it'd be great to see you." He shifts uncomfortably. "I just don't want to hurt . . . I mean, you're great, Jadie, it's just . . . long-distance relationships . . ." His gaze meets mine again for a mere flicker of an instant, then his eyes are off again, staring at some mythical object.

I'm trying not to look stricken. I want to appear like I'm fine with this, but I can feel the heat surging up my neck to my face, that all too familiar feeling of my throat tightening painfully, foretelling the imminent arrival of tears.

I am such an asshole. Of course I knew this was how the story was going to end. How else could it end? But I worked so hard at suppressing this knowledge, imagining a different end, that I succeeded utterly in fooling myself.

God. God. This is the oldest story in the world: girl meets boy. Girl falls for boy and convinces herself he's just as crazy about her as she is about him. Boy feels constrained by the fervor of the girl's ardor and does his best to get away with minimal, if any, discussion of what it all meant. How many times have I lived through phone calls that just stop coming without explanation? Then I leave pathetic, desperate phone messages while the guy has already moved on to another girl. His memories of me quickly become hazy and distant, while I have recorded everything about him in my journal, everything we did together, everything he said, how he looks when he laughs, comes, smiles, so I can analyze my time with him again and again like a precious gem that becomes even more interesting when examined closely from every angle in different shades of light.

"Sure. I understand. No problem," I say, doing my best to keep my voice steady.

I want to ask him what these last two weeks have meant to him, if anything, but that would be the in-person equivalent of leaving a pathetic phone message, and I already feel like an idiot. I want to take back the words "a writer can live anywhere," letting him know that I'm so interested in him I'd move across the country to be with him.

Two weeks. It sounds like nothing. Fifty weeks a year I live my life in a mindless routine of getting up, showering, going to work, having a drink with friends from time to time, living my life only partially awake because if I was totally awake, totally aware of how trivial and insignificant my life really was, the pain would be too raw, too intense. But here . . . sex, wine, dancing, laughter . . . There are so many new experiences, new tastes, new things to learn. The sleep is deeper, the smiles more real. Here I am part of something so much bigger than me. History. Tradition. Art. Culture. These last few weeks have packed more living in them than I've had in several years put together. It's only been a few weeks, but it seems much longer.

I wish Tate and Pete would come back to rescue me from this awkward silence.

But they don't come back, not for several agonizingly long minutes that I have to spend pretending to be just fine. At last Tate and Pete return.

"What do you want to do?" Pete asks. "When we were getting dinner, we saw a bar that looked—"

"Great. Perfect. Let's go there," I say, sliding off my barstool, throwing money on the table, and looking as cheerful as I can muster.

Tate is looking at me worriedly, so I do my best to avoid her gaze. Her concern for me is going to make me cry for sure.

The bar is several blocks away. Thank God for Pete, who can joke around endlessly about nothing in that way boys can. At least he fills the air with noise, and for that I am grateful.

At the bar, we order drinks and then Tate announces she has to go to the bathroom. She nods her head covertly backwards in the direction of the bathroom, giving me pointed looks, and I know she wants me to go with her, but I pretend like I don't notice.

"Jadie, come with me, 'kay? I've got to tell you something . . ."

Fuck. "Oh, sure."

So I follow her to the bathroom. As soon as we get there she asks me what's wrong.

"Nothing. It's stupid. I knew we'd go our separate ways . . . I just . . . I guess I thought maybe things didn't have to end . . . that maybe we could see each other when we were back in the States . . . it's just. . . . I feel more strongly about him than he does about me and . . . it hurts."

I manage, somehow, to reign in the tears. I refuse—*refuse*—to leave this bathroom with red, puffy eyes.

"I'm so sorry." She pulls me into a hug. The smell of her, the feel of her slight frame, her thin arms encircling me, is so comforting.

"I just feel so stupid," I say.

"No, don't think that. He seemed so into you."

That's true. That bastard. He massaged my stinky, sweaty feet. He bought me medicine when I was sick. He told me I was an amazing woman. Didn't any of that mean anything?

"Come on. Let's go back out there and be happy and have a good time," I say. She gives me a look. "Well, let's go out there and fake having a good time."

We return to the table and I force myself not to actually drink my beer—I know the slightest buzz will make me maudlin and the tears will come out in a deluge.

We get through the night thanks to Pete carrying on the conversation almost entirely by himself. Justin spends his entire night not looking at me and I spend the whole night sneaking covert glances at him, hoping to somehow catch him looking my way.

Eventually it's time for bed and Justin and I return to our room, undress like polite strangers, and get into bed, each of us so far off to our respective sides we are nearly falling off the edges.

I lie awake for a long time. I want him to tear my clothes off, fuck me raw, and tell me I'm beautiful and sexy and that he loves me—any lie I can comfort myself with. And I hate myself for wanting it.

It is a long and mostly sleepless night. I finally fall asleep just as the sun is coming up. I'm not sure how much later it is when I'm woken by the sound of Justin bustling around the room.

"So I'll see you off to the train station. Then I'll look for a train to Turkey."

What does he want me to say, that he's such a great guy for seeing me off?

"I'm basically packed so I just need to take a shower," is what I say instead.

I feel incredibly awkward when I emerge from the bathroom in my towel. Suddenly I don't feel comfortable naked around him, so I face away from him and put my underwear and shorts on under my towel and modestly put on my bra and T-shirt. I zip up my backpack and announce that I am ready to go.

Tate, Pete, Justin, and I walk to the train station beneath our backpack carapaces and find our train.

"We'll go find seats, Jadie," Tate says. "Justin, it was cool meeting you. Have fun in Turkey."

"I will. You have fun too."

"Justin, it's been real. Later, man," Pete says, shaking his hand. Then he and Tate climb aboard the train.

And now it's just the two of us. Justin and I stand facing each other, me expectant, he evasive. I want him to tell me this meant something to him, that I meant something to him.

I wait for him to give me his e-mail address or ask me for mine. I wait for him to lie to me and tell me he'll write, but he doesn't even give me that much, and I'm certainly not going to force my phone number and e-mail address in his hands and beg him to stay in touch.

"Well, have a good time on the rest of your trip," he says.

"Yeah, you too."

He gives me a chaste kiss that barely grazes my mouth

and a stilted hug like you'd get from a curmudgeonly, un-affectionate grandfather.

"Well, bye," he says.

"Bye."

And that's it, out not with a bang but a whimper.

How can this be it?

I get on the train feeling leaden and empty. Dazed. I almost walk right by Tate and Pete, but Tate shouts my name. It takes a moment to register that she's talking to me.

"Hey," I say. "Sorry, I didn't see you." Before I can hoist my backpack up onto the overhead rack, three guys from Spain come in and take the remaining three empty seats, talking loudly in Spanish.

I sit down and open my book, but the words are just a blurry haze of gray. I want desperately to be alone so I can cry. I want to be home. I want to know where I'm going to sleep tonight. I want to know where my next meal is coming from. I want to be able to use the bathroom any time I want without having to hike around for half an hour before I can find it.

As soon as the train leaves the station, I excuse myself and run to the bathroom so I can cry.

We have twenty-one hours until Budapest, twenty-one hours where I have nothing else to do but think about every second I spent with Justin. My internal monologue is siren loud, a clatter of competing thoughts. Such as:

Even though I know logically that the circumstances probably have as much or more to do with our splitting up as with Justin just not liking me enough, it still hurts because if Justin did care about me, he would have figured out a way to be with me. Did I love him? It sure felt like I was falling in love with him.

Will he miss me? Think of me? Remember me?

* * *

On my fourth visit to the bathroom to cry, there is a pounding on the bathroom door.

"Jadie, it's me. Open up," Tate says. Shit. She knocks again.

I open the door and she squeezes her way into a bathroom that's barely big enough for one person. I cry and she just holds me. We don't have to say anything. She doesn't tell me those annoying things you don't want to hear when you simply need to bask in being rejected. She doesn't give me any crap about how it was a learning experience or how it was all for the best.

When my tears go from a storm to a sniffle, I say, "I just . . . I have this love to give and no one to give it to."

"There's a guy out there for you somewhere."

"Where?"

"I'm not sure, but just think of all the places we haven't gone yet. Whole continents we haven't visited. Asia, South America, Canada, Russia, Africa, Antarctica—"

"My soul mate is not in Antarctica. He'd hate the cold as much as I do."

"Right, right, of course. I'm just saying, he's out there. We'll go home, you'll sell a book for millions, and we'll use that money to go back out there and find him. I have faith, Jadie—He's out there."

And I surprise myself by realizing I believe her.

9

Budapest, Hungary

Budapest is divided into two sections by the Danube: hilly Buda in the west and the plains of Pest in the east.

Even though I'm feeling glum, I still get a charge of excitement seeing a new city—the cobbled streets, the castles stretching up into the mountains, the stunning architecture. Tate, Pete, and I explore the city, and I'm grateful to have something to keep me distracted from my thoughts.

As evening falls, I tell Pete and Tate to have some fun on their own. They protest that they want to be with me, that they don't want to leave me alone in a foreign city, but I insist. It's not for their benefit, it's for mine. Watching them hold hands and give each other loving looks just hurts too much.

I find a small, dark restaurant that is completely empty, but the lights are on. Then I see a bored waitress standing in the corner. I push the door open. The waitress smiles at me and says in flawless English, "Welcome."

I'm momentarily irked that she pegged me so quickly for an American, although with my battered backpack, shorts, and sandals, my appearance is as American as you can get. She takes me to a corner table that is lined with a crisp white tablecloth that cascades down the floor like a ball gown. Wine glasses that reflect the warmly lit room sit atop the tablecloth next to gleaming silverware.

"Slow tonight, huh?"

She nods. "Very boring." She goes to hand me a menu, but I ask her just to tell me what vegetarian options there are, if any.

"We have two. We have a breaded cauliflower dish made with steamed cauliflower that is smothered with creamy parmesan cheese sauce and served with braised and seasoned red cabbage and parsley potatoes. We also have a dish called the mushroom paprika made of sautéed mushrooms and onions in light sour cream paprika sauce served over tiny homemade pasta dumplings with sautéed vegetables."

I order the mushroom paprika and a half liter of red wine. A few minutes later the woman returns with a small plate with thinly sliced cucumbers marinated in a light vinaigrette and two crispy puffs of fried bread with baked garlic cloves on top.

"On the house," she says. "You look like you need it."

Her smile is warm. She looks youngish—in her early thirties I'd guess—and she's very pretty, with clear skin and light brown curls that she's pulled back in a barrette. I rip off a small corner of the bread.

"You rub the garlic on the bread," she says.

"Ah, thank you." I do as she suggests. The bread is heavenly. "If you want, you can sit down."

She pulls a chair out and sits across from me.

"I'm Katalin."

"I'm Jadie. It's nice to meet you."

"You're sightseeing?" she asks.

I nod.

"What do you think so far?"

"Um, of Budapest? It's beautiful."

She looks at me. Her gaze is intense, and I can't figure out what she wants me to say.

"We just got here, you know, so we haven't seen much," I stammer on.

"Is everything okay with you? You seem sort of sad."

"Oh. It's nothing. Boy problems. It's no big deal. I'll get over it."

"What happened?"

"We met on the road a couple of weeks ago. We really hit it off—well, we really *seemed* to hit it off. We spent every minute together. I thought . . . I think I thought we were falling in love with each other or something. I even started fantasizing about moving across the country so I could be with him, but then, kind of abruptly, he said he was going to go his own way. It made sense—he was going to travel around for several more weeks. Then he's going to move to New York to take over his father's business. But the way things ended . . . he didn't even give me his e-mail address. It just seemed so odd. It all seemed so abrupt. We had this amazing time together, and I just don't understand how we could have been so completely not on the same page." I cringe at "same page," which is yet more corporatespeak that has wheedled its way into my vocabulary and is a particular favorite of Tina's. "I mean I think maybe he thought he was doing me a favor by not giving me hope when there wasn't any, and maybe in the long run he did do me a favor . . . but . . . it doesn't feel that way now. I just don't get guys at all. We spent twenty-four hours a day together for two weeks and laughed and talked and had a great time and then, poof! Off into the sunset."

"You said he was taking over his father's business . . . he's probably worried about his future."

"I get that. What I don't understand is how I could

have been so into things with Justin and he was thinking something so different about me."

"Did you ask him?"

She's got me on that one. "Not really. I mean no."

She smiles at me, she doesn't need to say anything; her point has been made.

"It's kind of ironic, actually. I'm a journalist, and I've spent these last few weeks interviewing people from all over the world. I feel perfectly comfortable prying personal information out of strangers, but can't talk about my feelings with a guy who's seen me naked."

"Why do you think you think that is?"

I shrug. "I don't know." I look down at my half-eaten piece of bread and take a sip of my wine. "You know, I don't want to talk about guys anymore. I've been talking about guys for the last few weeks. I don't want to talk about them for a while. Tell me how you learned to speak English so well."

Katalin and I talk for two or three hours. She tells me her life story, and it's a good one. While we talk, the restaurant gets just a handful of customers, and in between delivering food and drinks to the other tables, she comes back to sit with me.

She tells me about how her mother moved the two of them to the States when Katalin was ten. Her mother returned to Hungary a few years later, but Katalin stayed to go to college, where she fell in love with the man she thought she was going to marry. She was in her third year of medical school when her fiancé left her. He said she worked too many hours and that she was out of it even when she wasn't working.

"And the thing was, he was right, the hours were killing me. There were times when I thought I was losing my mind," Katalin says.

So she decided to quit med school and went to work as an editor for a publisher that published medical journals. She liked the job because it was relatively low stress but it still let her use her medical knowledge. Then, just as she was getting over the loss of the man she thought was the love her life, she got a phone call from her mother who told her she was dying of lung cancer. Katalin returned to Hungary to take care of her . . . and watch her die.

Katalin was depressed and confused and lost for a long time after that. She would come to this restaurant many nights, eating her dinner and thinking about whether she should return to the States or stay here, whether to return to medical school or pursue yet another career.

She and the cook/owner got to be friends, and he gave her a job as a waitress until she could figure out what she wanted to do. Over the next several months as she mourned her mother, she and the owner became better friends, then lovers, then husband and wife.

I look around the restaurant and see that all the other customers have left and it's just the two of us again.

"I could never have guessed my life would have turned out like it has," Katalin says. "It's certainly not what I was expecting. But you know, I don't think things could have possibly turned out better."

With that thought in mind, I leave the restaurant feeling surprisingly better then I did when I came in.

10

Someplace in Germany

Tate, Pete, and I get to Germany in the late afternoon. We try to find a restaurant we read about on the Internet that may well be the only vegetarian restaurant in the country, but we can't find the road it's allegedly on, so we become frustrated and give up. Instead we go to a typical German restaurant and Tate and I have a dinner of potatoes and bread and beer.

"This is a very nutritious meal," I say, spearing a potato.

"It's got to be hard being a vegetarian," Pete says.

"No, not at home. At home it's easy. There are tons of fake meat products there," I say.

"Like Tofurkey? I've heard of that. It sounds ghastly."

"Tofurkey is definitely not my favorite. But there are some really good things, like soy chicken nuggets and barbeque chicken patties. You know no chicken beaks or gross stuff was mixed in with your veggie nuggets," I point out.

"Still, think of all the meals you'll never experience," he says.

I shrug.

"What's the grossest thing you ever ate?" Tate asks him.

"Hmm. Oh, I know. One time my parents took me out

for my birthday to this seafood place. It was super expensive. I ordered the seafood platter with pasta. It cost $45, and when it arrived, there were three whole baby octopuses on it!"

"Ew!" Tate and I chorus.

"Octopuses have these little beaks on them—"

"Beaks? Really?" Tate says.

"Yeah. It was disgusting. But my parents were shelling out $45, so I felt obligated to eat them. It was like eating rubber. I could barely keep from throwing up."

We share more stories of gross things we've eaten or nearly eaten, like the time I ordered sweetbreads, thinking it was sweet bread, and instead it turned out to be entrails.

"It's all about the marketing," I say. "If they called it entrails, nobody would order it, but it's called sweetbread, so it sounds appetizing. It's very tricky."

After dinner we go to a loud, large beer hall. It being loud and large is about all I remember about it. I only have two beers, though they are enormous, and in no time I'm schnockered off my ass. I have vague memories of a cute German guy trying to hit on me as I made my way back from the bathroom to the table, but even drunk I'm in no mood for flirting. I have no need for any more mindless sex on this trip.

Tate, Pete, and I sleep at a hostel that has a bunch of bunkbeds in a big room. Fortunately or unfortunately, I'm drunk enough not to really notice how noisy it is to sleep in a room full of snoring people tossing about in their sheets. In the morning I wake up and feel like Frankenstein with steel bolts drilled into my temples, and I can't figure out why. I share with Tate and Pete the fact that my head feels like it spent the previous evening being been used as a battering ram and that I can't understand why I feel so ill.

"I mean I know the beers were big, but still, they were only about twice the size of regular beers, so that's only about four beers. Four beers shouldn't have made me so sick."

"Yeah, but the alcohol content is much stronger than regular beers. It's like twelve percent," Pete says.

"Twelve percent! Jesus! That's how much alcohol wine has in it! No wonder my brain feels like it's been sawed in half!"

I don't really remember what we spend our day doing. When I get the pictures back, then I'll find out. I imagine there are some photos of me smiling woozily in front of a castle or some other building of historical import, but I can't say for sure.

We get on the train for Amsterdam that afternoon. I'm looking forward to getting to Bacharach, which is known for its views of castles.

I'm so ill from the potent beers the night before that I fall right to sleep on the train, something I can almost never do.

When I wake, I ask Tate where we are. She tells me she's not sure, but that we just passed all these really cool castles.

"Shit."

I really wanted to see them, although I feel better after having gotten some rest. My body is so maddening, spending the hours when I'm supposed to be sleeping worrying about stupid things. But when I'm on a loud, crowded, uncomfortable train and I want to the see the sights, exhaustion steals me away from the land of consciousness like a Roman gypsy thief.

11

Amsterdam, Holland

Bicycles. Bicycles everywhere. Tall, blond, smiley people trundle along on them. The unmanned ones are chained to every conceivable thing they can be chained to. Welcome to Amsterdam.

We find a bed and breakfast to stay at and drop our bags off. Like most of the houses around us, our B&B is narrow and gabled and has steep staircases.

We walk around the streets lined with canals, then get bread and cheese sandwiches and sit at a park and watch the hippies.

I love how when you are really truly good and hungry, a simple meal of bread and cheese seems exquisite.

We walk around the city and stumble onto the red light district. Seeing the tired, bored-looking women in the windows trying to sell their bodies depresses the hell out of me. One woman has a bag of McDonalds behind her waiting for when she takes her lunch break, and I feel abruptly nauseated. Not that I didn't know this kind of thing existed . . . but the McDonalds bag, just sitting there behind her, makes it too real for me to bear.

I urge Tate and Pete along. We don't get far before we come upon a sex shop. The window showcases plastic penises, vibrators, leather attire and accessorizing whips, and a realistic woman's vagina in a frightening block form.

I can't get over the disembodied vagina. "Could you imagine dating some guy and finding one of those in his house? I'd freak."

"What are you saying? I love the one I've got at home," Pete jokes. "You just never know when you're going to need a block of vagina to keep you company."

"I can see how it'd be handy. If I wasn't in the mood, I could just let you have your way with the vagina block," Tate says.

We continue walking around, and I struggle desperately to get the images of the prostitutes out of my mind, but it's no good. I can't shake their bored expressions.

I'm still feeling bummed when we go to a coffee shop that offers a complex menu of marijuana choices. Pete and Tate order some, and I stare out the window as they roll up their joints.

I'm in my own world when I'm suddenly jolted back to the present when I hear Pete say my name.

"What?" I say.

"I was telling them about your research. They said they'd love to help out," Pete says, pointing to a table of three young, gorgeous blond women next to us.

I want to kill him. I'm in no mood to talk about love and romance right now.

"Oh, it's okay. I've probably collected enough information. Thanks though."

"No! No! Please. Ask us something. If you get famous I want to say that I helped you!"

The woman who says this is breathtakingly beautiful and I want to beat her gorgeous face in.

"Ah, okay. Why don't you tell me about your worst date ever."

"Oh, that's an easy one," she says, rolling her eyes. "I was at this party and I met this guy, and he was so handsome. We talked and he said that he really liked hiking

and biking and camping, that sort of thing. I do not like
doing any of those things, but when I was talking to him,
I said I loved it all. He asked for my number and a few
days later he called. We went out on a first date and had a
good time. He called me a couple of days later and asked
me if I wanted to go camping with him over the weekend.
What could I say? I'd told him I loved to camp, so I said
'yes.' That Friday night after work he picked me up. It
took us much longer to get to the campground than we'd
thought because we kept getting lost, and he was getting
really frustrated, because he was trying to . . . how do you
say? . . . impress? . . . impress me, but it was obvious he
did not know where he was going. At first I did not care
that we were lost because I was just happy to be with him,
but then we both started getting really hungry. We finally
made it to the campground, and it took forever to set up
the tent, mostly because I had no idea what I was doing
and the wind was blowing hard so we could not get the
tent to stay put long enough to get the . . . how do you
say?"

"Stakes?" Pete offers.

"Steaks?" she says, perplexed.

"We know what you mean," I say.

She goes on to explain how they finally got the tent up
but then it took forever to get the fire started, and by
then they were so hungry they didn't have the patience to
let their food cook all the way. They were cooking some
kind of meat or sausage, but I could not tell you for the
life of me what it was. I ask her three times to repeat the
word and the word clearly has no vowels and to pronounce it you have to act like you're coughing up a hair-
ball. Anyway, their grblbgrrrgrr or whatever was half
charred, half frozen, but they ate it anyway. It was already
pitch black outside. Then they went in the tent and she
turned off the flashlight and they started making out.

"Then he jumps up screaming like a little girl that something just ran over his skin. He was screaming for me to find the flashlight but I could not find it. I was feeling around the tent for the flashlight and I knocked something over. I realized it was my drink, so I said, 'Auk! I spilled the soda.' Then he got even more mad, yelling at me that all the bugs would come to our tent because there was orange soda everywhere. Finally I found the flashlight. I turned it on. We saw that there was a spider in the tent. I killed it. Jan was so angry that I had not remembered where I set the flashlight and that I spilled the soda."

"He was just upset that he looked like a wuss in front of you," I say.

"What is this, 'wuss'?"

"Just that he didn't look manly. He was embarrassed."

She nods her head, conceding that this might well be true. "It began raining so hard, and the wind was blowing. I told him that I was worried that the tent would blow away. Jan said this could not happen. A few minutes went by. The tent was flapping so hard—it began to blow away! Quickly we got our things and took the tent down. We set up the sleeping bags in the back of his van because it was raining too hard to drive through the woods in the dark. Finally we fell asleep, but in a few hours, I woke up, and I had to go to the bathroom. I opened the door at the back of the van and still it was raining so hard. It was so loud that Jan woke up. He was upset that I woke him. He asked me what I was doing and I said that I needed to go to the bathroom, but it was raining so hard and it was so muddy outside. He said I should just bend down and go out the back door. I said I was worried I would fall, so he said he would help me. I was like this." She stands up on her chair and squats like you do when you're just about to stand up on water skis. She balances on the edge of her chair but demonstrates how she was sort of teetering, peeing off the edge of the back of the van in the pouring rain in front of this guy she barely knows. "And then, it was so wet, my arms were wet, my feet were wet, and Jan lost hold of me. I fell back—right into the mud! My whole body!"

We all nearly bust a gut laughing. As dates go, that certainly ranks up there with one of the worst I've ever heard of.

"Did you ever see him again?" I ask.

She looks at me like I'm mad. "No!"

The second gorgeous woman tells a story of her worst date, which involved a guy who took an illegal drug and had to be rushed to the hospital to be treated for an overdose. He lived and everything was okay, but the way she tells the story, despite the seriousness of the situation, has me laughing so hard my stomach muscles actually hurt.

After her story about the drug addict, the conversation veers to a discussion on the merits of legalizing marijuana. I agree that while I'm not a fan of drugs, America's drug policies are largely asinine, which is a point we all agree on.

"But then where do you draw the line?" I ask. "Why aren't hard drugs legal in Holland, too?"

There are no right answers to anything we're talking about, but it feels good to be thinking about these things, to be *thinking* about issues instead of what I normally think about during the day: Needtogettoworkgoingtobelate. Needtogettomeeting. Needtogetprojecttimelinedone. Havetimeforthegym? Quickworkout. Rush! Rush through-shower. Panicatslowtrafficteryingtogetbacktothe-office. SomanythingsIcouldbedoingifIweren'tstuckintraffic. Grabquicklunch. Eatatdesk. Get to . . . got to . . .

This is what I'm meant to be doing with my life. Seeing new things, talking to people, learning, and sharing what

I see, hear, and learn with others. When I'm traveling and interviewing people, I feel happy and alive. I need to figure out a way to make a living from this. I want to feel this way all the time.

Pete sees us off to the ferry that afternoon. I stand a little ways back as he and Tate hug and kiss good-bye. They've already exchanged addresses, phone numbers, and e-mails.

"If you ever want to come to Colorado, you'd have a place to stay," Tate says.

"Colorado sounds like a place I'd love. Do you mean that, about the offer? I mean really mean it and aren't saying it to be nice?" he says.

"I really mean it. I'd love to see you again."

"I'd like to see you again, too."

I look away, trying to blink back tears, hoping neither of them notice I'm tearing up. Tate is getting the ending I wanted. I'm happy for her. And jealous as hell.

It's actually something of a relief for me to be on the ferry. It's nice to know there is really not much of anything I can be doing. I don't feel obligated to see any sights or improve my mind or learn anything about foreign cultures. I just sit on my ass and read my book and feel relaxed.

We finally get to England and then to the airport. We climb onto the plane and I slump into my seat, exhausted.

There are lots of great things about traveling, but I must say I can't wait to get home to my own place with a comfortable bed with soft, clean sheets and a bathroom I don't have to share with a bunch of strangers. If I want a snack or a glass of water, I can just go downstairs and get it rather than wandering around hoping to find a store or restaurant to buy food or drinks from. I won't get lost, I'll be able to speak the language, and I won't have to do my laundry in the sink. Heaven.

Although now that I'm thinking about it, I could really use a vacation to recover from my trip to Europe. Someplace like Hawaii. I won't sightsee at all; in fact, I won't see a damn thing except for the beach. I'll only walk from my hotel room to the chaise lounge—no more of this traipsing across a whole continent day in and day out. I will have a beach novel in one hand at all times and a piña colada in the other. I will be a slug, sleeping and sunning and lounging around for hours at a time . . .

As I fantasize about my trip to Hawaii, a pesky detail called reality intrudes on my thoughts. Specifically, the irritating problem of how to pay for it. My plot to meet a rich man who would take me away to his villa so I could write didn't quite work out as I'd hoped. Not that I really thought it would.

I know that nobody is just going to hand me a lucrative publishing contract. If I want it, I need to get it myself. No prince charming is going to put me up in his palace in Provence and pay all of my expenses as I thoughtfully pen articles and essays. I need to find a way to make the time to focus on my writing.

I pull out my notebook and I begin to write.

12

Denver, Colorado

Our friend Sylvia picks us up from the airport. I'm battling three equally ferocious desires: I long to go to my own bed and get some sleep, I'm starving and can't wait to eat, and I desperately want to shower and brush my teeth and scrub the grime of all this travel off of me. I form a plan in my head: food, shower, sleep, sleep, sleep.

"Tate, Sylvia, I'm famished. Do you mind if we stop for some lunch?"

"I'm starving. I'd love to eat," Tate says.

"Sure. I'll take you to Watercourse in Denver," Sylvia says.

We're approaching downtown Denver and are on Speer Boulevard, the main artery through town, when I see a half-built structure, lots of scaffolding, and several construction trucks.

"What's going on?" I ask Sylvia. "What are they building?"

"They're expanding the performing arts complex."

"What the hell are those?" I ask, eyeing a statue of two white, faceless creatures that are at least sixty feet high and look suspiciously like dancing aliens.

"It's public art, I guess."

"Public art? Of dancing aliens?"

Sylvia shrugs.

"Who thought this was a good idea?" I ask. "Why don't we just shine a spotlight to the heavens and say, 'Hostile alien creatures attack us here in Denver first, here are images of your people to show you the way.' " I try to make sense of the aliens stretching up into the skyline. I can't. "Italy gives us the Sistine Chapel and Michelangelo's statue of *David*, Paris gives us Monet and the *Mona Lisa*, and Denver offers the world dancing aliens. Great."

We turn near the library and there is yet more construction going on. I ask Sylvia what is going on here and she tells me they are expanding the art museum.

I can't even keep up with what's going on in Denver, which is forty minutes from where I live. How can I really ever know another country, other cultures?

Even if I had an endless amount of time and money to wander around the world, I'd still never be able to keep up.

Over lunch, Sylvia asks us about our trip and we tell her the highlights, which naturally don't include the stuff about seeing all the great art and monuments but about the guy walking into our room and having wet underwear thrown on his head, and Justin falling into the river on our rafting trip.

Sylvia is excited that we both met guys on the trip, but we tell her we don't have plans to see either of them again.

"They were just on-the-road-romances, you know?" I say in a voice that almost sounds convincing.

We laugh and talk and then I go home, skip the shower, and sleep for eight of the most beautifully restful hours of sleep I've ever had in my life.

When I wake up the next day, I tell myself, *okay, no more excuses, get writing*. I make coffee to kick-start my brain, and then I collapse on the couch and stare dazedly around my living room as if I'd suffered a brain injury.

I look at the wall above my couch. It's decorated with this banged-up frame that I'd salvaged from a neighbor's garbage can. There's no poster or painting in it, it's just a wood frame painted a Toulouse Lautrec shade of green. I hung it askew, thinking it looked kind of artsy (what can I say: poverty chic). I look at my colorful throw pillows, my extensive collection of aromatherapy candles in every color imaginable given to me by my mother, and I sink down a little farther into the cushions. Boy it's good to be home.

I finally manage to get off my butt long enough to put some laundry in the washing machine. This requires an epic amount of energy, so when I'm done I return to the couch to recoup my strength. Every other hour or so I'm able to muster the resolve to go do something productive—pay a few bills, get food from the grocery store, fold laundry. I look through the want ads to see if there is maybe a part-time job out there, or any jobs that don't sound awful, but all do. I hate that you have to pretend to like the idea of a "fast-paced environment" (meaning: you'll be expected to work your ass off) and be a "team player." Why can't someone just overpay me to work at a company with loose timeframes and a strong happy hour ethic and be done with it?

My ritual of looking through the classifieds for the secret to a new and better life both depresses me—there's nothing out there! and reinforces that I'm very lucky to have a job—there's nothing out there!

I throw the classified section of the newspaper down in disgust. Looking through it has exhausted me, and I need a nap to recover. I feel a twinge of guilt, but then I rest my head on a pillow and close my eyes. I decide to blame my stupor on jet lag and vow to become a productive citizen once my body has recovered from the demands of international travel.

It takes me three days to stop feeling like a comatose zombie, and then, of course, I have to waste my energy on going back to work.

When I get back to the office, my coworkers keep saying things like, "I thought maybe you'd been fired. You were away so long!" But it doesn't seem like it's been a long time to me. In fact, it doesn't feel like any time has passed at all. Things at the office are exactly the way they always were.

Ugh.

I do my best to keep my spirits high, telling myself how very lucky I am to have a job when so many people are unemployed right now. And the first few hours of work aren't bad at all because I spend the morning telling people about my trip. They only ask about whether I enjoyed my trip to be polite, but too bad for them. I tell them all about it in a gushing and enthusiastic manner.

Then comes my first meeting with the Stepford trio of Tina, Kelly, and Nadia. And my zeal disappears like my last lover: quickly and painfully.

Kelly is the liaison from the sales team, and Nadia works in enterprise accounts, a department whose purpose I never could discern.

"I hope you enjoyed your trip," Tina says in the same sort of tone you might use to say, "You just ran over my dog and totaled my car, you evil bitch."

"Yeah, it was great. We—"

"Things were a little crazy while you were gone. The sales team scored a major project with Olsen University to revamp their Web site."

"Olsen University?"

"It's a college that enables students to get their degrees online."

"Mmm," I say in a tone that I hope sounds enthusiastic and interested.

"And here's the thing, because the market is so tight now, in order to secure the contract, the sales team promised a rather aggressive timeline."

"How aggressive?"

"Six weeks."

I laugh. Nobody laughs with me. "No really, how long?"

"Six weeks."

"So the text and graphics must already be done then, right? The site must not be very extensive, right?"

"It'll be up to you to see what needs to be done exactly."

Translation: she has absolutely no idea what the project entails but has agreed to what is in all likelihood a ludicrous deadline anyway.

Figures.

I'm in a panic to find out more details about the project, or at least find out when I'll have enough information to get started, and I begin firing off questions. But somehow Tina manages to quickly change the subject around to something she's more interested in, namely, herself. She goes on and on about all the trouble she is having with her automatic sprinkler system. I keep trying to steer the conversation back around to the mammoth project that has just been dumped on my head, but she, Kelly, and Nadia go off talking about their big houses. They pretend to be complaining about all the burdens that being a home owner demands, but really they use the conversation as an excuse to let the others know the exact majestic square footage of their homes and how modern their remodeled kitchen now looks. They talk about lawn aeration and the merits of crown molding, and at some point their conversation somehow turns to a discussion of their engagement rings. Not having a lawn to aerate or a house to crown mold or so much as a boyfriend to give me an engagement ring, I have nothing to add to the conversation as usual, and I just swivel my head from one woman to another like a spectator at a tennis match. I feel like a feral child who has just recently been rescued from the depths of the jungles in Papua New Guinea, for all I know about the world these women live in.

"I made Ken get me a karat for each kid we planned to have. I just need to squeeze out one more!" Tina says. (Tina has two kids already.)

"Ah," I say.

"Dan and I went for quality," Kelly says, brandishing her left hand.

"We went for *quantity* and *quality*," Nadia says and brandishes hers. "Martin wants to have another kid. I'm not so sure. All that work!"

"Make him get you another karat on your ring!" suggests Tina.

"I don't think I could lift my hand if I did!" Laugh laugh (her), gag gag (me). "Actually, what I told him was that I'd consider having another kid if he bought me a Mercedes minivan . . ."

Oh my God. Tell me I'm not hearing this. A woman who doesn't want to have another kid but is willing to bring a human life into this world in exchange for . . . a minivan! A minivan, for God's sake! As I sit in the meeting, I send a silent prayer up to the heavens:

Dear God in heaven, I know I wasn't raised in a religious household, but please don't hold that against me—it really was all my parents' fault—and hear my plea: please let me make enough money as a travel writer that I can get out of the fiery, materialistic, consumerist hell that is corporate America. Amen.

A million years later the meeting ends, but Tina asks me to stay so she can talk to me. After Kelly and Nadia have left, Tina tells me in a sharp whisper to close the door, which I do.

Tina's expression is one of huffy importance as if she is about to tell me government secrets on which the lives of an entire nation depend.

"While you were gone, some things happened," she begins. "It's not important what, but because of certain events, I've had to initiate a new policy for my staff that I expect you to follow without fail."

I have to say, I'm intrigued about what this mysterious new policy could be.

"I don't want you to e-mail or talk to anyone outside this department unless I write the e-mail with you or am with you when you talk to them," she says.

I have to stifle the urge to laugh. "Are you . . . um, really? But Tina, my job is to manage all the different people who work on the different parts of the project, how can I make sure everyone is on track . . ."

"I don't want you to send any e-mail I haven't approved or talk to people outside this department if I'm not there," she repeats.

"But Tina, you're such a busy person . . ."

"We'll just have to modify our processes. It's imperative that I know everything that is going on in this department at all times. There have been some miscommunications . . . things that . . . *certain other executives* might try to wield to their advantage."

Tina sounds like she has a serious case of paranoia. It's best to treat unbalanced individuals delicately, so I say, "Okay. Will do."

* * *

I stop by the grocery store after work and pick up the pictures of the trip from the photo mat. I rush home and plonk down on my bed. I divide the double set of prints in two stacks as I go through them, one for Tate and one for me.

When I get to the first picture of Justin, the emotions swirl in my chest and my head in a tsunami sort of way— I smile at the same time I tear up, my chest feels heavy and my head feels light. I stare at the picture for a long time.

The picture is of Justin and me standing in the Boboli Gardens in Florence. It's a great picture of both of us— neither of us is blinking or making dorky, caught-off-guard expressions—and my hair actually looks good, which is no small feat as I have been experiencing what can only be called a bad hair epoch. Justin looks so damn cute with that smile of his and those green-brown eyes and that hair curling so adorably at his neck.

It makes me sad that he never gave me any way to contact him so I could send him a copy of this picture. Of all these pictures really. I would really love for him to have some memento that would force him to remember me from time to time.

The phone rings, and, ridiculously, my heart begins pounding at the thought it could be Justin. It's not, of course, it's someone from a local charity wondering if I have clothes I'd like to leave at the curb for them to pick up when their trucks are in the area on Friday. I tell them I don't have anything, and hang up, feeling a fresh wave of sadness about how things ended with Justin.

Technically, I know it's highly unlikely he'll ever call me, and there's no chance in hell he'll call me now since he's still in Europe. But I have this stupid fantasy that maybe he'll come home early or just change his mind about me and fork over a huge chunk of change to call me from Europe just to hear my voice. It wouldn't be all that hard for him to find me if he wanted to. My name is in the phone book so if he spent ten seconds on the Internet, he could find both my phone number and my e-mail address. I might be able to find his or his mother's address in Iowa that same way, but it doesn't matter, because he's not in Iowa anyway, and even if he was, I'd feel like a stalker, and I've humiliated myself enough.

I finally move on and look at the rest of the pictures, then I go back and look through the pictures from the beginning yet again, even more slowly this time. I smile, even though I feel sad. I've felt depressed ever since getting back from the trip—about Justin, about my job—but reliving the memories of Europe makes me feel better, even if it's just for a little while.

In the morning, I wake to my alarm at 5:30, make myself coffee, and turn on my computer.

I stare at the blank computer screen for a long time, unable to think of a single article to pitch or a single word to write. I sit blinking sleepily at the screen, sipping coffee, and waiting for the writing fairy to work her magic.

Nothing.

The writing fairy is asleep.

The muse of creativity is out on a coffee break.

Stumped, I open up an Internet browser and start searching various travel magazines and book publishers for inspiration. Unbelievably, I find some on the Web site of a publisher that produces nonfiction travel anthologies. They are accepting entries for a book that looks at the comedic side of travel—the mishaps and blunders that are teeth-grittingly frustrating at the time but can be highly amusing in hindsight. Pretty much every day of my trip was packed with blunders, so I figure I can definitely come up with *something* to write.

I bite my lip and ponder a few leads. I type a sentence, then delete it, then type a sentence, then delete it, then type a sentence and decide it's good enough to leave for now. Then I glance at the clock: 6:50. Shit! I'm going to be late for work!

I quickly and grumpily get ready for work, irritated that I have to go to the office just when I was finally getting into writing again.

I know it's a good thing we got the Olsen project because it means I have job security for at least a few weeks, but it's hard to get back into work mode after a month off and two months of having virtually nothing to do before that. My feeling is, *what do you mean I don't have time to play computer games all day? What do you mean I can't go out for a two-hour lunch?* But by the end of the week, I'm back into the habit of working for a living.

One morning, Tina comes marching over to my cube looking stern. I feel the way I feel whenever I'm driving near a cop car in traffic: guilty, even if I haven't done anything wrong.

She brandishes a printout of an e-mail exchange between Nadia and me. The e-mail, in its entirety, says this:

To: jadie.peregrine@pinnaclemedia.com
From: nadia.warner@pinnaclemedia.com

Your revised timeline looks good. I made a few suggestions; let me know if you'll be able to incorporate them.

To: nadia.warner@pinnaclemedia.com
From: jadie.peregrine@pinnaclemedia.com

No problem, will do.

Tina is staring at me like I've just burned her house down with all her loved ones in it, and I simply cannot figure out why. We sit in silence for an endless minute as Tina's glare bores holes in my head and I wrack my brains for what exactly my crime could be.

"Don't you remember our conversation the other day?" she finally hisses.

"Sorry, which conversation?"

"Do you or do you not remember me explicitly saying that I didn't want you communicating with any other department without my approval?"

"I remember that. I just thought—"

"If you have *any* e-mails to send to another department, I want you to work with me on writing the response."

"I'm sorry, I just want to understand this, you wanted me to work with you to coauthor the sentence, 'No problem, will do'?"

"Why do you work so hard to undermine my authority?"

Well, Tina, that would be because you're an idiot.

"I'm sorry, I didn't . . . I won't . . ."

"Just see that you don't do it again." She swivels on her high-heeled shoe and stomps away.

Later that afternoon I get an e-mail from John from IT who asks if the spec (specification) boards are due on Tuesday. The answer is "yes." I hit REPLY unthinkingly, and then I remember Tina's mandate.

My fingers burn to type in the three letters Y-E-S and then hit the SEND button, but I am terrified of Tina's wrath. I consider just walking to the other side of the office and whispering the answer to John, because at least then there will be no evidence she can print out and wield against me. I sit at my computer with my cursor blinking for at least two minutes, frozen with indecision.

I decide to cover my ass, and I call Tina, who of course is not at her desk because she's never at her desk because she's always in a meeting someplace. So I leave her a message saying that John e-mailed me to double-check the due date of the spec boards and I wanted her permission to write him back and confirm that Tuesday was the due date. I hang up the phone shaking my head at the police state that has become my work environment.

Hours later I'm absorbed in my work when I feel a presence hovering over me.

"Hi," I say to Tina.

"I'd like to read that e-mail from John."

It takes me a minute to remember what she's talking about, then I say sure and pull the e-mail up.

I swear to you, Tina and I spend the next twenty minutes composing a response that is so convoluted and evasive that it is pointless, even though the answer is still, basically, "yes." There is no way in hell I am going to be able to get anything done if I have to wait hours for Tina to be free to spend twenty minutes writing an e-mail that should take ten seconds to write.

Two weeks go by, three weeks go by, a month. Some mornings I write, many mornings I don't.

As I suspected, the Olsen account is a project that should take three or four months, not just six weeks. We're about to miss yet another deadline, so Tina says we, the members of the fulfillment team (meaning the people who do the work as opposed to people who sell our work), have to stay late to finish the design of the Web page templates and that she'll buy us dinner on the company, as if a five-dollar sandwich and a Diet Coke is a fair exchange for milking us out of what turns out to be seven hours of our lives. Yes, that's right, we stay till midnight: me, Tina, Ryan the graphic artist, Kathy the copywriter, and John from IT sitting around a computer going back and forth polishing the work we need to have done by our 9 A.M. meeting tomorrow.

I stagger home at midnight, open the front door to my apartment complex, get my mail, and schlep up the stairs to my place. Inside, I dump my keys and the mail on the kitchen table. Glancing down, I see that one of the envelopes has my handwriting on it—it's a self-addressed stamped envelope, the kind you send when you send out query letters to editors, the idea being that they'll send a response in the envelope. I sift through the rest of the pile of mail and there are two more self-addressed stamped envelopes. This is not a good sign. Most likely, if any of the magazines I'd queried had been interested in me writing the article I'd proposed to write, they would have called or e-mailed. I open the envelopes, and sure enough, inside are three form rejection letters. I sigh, throw the stupid rejections in the trash, and collapse on the couch still fully dressed and fall asleep, too tired to even be depressed.

I sleep in late, sprint through a shower, and dry my hair by sticking it out the window as I drive to work.

To get through the day, I practice my future exit interview speech to Tina in which I say all sorts of fiery things about her poor management skills. I've had a good two years of practice on this particular speech.

A few weeks ago I thought a trip to Europe would recharge me and get my life back on track. But the second I got home, everything was exactly the same as it always was. I still have a job I don't like, I still don't have a boyfriend, and I'm still making up excuses for not writing.

I'm exactly the same person that I always was. And I don't like it one bit.

13

Somewhere in Southern Colorado

I can't shake my feelings of listlessness. When I feel glum, the urge to hit the road is stronger than ever, my hope being that if I'm somewhere new I'll get a new perspective on things. I don't have any vacation time, though, so I only have a weekend to get somewhere and get my life in order.

I decide to visit my parents in Southern Colorado because it's only about a six-hour drive and it's been a while since I've seen them. I leave early Saturday morning with bottled water and an array of salty snack foods in the passenger seat for sustenance.

There are times when driving can feel like meditation, a kind of Zen zone where your body is basically working on automatic pilot and your brain is largely free of thought, and as I drive to my parents' home, this is how I feel. I've got my CD player blasting, and I feel the calm I always feel when I'm in the mountains. For some reason, I feel protected by them. It's not a logical feeling—what are they going to protect me from, enemy invaders? They are probably much more likely to bury me in an avalanche or dump boulders onto the hood of my car that will crush me dead. But safe is how I feel in them as I negotiate the perilously narrow, twisting mountain roads.

It's nearly one in the afternoon when I pull into my

hometown, which is on a mesa. It's the kind of place where residents frequently have to wait in their cars while a herd of sheep or cattle are moved from one pasture to another. There is no movie theater or coffee house here. Our one claim to modest fame is an airstrip that is all dirt and gravel and sees more high school parties than plane landings.

I drive to what passes for the commercial district. There are a handful of businesses and restaurants, including Mom and Dad's shop, which is now called Celestial Delights Hair Care and Furniture Repair. It used to be called Spiritual Awakenings, which was the worst marketing decision imaginable for a town filled with God-fearing people who thought my parents were trying to encourage communing with the dead, worshiping Satan, and participating in cult rituals that involved blood, animal sacrifices, and the selling of your soul to the devil.

My parents still attempt to sell a few crystals and tarot cards and various herbal remedies, but basically they've given up on their dream to bring the townsfolk into spiritual enlightenment via incense and aromatherapy candles; hence the name change.

I walk in the door to the front part of the shop, which is where the hair salon is. It's a cheery place, with big black and white tiles on the floor, two bright red cushy swivel chairs that are worn out in the main butt and middle back areas, and bright lights in a variety of primary colors hanging from the ceiling.

There are no customers in the shop, and my mother is sitting in one of the swivel chairs flipping through a magazine about holistic health care. The first thing my mother says to me is not "Good to see you!" or "Hello! You're looking well!" it's, "Your aura is looking off." Her face is a cloak of a concern.

"My aura and everything else."

"I'll get you some tea and a cookie, and then you tell me all about it."

Oh God, not one of my mother's bionic cookies. They look like hairballs and are less tasty. Their flavor, if you can use such a euphemism, is like unsweetened chalk mixed with sawdust.

She scoots off her chair to the "reception area," which consists of a battered green couch that I'm pretty sure was constructed before the dawn of mankind and a coffee table strewn with pristine copies of *Natural Healing* and *Alternative Medicine*. There is a table near the couch that has a pot of hot water brewing, a selection of caffeine-free teas, several white coffee cups perpetually stained brown inside, and a plate of bionic cookies. Every now and then a new customer will unwittingly take one of these cookies. The moment she or he bites into it, you can see her/his eyes widen in horror. It is hilarious to watch the lengths these unsuspecting victims will go to in an effort to distract my mother and then find some discreet place to hide the remainder of their "cookie."

Mom gives me a cup of chamomile tea and a bionic barfball. She smiles at me. Her kind face is framed by her long, dark, wiry hair that is turning gray. She is wearing a blindingly bright yellow cotton blouse and matching loose skirt.

I hug my mother. She has a reassuring plumpness to her. I want her to hug away all my sadness and insecurities. I want her to tell me exactly what to do with my life, how to fall in love and find riches and career satisfaction.

We each settle into a swivel chair and she says, "So. Tell me what's wrong."

"Work. My life. Everything."

"Start slow. What about work?"

I spill out everything that has been going on in my life. The words come out in such a rush I forget to breathe. I forget about punctuation and syntax, but my mother seems to understand me anyway. When I finally pour everything out, Mom says, "You know what you need?"

I feel such a tremendous rush of relief: thank goodness, some motherly advice that will clear up all this turmoil in my life.

"What?"

"You need The Empowerment Attainment Kit."

"The Empowerment Attainment Kit?"

"It comes with a variety of tools to strengthen the body, mind, and spirit. All the tools are energized with Seichim energy."

"Seichim energy?"

"The universal life force!" she thunders. She walks across the store to the display case that includes various organic hair products and the few remaining new age products Mom and Dad try valiantly to pawn off on townsfolk. While her back is turned, I take the opportunity to stash the bionic barfball in a tissue in my purse. I've known my mother for twenty-seven years: I came prepared.

I'm sipping my tea when she returns and hands me a basket wrapped in crinkly blue cellophane and tied with a matching cloth bow. "It has incense, a visualization candle, empowerment oil, a runic talisman, and a rhodonite stone."

I can imagine what the incense and candle are for. The empowerment oil sounds like something I'd like to use with my boyfriend if I ever got one, and I know the talisman is supposed to be imbued with magical qualities, but the stone's purpose is unclear to me so I ask, "The rhodonite helps in what way, exactly?"

"It brings you calmness, refinement, elegance, courtesy, and tact. Also, the incense, it has desert sage and lavender in it, and those will bring you peace and wisdom. It will cleanse your surroundings."

236

I would really, really like to believe that if I carry a rhodonite rock around with me, I'll be calm, refined, elegant, courteous, and tactful. I would also like to believe that burning a smudge packet of desert sage and lavender will cleanse my house and my inner spirit and bring me peace and wisdom. Unfortunately, I don't.

But I take the basket of stuff anyway, because at least it can't hurt.

"You still look glum, sweetie," Mom says.

I shrug. "I don't know. I went on the trip to Europe, and it was great. I had a lot of fun, and I learned a lot. I thought going on the trip would bring me some kind of peace, but instead it just made me more confused and restless than ever."

"Restless how?"

"Well, like . . . I thought the trip to Europe would scratch my travel itch, and it did, but only for about two days. You know how when you get back from a trip you suddenly appreciate little things like just how comfortable your own bed is, and how clean your toilet is, and how if you get hungry or thirsty you can just go to your fridge and get something to eat or drink?"

My mother nods.

"But after I got over the thrill of being back in the comfort of my own home, I started thinking about all the places we didn't get to see: Spain, Portugal, Ireland, Sweden, Norway. And how we didn't get to visit the smaller towns in the places we did see. And I wish we'd had more time to explore the cities we did go to. We just got a taste of them and I wanted a seven-course meal. And that's just Europe. There are six more continents I've barely begun to explore, if at all. And I feel like maybe if I'd had some more time, maybe then I would have been able to figure out how to get my life where I want it to be and I'd find the inspiration and motivation to write every day."

"Honey, you can't just go to some foreign city and pick up inspiration and motivation like souvenirs."

I sigh. "I know . . . but I thought going on this trip would get me all fired up to write again, and do you know what I did the other day instead of write? I cleaned the oven. It's my biggest goal in life to be a writer, but I would rather clean the oven than write. How does that make any sense whatsoever?"

"It makes perfect sense. Writing is hard work. Anything that's worth doing is hard work. You just need to make writing a habit like brushing your teeth. It takes six weeks to form a habit. So for six weeks, it might be really hard, but after that, it'll be like second nature."

I shrug. "I'll try. I just . . . I just wish I could just travel all the time. When I'm on the road I feel so alive."

"But honey, that's not how real life works."

I know my mother is right, but that doesn't mean I like it.

"Jadie, you've never been able to be happy with where you are and what you have. You need to learn to face reality."

I think about how I never asked Justin what he thought of me because I was scared that the truth wasn't what I wanted to hear. It's true, I've always lived in a dream world, imagining a better life in some place far away.

Bells jingle as the front door opens and Mr. Farley comes into the store. Mr. Farley is a farmer whose daughter Missy was (and no doubt still is) an Amazon of a girl who could outshoot the boys our age at the yearly town hunting trip (at least so I've heard—I wasn't allowed to go on the trip for obvious reasons). She always intimidated the hell out of me (and most of the boys, for that matter). Once, we both had a crush on the same boy, Russ Jenkins. Russ and I were assigned as lab partners in biology class, and it seemed liked he would sometimes give me loving gazes over the vats of formaldehyde filled with whatever pickled creatures we were supposed to be studying. One day Missy cornered me in a hallway and snarled at me that I'd better keep my hands off Russ Jenkins if I knew what was good for me. A few weeks later, when Russ asked me to the school dance, I said in a high-pitched squeak that I couldn't because dancing was against my family's religion. A few weeks after that, I'd heard a rumor that Missy had threatened to beat Russ up if he didn't go steady with her. I don't know how much of that story is true, but I did see a beaming Missy and a dispirited Russ eating lunch together every day in the cafeteria until the end of the school year, so I suspect there was at least some truth to the rumor.

I wait for Mr. Farley to give my mother one of those tolerant but wary smiles you'd give an old person with Alzheimer's, someone you knew wasn't a bad person but could act unexpectedly and might even be just a little bit dangerous.

But Mr. Farley's smile seems genuine.

"Just a trim today?" my mother asks. She slides off her chair and gestures to Mr. Farley to take her spot.

"Just a trim. Jadie, it's good to see you. Just here for a visit?"

"Yep."

He sits in the swiveling, cushioned chair and Mom drapes a purple polyester cape around him, snapping it at the neck.

"Your mother tells me you just got back from Europe."

"Yeah." What is it about this town that renders me monosyllabic?

"I saw some of Europe when I was in the Army. That was way back when. Haven't had a chance to go back since."

Mr. Farley and I share some of our favorite memories of our time in Europe, then we talk about some of our favorite places in the States. Then Mom talks about the road trip she and Dad took when they were about nineteen. Mom and Dad met at a Viet Nam War protest and fell in love, but Mom's conservative parents didn't approve of their daughter's whacky, long-haired boyfriend, so Mom and Dad took off in the paisley VW Bug, driving all over the States, trying to figure out what to do with the rest of their lives. "We were heading back to California when we stopped here in town—" Mom says.

"And it was so beautiful you couldn't leave?" Mr. Farley says.

"That, and we were sick of driving," she says, and we all laugh. "Well, I think that about finishes you up." She hands Mr. Farley a mirror and swivels him around so he can inspect the back of his head in the large mirror behind him.

"Top work as always, Linda. Top work." He slips her a ten that covers the cost of the haircut plus a two-dollar tip.

Not long after he leaves, Mrs. O'Connor comes in. She, too, seems happy to see my mother. I wonder what's going on here. Where are the looks of disapproval? Could it possibly be that the townspeople have finally warmed to my parents?

There is not a hint of condescension in her voice as she greets my mother and me. Mom asks her about her granddaughter's ballet recital and Mrs. O'Connor shares details excitedly while Mom trims her short, helmet-style curls. Mom's scissors zip around Mrs. O'Connor's head, snip, snip, snip, glints of silver metal flashing in the sunlight pouring in from the large store-front window.

I tell Mom I'm going to Dad's studio to say hi. I tell Mrs. O'Conner it was good to see her again and she tells me it was good to see me, too, and she actually sounds like she means it.

I walk through the door that leads to the back room where my father's workshop is. The workshop is ankle-deep in sawdust. The smell of wood permeates the air.

Dad is working intently at his work table.

"Hey, Dad, what are you working on?"

He claps his hands together, an expression of glee on his face, his balding-on-top Unabomber hairdo looking, as usual, like a dandelion at the seed stage startled from a sudden wind, half the white silken hairs blown off and the remaining hairs confused and askew. A million years ago he had the same honey-blond coloring I have, but now his hair is as white as cotton.

"Jadie! Jadie my girl! Good to see you." He wraps me in a tight hug. He smells of paint remover and sweat. It's a smell I find oddly comforting.

"Whatchya working on?" I ask again.

"Doorstops!"

"Doorstops?"

"Look, I've set up an assembly line. First, here's where I cut the wood into triangular shapes." He scoots down a couple feet or so, taking a recently cut piece with him. "Here's where I sand it." He scoots down another foot. "And here's where I paint them!" He gestures to a stack of doorstops painted highlighter yellow.

"An assembly line? That's interesting. Usually you associate assembly lines with situations in which there is more than just one person, so that's really . . . huh."

He doesn't hear me or pretends he doesn't hear me and continues, "I'm painting them florescent yellow—you'll be able to see them in the dark! I'm going to market them to fire departments."

"Why?"

"They'll be able to see them in the dark!"

"Right, but why do they need doorstops?"

"To hold the doors open!"

"So what you're thinking is they'll run around putting in doorstops as the building disintegrates around them in a fiery conflagration?"

"They can use them in the firehouses, too!"

This makes no sense whatsoever, but is, sadly, a typical example of my father's (lack of) business acumen. I think you can understand why we never became rich. Truly, it's amazing my family didn't live in a cardboard box when I was growing up (although to my parents' credit it would have been the most feng sheui-d cardboard box on the block).

Even though I've known my father my whole life, I still can't really believe he wants to launch a business making doorstops. At least the cost for the raw material is low. As I sit and watch him work, he asks me about my trip to Europe. I tailor my stories for my father-specific audience, leaving out the parts about Justin and talking to women about dating and romance and focusing on the history and architecture of the places we visited. When I'm done telling him about the cool amphitheaters in Greece and all about the Roman Forum, I ask him what's been going on in his life. He tells me about a desk he recently built, going into detail about the intricate drawers and nooks he put in it.

My father and I don't share feelings or experiences but activity reports. Still, as far as I can tell, our relationship seems to be a good one, at least as father-daughter relationships go.

My parents close their shop at four and I follow their VW Bug home in my car. Their Bug must have at least 200,000 miles on it. They don't drive it much anymore—just a couple of miles to and from their store every day.

When they take a road trip or drive up to Boulder to see me, they rent a car, knowing full well that the Bug's chances of making it aren't good. Still, I'm impressed by the Bug's longevity. I have no idea how it has held together for so long.

The house where I grew up is small and crammed full of things: paintings crowd the walls; vases, knickknacks, and pottery fill miles of shelf space; and the couches and chairs are piled high with bright pillows. The color scheme is royal purple and emerald green, and somehow it actually works.

The fall air is crisp and chilly, but we layer on sweaters and fire up the grill for a barbeque. Together the three of us chop, dice, and mix a meal of barbequed tofu sandwiches, grilled veggie skewers, roasted potatoes, coleslaw with pineapple dressing, and for dessert, poached fruit drizzled in a berry sauce. My parents may be pitiful at making cookies, but when it comes to fruit, veggies, and carbs, these people know what they're doing.

As I stand beside my parents in the kitchen making dinner, I watch the two of them flitting around each other in the tiny kitchen with practiced moves like ballroom dancers. They come in and out to and from the grill where the charcoal is sizzling and the rich scent of barbeque sauce fills the air. They call out requests for the other to bring him/her the tongs or to report on the status of how far along some portion of the meal is.

They make a great team, my parents. Watching them work together makes me smile. Sure, they've had nearly thirty years together to work out their routine, but their friendship and the kind way they treat each other makes me eager to find a guy I can spend the next thirty years—and the rest of my life—with.

It stands to reason that if these two crazy people could

have found each other in this great big world, there is a guy out there for me and I'll manage one day to find him, too. I find this to be an inordinately reassuring thought.

I get a good night of sleep in my childhood bedroom, and the next morning after breakfast, I go for a walk to stretch my legs. I walk along the side of a dirt road, my feet crunching through rust-colored leaves that have fallen to the ground.

As I come around the bend, I see a group of people straggling outside the church. It's obvious services just ended.

As I get closer, I squint, trying to make out a figure of a woman in a flowered dress and oversize cardigan holding a crying, red-faced toddler in her arms. The woman is screaming at a boy who is chasing another boy. It can't be . . . is that . . .

"Jadie? Jadie Peregrine?"

"Missy Farley?"

"Missy Coop—no, you're right, Missy Farley, duh." She slaps her free hand to her forehead. "I was Missy Cooper for a while, now I'm back to being Missy Farley again. Seems like me and Coop broke up just about the time I figured out my name, and now I have to remember my old name all over again!"

"Did you and Chris Cooper get married or something?"

"Not Chris Cooper, Mitchell Cooper. He's from Montrose. He's a few years older than us. You probably don't know him. We got married gosh, years ago. Seven years ago. We split up last year."

"Oh . . . I'm sorry."

She shrugs and sighs a deep, sad, tired sigh.

"These aren't yours, are they?" I ask.

"Yep, sure are. That little monster is Mitch Junior," she says pointing to a dirty blond boy who is terrorizing a snotty-nosed boy with the kind of hairstyle you associate with someone who has just been electrocuted, "and this is Clara."

"It's nice to meet you, Clara." The little curly haired girl begins a fresh wave of tears when I say this. She's wailing, really, as if I'd just run after her with a carving knife. Missy bounces Clara up and down and murmurs comforting words.

I'm flabbergasted by this sight. I can't imagine how I ever thought of Missy Farley as being Amazonian. She's tall, all right, and broad shouldered, but somehow all these years I had this image of her being this Goliath-type creature who could crush me using only her thumb. The brutish girl I knew growing up is gone and in her place is a gaunt, tired-looking woman. Her cardigan has a stain just above her breast and a hole on the side. Her eyes have dark circles the size of Oreo cookies under them, and I may be imagining it, but it seems like her hair is thinner than I remember.

"My dad says you have some fancy job up in Boulder. What is it again? Creative manager?" she asks.

"Creative project manager, yeah."

"Wow. Your parents must be so proud. Well, I'm not surprised, you always were the smartest girl in class. Everybody knew you'd be somebody when you grew up."

For a moment, I consider setting Missy straight on just how incredibly unimpressive my job actually is. But then I decide that what's the use of having a crap job if not to impress the people who tormented you all through grade school, junior high, and high school by confusing them with a fancy title?

"And Doug Swenson, he said he bumped into you in Boulder a while back and you told him about how you had a travel article published in a magazine!"

"Yeah," I shrug.

"A real live published writer! That's so great!"

"So how are things going with you?" I say, desperate to change the subject. I feel like such a phony.

"Well, you know, since Coop left, money's been tight. I got a job at the Dairy Queen, but that just doesn't quite seem to cover the bills. I was thinking about moving to my mom's place for a while, if I can put up with the I-told-you-sos . . ."

"Your parents' place by the creek?"

"No. Didn't you hear? My mom and dad split up . . . gosh, it's been years now. No, Mom lives in Telluride."

I am furious with my parents for not sharing any of this news with me. I don't understand the point of owning a hair salon if not to be the first person in town to hear the gossip and then pass it around. Maybe not to everybody, but certainly to your own daughter. Twenty-seven years I've had to train my parents, and still they insist on running amok, doing their own thing.

"For a while, I was living with Veronica Miller, you remember her, right?"

"Sure."

"Her guy left her with two kids too, but then she found a new boyfriend and moved out. I just can't quite pay the rent by myself." She blows a gust of air from the bottom of her lip to try to get her hair out of her eyes, but it falls right back. Her son is still screaming and running around like a banshee and her daughter is still crying, although now at a quieter and less outraged pace. I think these two thoughts, one after the other:

I have been so unbelievably lucky in my life—who the hell am I to complain?

And: thank *God* for birth control.

"I'm sorry, Missy."

"Mitch!" she bellows. "You get back here right now, mister! Don't you d—! I'm counting to three. You set that down if you know what's good for you. One . . ."

"Well, I guess I'd better let you get going."

"Two."

"It was really good to see you."

"I'm warning you!"

"So, I'll see you around, okay?"

"Three!"

I watch Missy charge after her son, and I creep backwards practically on tiptoe, as if I'm leaving the scene of the crime or something.

As I walk back to my parents' place, Missy's words reverberate through my head. *You always were the smartest girl in class. Everybody knew you'd be somebody when you grew up. You always were the smartest girl in class. Everybody knew you'd be somebody when you grew up.*

Is that really what they said about me? But I thought they thought I was Weird Girl. I thought they thought that the only thing that would ever become of me was that I'd end up in an asylum knitting sweaters made from cat hair or something. They thought I was going to be somebody when I grew up?

Is it possible that no one was ever really judging me? That I was just judging myself?

For the entire six-hour drive home, I think about these things. My thoughts and my mind are all jumbled. It's like looking at my life as a Cubist painting, and I can't figure out which angle is the right one.

14

Boulder, Colorado

Monday morning I wake up early and write for an hour. Then I spend twenty minutes stretching and doing yoga. I leave for the office feeling centered and serene. I am determined to focus on all the good things about my life all day long. I will not allow myself to get down. Over lunch I will go outside and take deep breaths of the fresh air. I will savor my lunch slowly rather than scarfing it down like a pack animal with a fresh kill. I will focus on the miracle of life and being alive.

And then I get into the office.

No one is working. Everyone is clustered around in various groups, whispering to each other. The office is abuzz with the kind of gossipy murmurings that make it clear something has gone down.

"What's going on?" I ask Ryan, the graphic designer.

"Tina fired Kathy."

"What do you mean she fired her?"

"Apparently Kathy told Tina she was a paranoid, talentless dictator."

My mouth falls open. Damn it! Why couldn't I have said it first? Then I have to stifle a laugh. Then Ryan laughs, and there's no way I can control my mirth. We do our best not to fall on the floor cackling loudly, trying to reign in our laughter to something office appropriate-ish, but we begin laughing so hard we can't control the fat tears popping out of our eyes and rolling down our cheeks.

We laugh good and hard for at least five minutes, and then the full meaning of what has happened hits me, and I abruptly stop laughing.

"Wait a minute. Who's going to write the copy for the Olsen site?" I ask.

Ryan dries his tears, gets control of his laughter, and gives me a pointed look. My heart sinks. And then: Tina's shrill voice across the crowded office, "Jadie, can I see you in my office?"

Oh shit.

"Sorry, man," Ryan says, shaking his head.

I walk down the hallway, a death row inmate traveling from prison cell to gas chamber.

"Close the door," Tina commands when I get to her office.

I do as I'm told. Tina gestures for me to sit down. I do that, too.

"As you may have heard, I had to let Kathy go. Her writing skills just weren't up to snuff. You do some kind of writing, don't you?"

"Travel writing. It's really very different than—"

"Good. I knew I could count on you. Here are the pages I need you to rework."

"But Tina, the thing of it is, I'm swamped just with doing my regular—"

"I know. This is not a situation any of us want to be in. We all have to pull together as a team to get through this difficult time."

"But I have no exper—"

"Jadie, I know you can do it. Get me a revised draft by noon."

"By noon *today*?"

"Sooner, if possible."

I stand. In a shaky voice I say, "Okay."

I spend all morning rewriting Kathy's text. Tina spends all afternoon ripping my efforts to shreds, telling me everything I did wrong. As it turns out, the only thing writing travel articles and writing marketing copy for the web have in common—at least for my purposes—is that they both use the English language.

I spend the next morning reworking the copy, and then I give it to Tina to rip up again. As she's destroying my copy with a red pen, I try to keep on top of the job I was actually hired to do.

Just before lunch, Tina dumps the pages of text on my desk and asks me to type in the changes, which I do. One of her comments is that I need to, "Inject more exclamation points! People need to get excited!"

She doesn't understand. I'm a writer. I take my punctuation very seriously. I can't use exclamation points so promiscuously. I just don't have it in me.

And she wants me to put quotation marks around the words "real-life" in the sentence "Our courses teach you the real-life skills you need to succeed in today's job market." I don't get it. Why the quotation marks? Quotation marks in this case essentially mean "so called," as in "so-called real-life skills." And what is "real" life anyway? I would say real-life skills means the ability to learn how to have a better relationship with your friends and family and how to lead a happy life, but from the context here, it's clear when they say real life, they mean the nine-to-five grind. As if your day job is what's real and everything else isn't.

I'm twenty-seven years old. That leaves thirty-eight years until retirement. I'll never, ever make it.

15

Hell (aka Corporate America)

I look at the clock, unbelieving. How could it possibly not be five o'clock yet?

Why is it that every Friday afternoon the entire world falls into a time warp where every minute drags on for days?

It is 4:28.

It is still 4:28.

It has been 4:28 for twenty years. For the love of God, will this day never end?

I cannot wait to get out of the office. My home is calling to me.

I look at the calendar. It is October 28. I read somewhere that by the end of October, Americans have worked more hours than Europeans work all year.

I am so ready to go home.

My couch is calling to me. I simply cannot wait to change into my pajamas. I can't wait to order some Chinese takeout, watch a sappy video, and snuggle up beneath an afghan. I can't wait to get away from Tina. I live in constant fear of doing anything because she is so ready to scream at me for things that are so unbelievably ridiculous I'm starting to believe that maybe she's not the insane person, I am. Listen to what she yelled at me for yesterday: one of the guys in the sales team asked if a certain part of the Olsen project was done yet. I said, "We're working on it." Somehow this got back to Tina, and she yelled at me, saying we don't want to make promises we can't keep. I pointed out that I hadn't actually made any promises. She asked why I had to fight with her every step of the way.

So now I'm afraid to leave my desk in case a coworker says something potentially controversial to me like, "Good morning," and I'll say something potentially incriminating back like "Good morning to you, too." And this will get back to Tina and she'll scream at me again. I feel like an abused dog that is afraid to come out from cowering in a corner lest I get beaten again. I haven't written a single word for myself for the last two weeks. I've been too busy working fourteen-hour days as I try to do the work of two people under a preposterously tight deadline. Every now and then, just before I drift into an exhausted sleep, a little voice in my head asks, "Why are you doing this?"

My phone rings. It's John from IT who asks me if I can come meet him and the other guys on the programming team to look through the part of the site they've finished developing.

"Right now? Ah, how long do you think that might take?"

"It could take all night. All weekend. We're way behind deadline. We have to log the hours to get the project done."

All night? All weekend? But my couch, my pajamas, my Chinese food, my sappy video, these things need me, I need them. And most of all, what it comes down to is this: I don't want to spend my weekend working.

I ask you, when does anyone on their deathbed say, "Boy, I really regret not having worked more hours at the office. If only I'd worked a few more weekends..." Never, that's when.

But what I say is, "I'll be right there."

I walk down the hall to the where the IT department is located and bump into Ryan, who is walking in the same direction I am.

"Did you get drafted to meet the IT group, too?" he says.

"Who the hell calls a meeting at 4:30 on a Friday afternoon? Don't these people have families to go home to?"

We approach the IT department and see the five members of the Web development team standing around John's desk, looking at the Olsen Web site. Ryan points to one man after another, "Divorced, divorced, divorced, divorced, single."

It explains a lot.

I get home at 9:30 at night, change into PJs, snuggle up underneath an afghan on the couch, and turn the TV on. I have no idea what's happening on the TV, though, because my head is too crowded with thoughts. I can't stop thinking about what my mother said, "But Jadie, that's not real life," and about the quotation marks Tina wants me to put around the words "real life." What is real life anyway? I know real life is not the fantasy that some rich man is going to come along and make all my dreams come true. But I'm not convinced that real life has to mean spending my days working too many hours at an unfulfilling job, either.

Saturday night, I meet Tate for dinner and drinks. She's waiting for me outside the restaurant. We hug by way of greeting. I follow her inside and slide across from her in the booth.

"How are things?" she asks me as the waitress hands us our menus.

I roll my eyes. "Not that great. Things have been really crazy at work and my life has just been really blah. I think there might be some kind of mental illness that people get when they come back from trips and I have it."

"What disease is that?"

"Well, since I made it up it doesn't have a name. I'll call it The Blahs."

"Symptoms?"

"General feelings of listlessness and boredom."

"Causes?"

"When I'm on a trip, I'm constantly learning new things and seeing new things and my days are filled with all this stimulation. I write pages and pages in my journal because there is so much to report on. Since I've gotten back, I've barely written in my journal at all because all I write are complaints about how boring my life is. Life just seems so dull by comparison to the trip."

Tate studies me. "I'm sorry. I wish I could do something."

I shrug just as the waitress returns to take our orders. We each order beers and I order a hummus sandwich with a side salad while Tate gets a veggie burrito.

"So, how are you?" I ask after the waitress has left.

Tate smiles. "Awesome."

"Yeah?"

"Pete has been e-mailing me. We've been e-mailing each other."

"That's great! So what has he been saying?"

"You know, just telling me about the places he's visiting, that kind of thing. And . . ."

"And?"

She smiles even harder. "He said he thinks he loves me."

I immediately sigh and clap both my hands to my heart.

What can I say, I'm a sucker for romance. "Tate, that's so wonderful. Tell me how he said it. What did you say? Tell me everything!"

"Well, he can't e-mail me every day since he's on the road, but he said that he writes me every chance he gets, every time he can find an Internet café. And he said that I should know that even if he's not writing, he's thinking about me. He said he thinks about me constantly, and he's never been so crazy over anyone, and he thinks he may be falling in love with me."

"Tate, that's so wonderful! What did you say? Er, write I mean."

The waitress brings our beers. I take a sip of my amber, and the toasty malt flavor washes over my tongue down my throat.

"Well, I didn't write back right away. I was too busy freaking out. My heart was just pounding like mad, you know?"

I nod.

"But I thought about it, and I thought, you know, it's crazy, but I think I love him too."

I clap my hands over my heart again.

"So I wrote him back saying that, but I also wrote, you know, how could we love each other? We only knew each other two weeks."

"But think about that French woman, Adèle. She fell in love in just one night. When it's right, it's right."

"That's basically what he said."

"So, when are you going to see each other again?"

"We're talking about meeting in Australia in a few months and traveling all around there. We'll go to New Zealand and Tasmania."

"Oh! That's the most romantic, exciting thing I've ever heard. I'm so jealous I could spit."

"I'd want you to come with me."

"Don't be ridiculous. You don't bring a girlfriend on your romantic trip with your new boyfriend."

"You'd meet a guy."

"Yeah, because meeting a guy on the road worked out so well for me last time."

"Well, even if you didn't meet anyone, you wouldn't be in the way. Pete likes you, I like you, you like me and Pete, it'd work."

Just the prospect of hitting the road again makes me feel better. Maybe that has been the real reason for my case of The Blahs—not having anything to look forward to.

"We'd have to save money like crazy," I say.

"For sure. So you'll come?"

"You never have to twist my arm to go on a trip. I'd love to go."

Tate smiles and takes a sip of her beer. We spend the rest of the night talking about Pete and our trip. I feel that pre-trip excitement bubbling up in me, and I couldn't be more thrilled.

Monday morning I get a message from Tina, asking me to ask Ryan when the revised graphics for the "About Us" section of the Olsen Web site will be ready.

I hit the FORWARD button so my email to Ryan includes Tina's question.

To: ryan.decsher@pinnaclemedia.com
From: jadie.peregrine@pinnaclemedia.com

Can you please answer Tina's question? Thanks.

Two seconds later I get the reply.

To: jadie.peregrine@pinnaclemedia.com
From: ryan.decsher@pinnaclemedia.com

This afternoon at the latest.

Once again I hit the FORWARD button.

To: tina.hayes@pinnaclemedia.com
From: jadie.peregrine@pinnaclemedia.com

Here's the answer.

Why did she have to get me involved in that little exchange? Did it save her one second of time to have me forward two e-mails instead of her sending the e-mail directly to Ryan? No. It was just because she feels the need to delegate whenever possible. It's all about her maniacal obsession for authority.

I try to go back to what I was working on, but I can't stop thinking about how annoyed I am about the e-mail thing. She's done this before to me lots of times, and it's always annoyed me, but today, the more I think about it, the more irritated I get. I sit at my desk getting angrier and angrier, until I'm clenching my teeth and my entire body feels taut as a stretched rubber band. This incident isn't any different than thousands of instances where Tina wielded her authority simply because she could, but it is the incident that makes me decide once and for all, *I can't take this fucking job anymore.*

I march into Tina's office and tell her that I quit, and that my last day will be two weeks from today.

"What? No! You can't leave! Not now! Not in the middle of the Olsen project!"

"I'm sorry Tina, but my last day will be two weeks from today."

"What is it? Do you want more money? We can talk about a raise."

No amount of money is worth the psychological abuse I put up with here everyday. No amount of money is worth working long hours and sacrificing my weekends and my dreams so I can work my ass off to help make a few rich stockholders and executives even richer than they already are.

The flinty-sharp exit interview I've practiced for the last two years begs to be set free. I long to open my mouth and point out every one of her managerial flaws. But then I won't be able to use her as a reference for my next job—and that reference will be hugely important for me to ever get another job—and anyway, Tina is not going to change, so what would be the point?

"It's not about money, Tina. I just . . . it's time for me to move on to new challenges."

It is remarkable the bullshit skills you learn working in corporate America.

16

Boulder, Colorado

Four Months Later

Brent—another waiter—Tate, and I finish cleaning up after our shift. As I scrub down the tables, I admire the definition that has returned to my arms after four months of carting big plates of food around.

We count our piles of singles, close the Greenhouse up, and run across the street to an Irish pub where we meet Sylvia and her husband, James. There is a good-looking guy standing beside them with dark eyes that are as shiny as pools of black ink and an easy smile that he flashes in my direction.

"Jadie and Tate, this is our friend Adam," Sylvia says. "He just moved here from Wisconsin."

"It's nice to meet you," I say. "The call of the mountains was just too strong, huh?" I sit across the table from him.

"I was always wishing I could spend my weekends climbing or hiking instead of working at the office," he says. "And I thought that instead of just visiting Colorado whenever I could, I should just move there."

"That's great. How long have you been out here for?"

"Two weeks. I found a place to live, and now I'm spending some time squandering my savings, hiking and biking, all that good stuff. Eventually I'll start looking for a job, but first I have to decide whether I want to stick with law or do something else completely or maybe be something in between—become a law professor or something."

I don't notice the waitress standing there waiting to take our order until Tate elbows me in the ribs.

"What? Oh. Um, a Boddingtons please."

Adam orders a Guinness, then returns his gaze to mine. "How about you? What do you do for a living?"

"Actually, I just quit my job recently. Tate and I went to Europe, and after that . . . I went back to work for a few weeks and I just couldn't take the insanity of the place anymore. I was working such long hours I didn't have time to pursue my real dream, which is to be a travel writer, so one day I just upped and quit. I had no job lined up and no health insurance and no savings, but the moment I said the words 'I quit,' I felt this enormous relief. Like there had been this cloud over me—kind of *in* me— that disappeared. I felt *serene*. I never feel serene. For about two weeks, I just wrote nonstop. One query letter after another, one essay after another, one article after another. I came up with just tons and tons of ideas for things to write. But after about two weeks into being a layabout I got my credit card bill and panic started to set in. So I talked to Jack, the owner of the Greenhouse, which is a restaurant across the street, and asked him if I could get my old job back. He didn't really need me, but he went ahead and hired me anyway. At first I wasn't getting many shifts because they were fully staffed, but it was great because I just worked on writing. After a month, one of the waiters graduated and quit, so I was able to go full time. I took a big pay cut, but I cashed out my 401k and sold my car, so that will tide me over for a while, and, I'm happy to report I have sold three articles and I have an essay coming out in a few months in an anthology."

"That's great."

"Yeah. It is great. I made eight hundred bucks between the articles and the essay. It was the happiest eight hundred bucks I ever made."

"What are your pieces about?" Adam takes a sip of his beer. His dark eyes peering over the top of his foamy glass are filled with interest.

"Well, when I went to Europe I had this idea that I would interview all these women about how guys, romance, dating, and marriage are different in different parts of the world, which I did. So one of the articles I sold was to this magazine called *Colorado Bride*, and it's about how wedding ceremonies are different in different parts of the world. It offers tips for how brides can incorporate some of these traditions into their ceremonies. When I was in Europe I'd talked to several women about various wedding traditions, but I still had to do a bunch more research. Doing the research was so much fun. I read several books and I e-mailed some of the women I spoke to in Europe and they gave me names of some of their friends who lived in different parts of the globe, so then I e-mailed *those* women. The whole thing was just a blast, and on top of all that, I got paid to do it. Who would have thought it was possible to get paid for doing something you actually enjoy doing? It's like living a fairy tale."

"Good for you. That's great. Really great."

"Thanks. Another one of the articles is for this magazine called *Making Tracks* and it's about this camping spot in Southern Colorado that not many people know about. A bunch of us were planning to go for the weekend a couple of weeks from now so I can do more research. It's basically going to be everybody at this table. You're welcome to come if you're interested."

"I would love to."

Maybe he just means that he'd love to come just as a

friend, but the way he says it makes my heart beat a little faster.

"Being a travel writer would be one of the best jobs I could think of," he says. "I love traveling."

"What countries have you gotten to see?"

It turns out that Adam took a year off after graduating from his undergraduate alma mater to travel. He visited Thailand, Morocco, Egypt, and Zimbabwe. He tells me about nearly getting gored by a hippo in Africa.

"My God. Were you terrified?"

"That was scary, but what was worse were the carpet salesmen in Morocco. You don't know tenacious until you've tried to dodge one of these guys. They have more tactics than a war commander to get you to buy a carpet. These guys are relentless. They speak dozens of languages flawlessly and they start out subtle, asking things like what you do for a living to get an idea of how much money you make. Once they glom onto you, you can't shake them. They get you when you're in a public place and try to hustle you back to the store. I was literally running from this little carpet salesman through the streets of Marrakesh. I was like doing a hurtle relay over baskets of goods being sold in the streets trying to shake this guy."

I laugh. I love his adventurous spirit. I like to travel, but I'm definitely not an adventure traveler. I like art and culture and peeing in toilets as opposed to a hole in the ground if at all possible.

"But I haven't taken a big trip overseas for a while now. What about you, do you have any other big trips planned?" he asks.

"Actually, yes. Tate and I are planning to go to Australia in a couple months. When we were in Europe, Tate met an Australian named Pete. He's working in England right now trying to save money. Australians can do that since

Australia is, watchyamacallit, part of the commonwealth of England or whatever."

"Yeah, sure, of course."

"Anyway, we're going to meet him over in Australia, and tour around there for a while, and if things work out, I think he might come to the States with us."

"That'll be a blast."

For a moment, we just sit there nodding and smiling at each other. Then he says, "So do have some boyfriend you'll be taking with you to Australia or are you leaving him behind?"

"There is no boyfriend in my life to take with or leave behind."

"How is that possible?"

"Let me tell you." I tell him about Jeff, the bitter divorcé; the lesbians; and the socially inept engineer. I don't mention Justin because I don't have any funny stories to share about him, just the occasional lingering feelings of heartache.

By the time I get to the exhibitionist engineer, Adam is laughing so hard his face is red and he can barely breathe.

" 'No, I willy was bruffing my teef,' " he repeats, and this renews his hysterics. I repeat choice bits of my tale, making a two-minute story last twenty minutes, and Adam keeps roaring the entire time. I decide I like Adam very much.

When I have finally good and truly wrested out every last bit of humor from stories of my dating woes, I ask him about his dating life and learn that he's been single for the last several months. He decided to make the move to Boulder before he fell for somebody in Madison.

"I have to say, I'm really happy nobody's snapped you up yet," he says.

"Do you . . . think maybe you'd like to get together before that camping trip? I promise not to take my clothes off while you're in the bathroom brushing your teeth. You know, unless you want me to."

"That'd be great. The getting together part. I'm still having post traumatic flashbacks whenever I brush my teeth, so we should probably play that part by ear."

I smile at him, and he smiles back. I realize just how truly happy I am right now.

I know that not all of life can be a trip to Paris or Hawaii or Rome. Not all of life can be first kisses and roller-coaster highs of falling in love. I know that laundry needs to be done, beds need to be made, and groceries need to be bought with money earned somehow. But there's nothing wrong with wanting to live a fairy tale life. Sure, the odds are good that not every day will be photo-op fascinating or worth detailing for dozens of pages in your journal, but to try to live a life that's as full as those kind of days as possible—who can argue with that? Because what is "real life" anyway?

All I know is that as I sit across the table from Adam, every part of me pulses with electric energy. Every synapse is firing, every part of me is alert, awake, and what I think is that this, this feeling, *this* is real. This feeling of being absolutely alive, absolutely in this moment, this is as real as it gets.